RENEGADE RANGER

Center Point
Large Print

Also by James J. Griffin and available from
Center Point Large Print:

Death Stalks the Rangers
Death Rides the Rails
Ranger's Revenge
Texas Jeopardy
Blood Ties

**This Large Print Book carries the
Seal of Approval of N.A.V.H.**

RENEGADE RANGER

A Texas Ranger Jim Blawcyzk Story

James J. Griffin

CENTER POINT LARGE PRINT
THORNDIKE, MAINE

The text of this Large Print edition is unabridged. In other aspects, this book may vary from the original edition. Printed in the United States of America on permanent paper. Set in 16-point Times New Roman type.

ISBN: 978-1-64358-132-3

Library of Congress Cataloging-in-Publication Data

Names: Griffin, James J., 1949- author.
Title: Renegade ranger : a Texas Ranger Jim Blawcyzk story / James J. Griffin.
Description: Center Point large print edition. | Thorndike, Maine : Center Point Large Print, 2019.
Identifiers: LCCN 2018059093 | ISBN 9781643581323 (hardcover : alk. paper)
Subjects: LCSH: Large type books. | GSAFD: Western stories.
Classification: LCC PS3607.R5477 R46 2019 | DDC 813/.6—dc23
LC record available at https://lccn.loc.gov/2018059093

For Patricia and Nicholas Fiondella

As always, thanks to
Texas Ranger Sergeant Jim Huggins
of Company A, Houston,

and Karl Rehn and Penny Riggs
of KR Training, Manheim, Texas for their
assistance, advice and expertise.

Chapter One

The two gunmen stood slightly crouched, hands hovering over the butts of the Colts hanging on their left hips. Both men's eyes glittered like chips of blue ice while they sighted on their targets.

As one they grabbed for their guns, their hands a blur when they lifted the weapons from their holsters with blindingly fast speed. Gunfire shattered the quiet afternoon and powder smoke filled the air.

As quickly as it had begun, the firing stopped, silence descending once the gunmen had emptied their weapons. A gentle breeze slowly cleared the clouds of gun smoke, revealing their bullet-punctured victims. Out of twelve tin cans, one lone survivor remained standing.

"Not bad shootin', Dad. Eleven out of twelve. You got all six of yours, and I got five out of six. Pretty good, eh?"

"It's good, all right, but not good enough."

Texas Ranger Lieutenant Jim Blawcyzk slid a cartridge into his heavy Colt Peacemaker, leveled the gun, and fired, blasting the sole remaining can off its fencepost.

"That one you missed could've been the renegade who drilled you right through your guts, Charlie," he concluded. "Bet a hat on that."

"Are you tryin' to tell me you've never missed a shot, Dad?" Charlie retorted.

"Nary a one," Jim replied, grinning.

"Dad, you're a ring-tailed liar," Charlie exclaimed. "If you've never missed, how do you explain all those bullet scars your hide's carryin'?"

"Those aren't bullet scars. They're hornet stings," Jim answered.

"Sure they are, and I'm the Governor of Texas," Charlie shot back.

"I'm just tryin' to make sure you're absolutely as prepared as possible when you join the Rangers in a few years," Jim answered. "That one bullet . . ."

"I know. That one bullet could be the difference between me or some outlaw lyin' dead in the dust," Charlie finished for his father. "Besides, I'm joinin' the Rangers next year, soon as I turn eighteen, not in a few years. You and Mom know that."

"Long as you don't get too big for your britches you can join the Rangers next year," Jim corrected.

He reached up to knock the dark brown Stetson off Charlie's head and tousled his hair, as he'd been doing since the boy was a toddler. At the age of seventeen, Charlie had shot up in height over the past several months and now stood two inches taller than his six foot plus father. With a thick shock of blonde hair, clear blue eyes, and the same lanky frame, he was the spitting image of his Texas Ranger dad.

Charlie picked up the hat and jammed it back on his head.

"Dad, ain't I gettin' a bit old for you to be mussin' my hair?" he complained.

"You'll never be too old for that . . . or for a swat on your behind, either," Jim warned. "Bet a hat on it. What's wrong? You afraid your hair won't be just right for Mary Jane Jarratt at the church social come Saturday night?"

"Dad . . . ah, never mind." Charlie quickly changed the subject. "We gonna practice some more shootin'? After all, you're leavin' in the morning. Who knows when you'll be back?"

"Not right now, since it's almost suppertime. We'd better clean up, then see if your Mom needs any help settin' the table."

"Okay, Dad."

Jim and Charlie headed for the house. Julia, Jim's wife and Charlie's mother, was in the back yard removing sheets from the clotheslines.

"You want some help getting those off the line, Julia?" Jim called.

"There's no need, I'm almost finished. You two are lucky the wind was blowing away from the house. If it hadn't been and my clean sheets smelled of gunpowder, it wouldn't have been

9

just the tin cans which would have had holes in them," Julia scolded. Her brown eyes held a mischievous sparkle.

"I think Mom means we'd have had trouble sitting down for a spell, Dad," Charlie laughed.

"I got her drift," Jim chuckled. "Honey, what about the table? You want us to set it after we wash up?"

"I'd surely appreciate that," Julia answered.

"All right; we'll handle that. Let's go, Charlie."

While Julia finished emptying the clothes-lines, Jim and Charlie headed for the pump and wash bench back of the house. They stripped off their shirts and ducked their heads into the shallow trough, quickly washed and toweled off, then slid back into their shirts. By the time they were done, Julia had carried a basketful of sheets inside, set it down, and was removing a roast from the oven.

"Everything's ready. It's just waiting on you two to set the table," she said.

"Have it done in a jiffy," Jim replied. Shortly, the table was set and the family sat down to a supper of roast beef, boiled potatoes, green beans, bread and butter.

"Charlie, you lead Grace tonight," Julia requested.

"Sure, Mom." Charlie folded his hands and bowed his head, while his parents did likewise.

"Bless us O Lord, and these Thy gifts, which

we are about to receive from Thy bounty, through Christ our Lord. Amen."

"Amen," Jim and Julia echoed.

While they ate, Julia told her husband of the latest sale of one of their foals. Their small horse ranch, the JB Bar, had become quite well known for its quality horses, most of them paints. Jim had ridden paints throughout all of his Ranger career. Although most ranchers, cowboys, and indeed the majority of his fellow Rangers favored solid color mounts over what many of them disdainfully called "Indian ponies," Jim had a special fondness for the paints and their colorful white splotched coats.

"Jim, I sold Chekotah's colt today. Ben Bradley over at the Triangle BB's buying him. Ben's positive he'll make a good stock horse, plus he's planning on breeding him to some of his mustang mares once he's old enough. He thinks that will make a good combination, the toughness of those mustangs crossed with the conformation and color of Chekotah's and Sonny's bloodlines."

"You sold Dallas?" Jim replied, doubt in his voice. "I was kinda thinkin' of keepin' him."

"Jim, you want to keep every foal born on this ranch," Julia answered, not quite able to hide completely the exasperation in her voice. "If it were up to you, we'd never sell any at all, even though we're practically overrun with horses as it is. If I listened to you, we'd be horse poor for certain. That's why I ask you not to name any of the babies, even though you never listen. You get too attached."

"I know," Jim sighed. "It's one of the reasons I asked you to take charge of the ranch years ago. I just can't bring myself to let go of any of the foals. Never could. You've got a much more level head than I do, that's for certain. Besides, my bein' gone Rangerin' so much makes it impossible for me to help out enough around here. I'd have plumb starved to death years ago if it hadn't been for you, Julia. You've always done a fine job runnin' this place."

Jim's great passion in life, besides his family and the Texas Rangers, was horses. He had an almost mystical connection with them, and often stated he preferred the company of equines to that of ninety percent of the humans he met.

"Ben's also a good man. He'll take excellent care of Chekotah's foal, so you needn't worry about that," Julia tried to reassure him.

"You're right there," Jim agreed. "Dallas'll have a fine home, that's for certain."

"That's enough talk about horse tradin'," Charlie broke in. "Dad's leavin' in the mornin', while Ty Tremblay and I have gotta move that stock outta the Four Ts' back pasture and fix the fences along the creek. If you keep Dad talkin' about horses, we'll never finish supper and before mornin' comes, I'd purely like to have a big chunk of that chocolate cake you baked, Mom."

"The boy always did have more sense than me," Jim laughed. "Sure, Charlie. Let's cut the cake."

Since Jim and Charlie both needed to be awake with the sun the next morning, once supper was finished and the dishes washed, dried, and put away, everyone headed straight to bed. Charlie was asleep almost as soon as his head hit the pillow.

Jim and Julia had said their evening prayers and were now lying side by side. Julia had her head resting on Jim's chest, while he had one arm wrapped around her and was stroking her long, dark hair. To Jim, she seemed uneasy, her body a bit tense.

"Julia, is something troubling you?" he asked. "I know you worry whenever I'm on the trail, but it seems like something more is on your mind tonight."

"I'm just a bit preoccupied, that's all," Julia murmured.

"About what?"

"Charlie. You and he practicing shooting today reminded me how fast Charlie's growing up. He'll turn eighteen next year, and no doubt will want to sign up with the Rangers the day he does. I remember when he was a little boy who used to chase fireflies and lizards," she said wistfully. "It won't be all that long until he's chasing outlaws instead."

"I've never encouraged Charlie to become a lawman like me," Jim pointed out.

"I know that," Julia answered. "But he's always looked up to you, and you've never discouraged him, either. We've both known for a long time that one day our son would follow you into the Rangers."

"Do you want me to try and talk him out of it?"

"Not at all. Besides, neither one of us could change his mind, and I know how proud you'll be when Charlie pins on that badge. I will be, too. It's only that then I'll have two of you to worry about, rather than just one."

"That, and you'll be alone most of the time. I understand why you're troubled," Jim answered. "Maybe by the time Charlie joins the Rangers I'll be ready to retire."

"Jim, don't try and kid yourself, or me. We both know the only way you'll quit the Rangers is when you can no longer climb into the saddle, or if . . ." Julia hesitated.

". . . if I'm killed or shot up so bad I can't keep Rangerin'," Jim concluded.

"Yes."

"Well right now I'm here, and a year is a long time. Who knows? Charlie might just decide he wants to stay home and be a rancher after all,

14

particularly if Mary Jane Jarratt has anything to say about it. For tonight, I know how to get all this off your mind," Jim finished.

"How?"

"Like this."

Jim rolled onto his side, pulled Julia more tightly to him, and pressed his lips to hers.

Chapter Two

An hour after sunup the next day, Jim and Charlie had already eaten a huge breakfast and were now in their saddles, preparing to ride out. Jim was on Sizzle, his big sorrel paint, with Sam, his ill-tempered former trail horse, trailing alongside. Sam was a palomino paint who'd been badly injured several years previously when outlaws had attacked Jim's ranch, leaving Jim and his family for dead. Since Sam could no longer carry the Ranger's weight, he now served Jim as a pack horse. Charlie was on Ted, the buckskin paint he'd been given by Jim while the boy was still a toddler. He would ride along with his father as far as Mark and Michelle Tremblay's Four Ts ranch.

Jim leaned from his saddle to give Julia a last farewell kiss.

"Jim, please be careful," Julia pleaded. "You know how I worry when you're gone."

"I know," Jim replied. "There's no need to fret about me this time, though. I'm just goin' to Mason to make sure things stay quiet until after the election. Folks down there sure don't want a repeat of that feud they had a while back, so Jake Cooper, the Mason County sheriff, asked for a Ranger to help keep the peace. Coop's a real good lawman, so I'm not expectin' much trouble, if any. This'll be a short assignment. I'll be home in a couple of weeks."

"Dad, we'd better get goin'," Charlie urged. "Me'n Ty have a lot of fence to fix before the day's out."

"You mean Ty and I," Julia gently corrected.

"Either way, it's gonna be a long day, Mom," Charlie grinned.

"All right; let's get movin', Charlie," Jim agreed. "Julia, I'll be back before you know it."

"And I'll be home for supper," Charlie assured her.

"It will be waiting for you," Julia promised. "I'm goin over to the McCue's to visit with Cindy for a bit, but I'll be home by late afternoon at most. Jim, don't forget to give Captain Trumbull those molasses rum cookies I baked for him. Don't you dare go eating them yourself."

"I'll do my best, but you know how much I love those cookies," Jim replied. "Someday I'm gonna be accused of havin' too many drinks, but it'll only be your molasses rum cookies to blame."

Jim never drank anything harder than sarsaparilla.

"I mean it, Jim," Julia warned. "There's two packages, one for you, one for the Captain."

"Don't worry, honey," Jim assured her. "Captain Trumbull will get his cookies. Bet a hat on it. Charlie, let's go."

Jim and Charlie turned their horses, heeling the

mounts into a jogtrot. Julia watched them until they faded from sight.

Two hours later, Jim was looping his horses' reins around the battered hitchrail in front of Ranger Headquarters in Austin. As usual, he gave each gelding one of the peppermints he always kept in his hip pocket for them.

"You just take it easy a spell. I won't be all that long," he assured the paints. "After that we've got five days travelin' ahead of us." He patted each horse's muzzle, then headed inside.

Jim strode down a long, wainscoted corridor to Captain Hank Trumbull's office at the end of the hall. Trumbull had his back turned to the door while he studied a large map of Texas on the far wall.

"Howdy, Cap'n," Jim softly drawled as he entered the office.

Trumbull turned at the sound of the Lieutenant's voice.

"Howdy yourself, Jim. I thought it was about time you were showin' up," he said, smiling. "Usually you're here waitin' for me."

"I figured since I already know where I'm headed, I'd take it a mite easy and spend a little more time with Julia and Charlie before I left," Jim explained. He took a tin mug from its shelf, then headed for the stove in the corner. He picked up the battered coffee pot Trumbull always kept simmering and filled it with the thick, black brew. That done, he settled onto a worn leather chair opposite Trumbull's desk. While Jim was getting his coffee, the captain took out a well-worn pipe, filled it, lit it, took a long puff, then blew a ring of smoke toward the ceiling.

"I can't blame you for that," Trumbull answered. He signed deeply. "Family is always important. Lord knows I sure miss mine."

Trumbull's wife Maisie had passed away several months previously. Their three children had all died earlier, their daughter Josie of influenza, while their two sons, Jeremiah and Michael, had both died fighting at Antietam.

"I know it's gotta be difficult being without Maisie," Jim sympathized.

"Boy howdy, you've sure got that right. You don't know the half of it," Trumbull agreed. His frosty blue eyes held a tinge of great loneliness. "The house just seems empty without her, which is why I find myself spendin' more and more time here or at the Silver Star. Keeps my mind off things. But I can't complain all that much, for despite all our troubles, the Good Lord gave Maisie and me a long time together. We had a fine life, all things considered. My only regret is not bein' able to see our kids live long enough to raise families of their own."

"I reckon that's so," Jim answered. "Charlie's sure growin' up fast. Seems like only yesterday

19

he was knee-high to a grasshopper, and now he's already planning on joinin' the Rangers soon as he turns eighteen. In fact, that's pretty much all he talks about."

"That'll be next year, won't it?" Trumbull said. "Well, the Rangers'll be glad to have him, that's for certain, but what about Julia? How does she feel about her only child joining the Texas Rangers?"

"She's not all that happy about it, truth to tell, but she won't stand in his way either," Jim replied. "We talked about that just last night, as a matter of fact. Julia says she'll be as proud as I am when Charlie pins on the badge. Bet a hat on that."

"I don't think she or anyone else can possibly be as proud as you'll be, Jim," Trumbull noted. "However, I'm glad to hear she'll accept Charlie's decision. Well, I reckon we've spent enough time palaverin'. Time to hand over your papers and get you on your way, Lieutenant."

Trumbull turned to the file cabinet alongside his desk, pulled open the third drawer, and took out a thin manila folder. He removed a letter from the file and passed it to Jim.

"Here's your authorization to assist Sheriff Cooper of Mason County to keep the peace until after the upcoming election, per his request. He doesn't want a repeat of that feud, and neither do most of the folks down there. I don't need to remind you of what could happen down that way if there's not enough law to maintain order."

"You sure don't," Jim agreed.

"With luck, you won't have any work to do at all," Trumbull continued. "Cooper and his deputies will still be the main officials in charge. Your role is strictly to assist the local law, unless things get out of hand. In that case, your position as a Texas Ranger takes precedence over all local and county law officers, and you are to take any and all steps necessary to assure any trouble is nipped in the bud, and a fair and honest election held. Is that clear?"

"As crystal," Jim answered. "Like you said, I don't expect much trouble. Jake Cooper's a fine lawman, and most of the folks around Mason are pretty tired of troublemakers after all the feudin'. I'm figuring on a nice easy assignment for once."

"I hope you're right, but don't take anything for granted, Lieutenant," Trumbull warned. "To borrow your favorite expression, I wouldn't bet a hat on it."

"I never do," Jim replied, as he folded the letter and slid it inside his vest pocket, then stood up. "Reckon I'll be ridin'. I'll see you in a couple of weeks, Cap'n."

"Adios, Jim."

When Jim headed out to his waiting horses, he found another Ranger tying his black gelding alongside Sizzle.

"Tom. Tom Foley!" Jim called.

"Jim Blawcyzk. Well I'll be. Howdy, Jim. It's been quite a spell since I've seen you. 'Bout a coupla years, ain't it?"

"At least that long," Jim replied as they shook hands. Foley was about the same age as Jim, two inches shorter and about thirty pounds lighter. His hair and eyes were dark brown, and he sported a bushy mustache of the same hue. Foley's rugged good looks had always made him irresistible to the ladies. He was probably as fast and accurate with the Colt .45 he wore in a crossdraw holster on his left hip as any of his fellow Rangers.

Foley had been a chuckline riding cowpoke until the day he had chanced upon a beleaguered Blawcyzk, who'd been wounded and pinned down by the gang of outlaws he was pursuing. Foley had come to the aid of the hopelessly out-numbered and surrounded Ranger, his unexpected attack routing the suddenly unnerved renegades. Most of the gang fell to Foley's and Blawcyzk's accurate shooting, with only five survivors able to flee into the badlands. Foley, having also taken a slug through his shoulder and a bullet slash across his scalp, had let them escape so he could tend to the badly shot-up Blawcyzk, who had by then passed out from pain and loss of blood. He patched up the injured Ranger, cared for his own wounds, then headed for the nearest ranch. With the assistance of the rancher and his family he nursed Blawcyzk until the Ranger was strong enough to reach the nearest town with a doctor, so he could receive proper medical attention. While recuperating, Jim had convinced Foley to join the Rangers. They'd ridden together on several occasions in the past, mostly as members of Company D along the Rio Grande. Foley had proved a more than capable lawman, always cool under fire, seemingly unflappable no matter what the circumstances.

"Where you ridin' in from, Tom?" Jim asked.

"Big Bend country, where else?" Foley shrugged. "Seems like I spend most of my time there, or somewhere along the border. Say, remember when the two of us rode after that gang of Mexican smugglers down that way? We must've chased 'em for a month of Sundays before we cornered them along Blue Creek."

"As I recollect, it was more like the other way around. They had us pretty well trapped, I seem to recall," Jim replied.

"Yeah, but we shot our way out of that trap," Foley answered "Recovered a whole bunch of stolen goods and lots of 'dobe dollars, too."

"And also some chunks of lead, which we carried in our hides," Jim laughed.

"I reckon you're right," Foley agreed, chuckling. He leaned against the hitchrail to roll and light a quirly. When he did, Sam lunged at him, baring his teeth. Foley jerked back just in time to avoid having a piece of flesh torn from his forearm by the ill-tempered paint's wicked yellow teeth.

"Easy, horse. I'm a friend, remember?" he said to the gelding.

"I see ol' Sam's as ornery as ever," he continued to Jim. "He'll never change, bet a hat on it," Jim agreed. "I notice you're ridin' a new mount. He's a good lookin' animal. What happened to Buckeye?"

"I had to put him down," Foley replied wistfully. A trace of sadness flickered across his face. "Age finally caught up to Buck. His joints had gotten so stiff it was hard for him to even walk. One mornin' when I went out to his stall he was lyin' on his side and couldn't get up. I knew right then I had to put him out of his misery. Hardest thing I've ever had to do."

"I know what you mean," Jim sympathized. "These horses sure are our pardners, ain't they?"

"Boy howdy, they are indeed," Foley concurred. He took a puff on his quirly. "Indigo here's one of the best I've ridden. Don't know how much longer it'll matter though. It won't be too many years before we won't be ridin' horseback at all."

"I don't even want to think about that," Jim objected. His aversion to almost all forms of machinery was well known.

"Mark my words, it's true," Foley insisted. "Look at the railroads—layin' tracks in every direction all over the state. More'n more we're usin' them rather than our horses to get from one point to another, especially if we've got a long distance to cover from Austin to our next assignment. Then there's that contraption of Alexander Graham Bell's, the telephone. If it does what everyone claims it can, it'll soon render Western Union and the telegraph obsolete."

"Now that one I can live with," Jim answered. "Just imagine bein' able to reach a county sheriff with one of those, to let him know some renegade we're after is headin' for his territory. He'd be able to capture that hombre for us before we got there, so all we'd have to do is rustle him outta jail and bring him back for trial. I've gotta agree with you, the days of the telephone are comin' fast. Ever since Colonel Belo over in Galveston hooked up a telephone line from his house to the office at his newspaper, the Galveston News, back in '78, folks have been clamorin' for one. Besides Galveston, Houston's got an exchange now, and there's plans for plenty more."

"I hear tell Galveston's already workin' on producin' electricity, too," Foley responded. "Before we know it most buildings' light'll be comin' from those new-fangled bulbs of Edison's, rather than gas lights or kerosene lamps. Why, someday we might even use machines to fly like the birds."

"I reckon," Jim sighed, "But I'd sure hate to

see that day come. The world's startin' to move way too fast for this ol' boy. Give me a good horse and saddle any day of the week. Bet a hat on it."

"I dunno. I could get used to easier travelin'," Foley mused. "It gets danged uncomfortable forkin' a bronc all day, then sleepin' on the hard ground all night."

"Tom, you've done much more sleepin' in a soft bed with a soft woman than you've ever done alone on the hard ground," Jim objected, with a smile.

"I can't argue with you there, that's for certain," Foley admitted. He took a last drag on his cigarette, ground it out on the rail, then dropped the butt to the dirt.

"Well, I figure I've kept Cap'n Trumbull waitin' long enough. Might as well find out where he's sending me next. Good seein' you again, Jim."

"Yeah, I've killed enough time too. I'd better get movin'."

Jim tightened his cinches, untied both his horses, then climbed onto Sizzle's back.

"Where you bound?" Foley questioned.

"Should be an easy job for once. I'm headed down to Mason County to help Sheriff Cooper keep an eye on things until after the election. I'll only be gone a couple of weeks," Jim explained.

"You take care nonetheless," Foley advised. "Adios."

"Always do. You make sure and do the same," Jim answered. "Adios, Tom."

He backed Sizzle away from the rail and put him into a slow jogtrot, sending him down Congress Avenue, Sam alongside.

Jim had gone about three blocks when he pulled back on the reins, hauling Sizzle up short.

"Blast it!" he exclaimed. "I plumb forgot to give Cap'n Trumbull the cookies Julia baked for him. She'll have my hide if I don't give the cap'n those cookies . . . not to mention if he ever found out I had cookies for him but saved 'em for myself I'd be busted down to private and kept patrollin' the Border for the next ten years. C'mon, Siz, let's head back."

A moment later, Jim was dropping Sizzle's reins back over the rail at Ranger Headquarters. When he swung out of the saddle, both horses nuzzled at his hip pocket, begging for a peppermint.

"Oh no, not this time, Jim chuckled. "I'll only be a minute. You two wait right here."

Sam snorted indignantly and buried his muzzle in Jim's belly, driving air from the Ranger's lungs. Jim grunted with the impact.

"Try that again and you won't get any peppermints for a week," Jim warned the horse, with a friendly slap to Sam's neck. He ducked under Sam's neck and returned to Sizzle's right side, stopping alongside the big paint to open his saddlebag. Just as he unbuckled the straps, three gunshots rang out from inside the Headquarters building. Jim whirled, yanked his Colt from the holster on his left hip, and raced inside.

Tom Foley was just emerging from the corridor leading to Captain Trumbull's office, his smoking six-gun in his hand. An expression of surprise mingled with disbelief crossed his face when he spotted Jim.

"Tom! What happened?" Jim called.

Foley's answer was to thumb back the hammer of his gun and pull the trigger, putting a bullet into Jim's belly. Jim clawed at his middle, struggling to keep his balance as his knees buckled. He staggered, trying futilely to find enough strength to bring his gun level with Foley's stomach and pull the trigger.

Foley fired again, this bullet taking Jim in the chest and slamming him into the wall. Jim hung there for a moment, then slid to the floor and toppled to his side, his Colt spilling from his hand. Foley stepped over Jim's outstretched legs and hurried outside, mounting his horse, yanking him away from the rail and spurring the powerful black into a dead run.

Wracked with pain, Jim felt someone gently rolling him onto his back. Through blurred vision, he recognized the face of his long-time riding partner, Smoky McCue.

"Jim! Who shot you?" Smoky cried.

"Tom . . ." Jim's voice was barely a whisper.

"I can't hear you, Jim," Smoky said. He knelt alongside his downed friend and leaned close to catch Jim's barely audible words.

"Who did this, Jim?" he repeated.

"Tom . . . Tom Foley," Jim gasped.

"You mean Ranger Tom Foley?" Smoky demanded, not able to believe what he was hearing.

"Yeah. Yeah," Jim stammered. "Think . . . think he shot . . . Cap'n Trumbull, too. Dunno . . . Dunno why . . . he plugged me. Got me . . . good. Reckon I'm . . . done for."

"No you're not," Smoky retorted. "Doc Talmadge'll fix you up in no time. Just take it easy until he gets here."

"Sure. Whatever you . . . say, Smoke," Jim replied. "Take care of the . . . cap'n first . . . though."

"All right, Jim," Smoky agreed. "I'll be back quick as I can."

"I'll be here . . . not . . . goin' anywhere." Jim managed a wan smile.

"Someone go for Doc Talmadge, now! Tell him don't waste any time," Smoky shouted.

Smoky's frantic demand was the last thing Jim heard before he drifted into a sea of black.

Reluctantly leaving Jim, Smoky headed for Captain Trumbull's office. Two other Rangers,

Mal Healy and Seamus O'Toole, were already in the room. They looked at Smoky and shook their heads.

Captain Trumbull was behind his desk, sprawled face-down on the floor with three bullets in his back. The captain would never issue another order.

"Mal, you and Seamus take charge here," Smoky commanded. "Jim Blawcyzk's also been shot real bad. He claims Tom Foley did the shootin'. Soon as the doc gets here, round up a couple more men and get on Foley's trail."

"Sure, Smoke," Healy readily agreed. "What about you?"

"I'm headin' to Jim's place. Someone's got to tell his wife and boy what's happened. I reckon that falls to me. Once I take care of that chore, I'll be takin' up Foley's trail too, unless you've managed to track him down first. I'll follow him to Hell and back if I need to, even Mexico, but I'll bring him in. As Jim would say, bet a hat on it."

"All right, Smoky," O'Toole answered. "However, if I get my sights lined on Tom Foley's back, you won't have to worry about bringin' him in. I'll leave his worthless carcass for the buzzards."

"Reckon that goes for me, too," Healy added.

"That's enough of that kind of talk. I want Foley brought in alive if at all possible. We'll have a trial, then a hangin' . . . but we'll do this legal and proper. Is that clear?"

"It's plain enough, Corporal," O'Toole grudgingly answered.

"Good. I'm headin' out. Take Captain Trumbull, put him on the couch, and cover him. Have Doc Talmadge send for the undertaker. I'll catch up with you soon as I can."

"We don't have any idea which way Foley went," Healy pointed out.

"Doesn't matter. There's no place on this Earth he can hide," Smoky answered. "Just get after him."

Doctor Calvin Talmadge, one of the Ranger surgeons, arrived just as Smoky stepped outside.

"Corporal, Ranger Morton tells me you have at least one badly wounded man here, maybe more," he stated.

"That's right. Jim Blawcyzk's just inside. He took a bullet in the chest, another in his gut. Do what you can for him, Doc."

"Of course," Talmadge replied. "Is there anyone else?"

"No one else," Smoky said. "Captain Trumbull was shot too, but there's nothing you can do for him."

"You mean the Captain's dead?" Talmadge asked, clearly shaken.

"I'm afraid so," Smoky confirmed. "He was shot three times in the back."

"Doc, hurry," O'Toole called from the doorway. "All right."

Talmadge rushed to his patient, while Smoky hurried for the stable where Soot, his steeldust gelding, had been stabled for the night. He hurriedly threw his gear on the horse and mounted. Smoky forced himself to allow the dark gray to walk and trot for the first half-mile, warming up, then pushed Soot into a full gallop.

Chapter Three

"Soot, I'm sorry. I'll make it up to you, I promise. You'll get a good rubdown and extra grain once all this is over," Smoky apologized to his horse as they neared McCue's Box MQ spread. Soot was covered with lather, his breathing labored and stride faltering. Smoky had pushed the steeldust hard all the way from Austin, covering the twelve miles to San Leanna in little more than an hour. He'd decided to stop at his place and get his wife before heading to Jim's JB Bar. It would be far easier to have Cindy along to help him break the news of Jim's shooting to Julia.

Smoky muttered a curse when he topped the low rise overlooking his ranch and recognized the paint mare lazing in the shade of the cottonwood tree in his front yard. He pulled Soot to a halt for just a moment.

"Julia's here, of all the rotten luck. That's the three year old she's been trainin'," he said. "She must've decided to ride over and visit Cindy, so now I've gotta tell them both at the same time. Well, there's no use puttin' it off. C'mon, Soot."

He heeled the tiring gelding into a lope once again.

Smoky slowed his mount before he reached the gate, not wanting the hoof beats of a galloping horse to alarm the women inside the house. He walked the steeldust up to the porch, eased out of the saddle, and looped Soot's reins over the rail.

"I'll give you a drink soon as I can, Soot," he promised the steeldust, patting his neck. Soot nuzzled his hand and nickered. Smoky climbed the stairs, crossed the porch, and quietly opened the door.

Cindy and Julia were in the parlor, working on a patchwork quilt. Cindy looked up in surprise, a wide smile spreading across her face at seeing her husband enter the room.

"Smoky, I didn't expect to see you until tonight. I thought you'd be testifying at Malachi Quention's trial most of the day. I'm certainly . . ." She stopped short when she noticed the morose expression on his face.

"Smoky, what's wrong?" she exclaimed.

Smoky crossed the room and took Julia's hand.

"Julia, Jim's been shot," he said. "You need to go to Austin, right now."

"Jim's been shot?" Julia echoed, not quite sure of what she'd just heard. "Are you sure?"

"I was there right after it happened."

"Oh no!" Julia cried, stunned. "My Jim. How bad is it, Smoky?"

"Very bad, I'm afraid," Smoky answered. "Captain Trumbull was also shot. He was killed. Doctor Talmadge was with Jim when I left him, so he's in good hands. If anyone can pull that stubborn cuss of a husband of yours through, it's Doc Talmadge, but there's no time to waste. We need to get started right now."

Julia's eyes were moist as she fought to hold back tears and keep her emotions in check.

"Captain Trumbull's dead?" she repeated. "That doesn't seem possible. I gave Jim some cookies for him just this morning."

"I don't want to believe it either, but it's true," Smoky answered. "Julia, right now you have to worry about Jim, no one else. You need to be with him as quickly as possible."

"Of course. Myra's right outside and already saddled. I'll leave immediately." She started to cry.

Cindy moved alongside Julia and wrapped an arm around her shoulders.

"Julia, Jim will be just fine, you'll see. I'm going to saddle Dolly and ride to Austin with you, all right? Just give me a couple of minutes to get her ready."

"Of course I'd like you to be with me," Julia answered, regaining her composure somewhat. "But what about you, Smoky? Oh! Someone needs to let Charlie know what's happened."

"That's what I'm planning on doing," Smoky explained. "I was heading for your place but decided to stop here first and get Cindy, so she would be with me when I gave you the news about Jim. I'll go find Charlie as soon as you start for Austin."

"Charlie's not home," Julia answered. "He's helping Ty Tremblay move stock out of the back pasture and fix fence at the Four Ts. You'll find him there."

"All right, I'll help Cindy with Dolly while you check Myra and tighten your cinches. As soon as you're both ready to leave and I let Soot have a drink I'll start for the Tremblay place. Once I find Charlie we'll head back to Austin, and then I'm going after the man who did this."

"You know who killed Captain Trumbull and shot Jim?" Cindy said. "Who was it?"

"It was another Ranger, Tom Foley."

"Another Ranger! Are you certain of that, Smoky?" Julia asked.

"That's what Jim told me just before he lost consciousness," Smoky answered.

"That doesn't seem possible," Cindy said.

"I know," Smoky agreed, "but apparently it is."

"Jim shot by one of his fellow Rangers," Julia murmured. "I always feared he'd be killed by an outlaw, but for him to be gunned down by one of his friends . . ."

Her voice trailed off.

"Julia, don't think about that," Cindy advised. "All you have to be concerned about is Jim's recovery. From what Smoky says, he'll need your strength and love more than he ever has before."

"Cindy's right," Smoky added. "So let's get the horses ready and get you on your way."

Cindy's bay mare Dolly was swiftly saddled and bridled, while Julia checked the gear on her mare Myra and slipped the bridle back over her head. Soot had nibbled on some dry, stunted grass while he was awaiting his rider and now, after the brief rest and a short drink, was ready to go a few more miles.

"I'll have Charlie in Austin with you as quickly as possible, Julia," Smoky reassured her.

"I know you will, and thank you for everything, Smoky."

"Save your thanks until I round up Tom Foley and bring him in for a hangin'," Smoky replied. He climbed into his saddle, pointed Soot toward the Four Ts ranch, and put him into a long-reaching lope.

Smoky bypassed the main buildings at the Four Ts ranch, heading instead directly for where Julia had indicated Charlie and his best friend, Tyler Tremblay, would be working. At the far west boundary line of the ranch, he found a newly repaired stretch of barbed wire fencing.

"Looks like they're done fixin' this section, Soot. That means we should find 'em shovin' cattle back across the creek a bit further on."

He put the horse into a gentle trot, conserving Soot's strength for the hard run back to Austin.

He followed the fence until they came to a rough cattle trail, then turned down that, heading for the creek which traversed the Tremblay ranch. Once he reached the creek, he turned Soot upstream, following the brush-strewn bank.

When he came to a spot where the creek widened and deepened, Smoky noticed Charlie's and Ty's horses, unsaddled and picketed where they could graze on the lush grass bordering the water. The boys' hats, boots, clothing, and gunbelts were piled haphazardly on the creek bank. Evidently they had decided to take a break from their work with a cooling swim, for Ty and Charlie, dripping wet, were standing on a boulder in the middle of the stream bed, pushing and shoving. Their shouts and grunts drifted across the water as each strained to knock the other off the rock and into the creek. So engrossed were they in their struggle they failed to notice the approaching Ranger. Smoky lifted his Stetson over his head and waved it back and forth, trying to get their attention.

"Charlie!" he shouted. "Charlie!"

"Uncle Smoky?"

Charlie looked around, startled. When he did, Ty put both hands in the middle of Charlie's chest and pushed hard, knocking him off balance to send him tumbling into the creek.

"Reckon I won that time, pardner," Ty chortled

when Charlie surfaced, spluttering and gasping for breath.

"Ty, you . . ." Charlie began, but stopped short when Smoky called again.

"Charlie, get over here!"

"Somethin's wrong!" Charlie exclaimed. He started swimming for the bank with smooth, powerful strokes. Ty plunged in after his friend, both boys churning the water as they raced toward the creek's edge.

Charlie reached the bank first, lunging from the water and scrambling up the slope to where Smoky was just dismounting. He stopped for breath, chest heaving as he pulled air into his lungs. Worry tinged his blue eyes. While the youth stood there, Smoky was struck once again by how much he resembled his father.

"Uncle Smoky, what're you doin' here?" Charlie demanded. He'd been calling his father's Ranger partner and friend "Uncle Smoky" all his life. "Somethin's happened to my dad, hasn't it?"

Smoky hesitated for just a moment, until Ty reached Charlie's side.

"I'm afraid so, Charlie," he solemnly replied. "There was a shooting at Ranger Headquarters. Captain Trumbull's been killed, and your dad was badly wounded."

"How bad?" Charlie interrupted.

"Real bad. I'm not gonna try and sugarcoat things for you, Charlie. He was shot in his chest and belly. Doc Talmadge is doing everything he can for him, but he may not pull through."

Charlie gasped as if he'd been kicked in the gut.

"I can't believe it. You can't be right, Uncle Smoky."

"I wish I weren't," Smoky answered.

"Charlie, I'm bettin' your dad will be fine," Ty tried to reassure his friend. "He's as tough as they come. You know that."

"My Mom! Does she know what happened yet?" Charlie questioned.

"Yes, she does," Smoky replied. "She's already on her way to Austin. Luckily, she's not alone. I found her at my place, so Cindy is with her. Right now you'd better get dressed and get those horses saddled. We don't have any time to lose."

"Sure. Sure, Uncle Smoky."

Charlie and Ty hurriedly dressed, then saddled and bridled their horses. Once they had mounted, Charlie turned to Smoky and asked, "Uncle Smoky, do they know who shot my dad?"

"We believe so," Smoky replied. "Your dad told me who it was just before he lost consciousness. You'll find this almost impossible to believe, but Jim claimed it was another Ranger, Tom Foley."

"Another Ranger! Tell me he's in a cell waitin' to be hanged, or that he's already dead, shot down like he shot down my dad," Charlie replied.

40

"I honestly don't know," Smoky explained. "He already had a fairly good start before anyone realized what had happened. There were some men on his trail when I left Austin, but I have no idea of whether or not they've caught up with Foley."

Charlie's eyes turned to chips of blue ice when he fixed his gaze on Smoky. A chill went through the veteran Ranger at those eyes. They held the same grim determination as Jim's, but there was something in their depths Smoky had never seen in his partner's eyes, not even when Jim was on the trail of the outlaws who had beaten and raped his wife, shot him and his son, and left them all for dead. While Jim's could be cold with anger, Charlie's eyes glittered with an unholy fury. Smoky shuddered slightly, then had to turn away.

"I hope they haven't caught him," Charlie declared. "I want to take care of him myself. I'll fill his lousy guts full of lead, just like he did to my dad."

"Now's not the time to think about that," Ty admonished his friend. "All you need to think about right now is your dad and his recoverin'. Plus don't forget your mom's gonna need your help more'n ever until this all plays out. Far as that goes, I'll leave you when we get to the turnoff for my place. I'll let my folks know what happened and we'll take care of your animals, so don't worry about your horses or the rest of

41

your stock. First chance I get I'll ride into Austin. Meantime, my prayers are with your dad."

"That's good advice," Smoky added. "You should listen to Ty, Charlie. Now let's get movin'."

Not giving Charlie the chance to retort, he touched his spurs to Soot's flanks, putting him into a gallop.

Chapter Four

Charlie headed straight for Doctor Talmadge's small private hospital, which was located a couple of blocks from Ranger Headquarters. He found his mother and Cindy waiting anxiously in the front room. He hurried to Julia and hugged her.

"I got here as quick as I could, Mom. How's Dad?"

"We don't know yet, except that he is still alive," Julia explained. "Doctor Talmadge is working on him. He's come out a couple of times to keep us informed as much as possible, but hasn't given us anything definite. I'm certainly glad you got here so quickly Charlie, just in case . . ."

Her voice trailed off.

"Julia, don't even think that way," Cindy admonished her. "Jim's not going to die. He's too stubborn for that, and Doctor Talmadge is the same. He hates to lose a patient, so he won't give up on your husband without a fight. You need to have faith."

"Cindy's right, Mom," Charlie added. "Besides, I have a feelin' the Good Lord's not quite ready for Dad yet."

"See, Julia. That's the same thing Reverend

Baker said when he came by," Cindy continued, referring to one of the Ranger chaplains. "When God's ready to call Jim home, it will be on His schedule, and there's nothing any of us can do about that. All we can do is pray that His will be done."

"I realize that, but it's so difficult," Julia answered.

"Of course it is," Cindy sympathized.

"Did Doc Talmadge give you any idea when we can see Dad?" Charlie asked.

"Not yet. Evidently he's still trying to stop the bleeding," Cindy answered. "Charlie, where's Smoky?"

"He had to go by our place and pick up a fresh horse. Soot was plumb done in," Charlie replied. "He'll be along shortly, since he wants to get on the trail of that renegade Ranger who shot Dad and killed Captain Trumbull as badly as I do."

"Charlie, you can't even think about that," Julia objected. "You're not old enough to join the Rangers. Leave that up to Smoky and his partners."

"I didn't say anything about joining the Rangers," Charlie retorted. "I said I'm goin' after the man who did this, and nothing or nobody can stop me."

"Julia, Charlie, this isn't the time to argue over that," Cindy cautioned. "Let's just worry about Jim. Once we know for certain he's going to recover, then you can discuss what to do about the man who shot him."

Before either could answer, the door to the back room opened and Doctor Talmadge appeared. He was tall, with a full salt and pepper beard and hair. Spectacles covered his soft brown eyes, which reflected his kindly nature.

"Doctor, is Jim . . ." Julia began.

"He's stable for now," the physician began. "I can't promise you what his prognosis will be."

"Can't you give us anything more than that?" Charlie questioned.

"I was about to, if you'll let me continue," Talmadge answered.

"Of course, Doctor. Please go on," Julia urged, with a warning glance at her son.

"Thank you. As you're aware, Jim was shot in his chest and abdomen at fairly close range. I was unable to remove the bullet in his chest without endangering the chance for Jim's survival even more. That slug will have to remain inside his chest for the rest of his life. Fortunately, it did miss his lungs, and with any luck it won't bother him all that much once the scar tissue finishes forming around it."

"What about the bullet in my dad's gut?" Charlie demanded.

"Charlie, please," Julia said.

"I'm coming to that, son," Talmadge continued. "Obviously that's the more serious wound, and the one I'm most concerned about. It appears, as best I can tell, that the bullet did miss your father's intestines, which is really good news. I'm sure you're aware that if the bullet had penetrated his intestines, Jim's odds of survival would be nil."

Talmadge paused, then continued.

"The bullet went completely through Jim's body and exited from his back. From the path it took, my best opinion is it went straight through his liver without hitting any other vital organs. That's important, because medical science has learned quite a bit in the last several years. One thing we now know is that the liver is fairly good at repairing itself in a relatively short amount of time. However, clearly there is still a great chance of infection. In addition, there are several other organs quite close to or even shadowing the liver, including the kidneys, intestines, and lower lobe of the right lung. I have no way of knowing for certain whether the bullet nicked or pierced any of those organs. Truthfully, it would be miraculous if it didn't. In addition, just the shock from the impact may well have caused injury to these. Again, how serious the damage might be I have no way of knowing. Only time will tell."

"How soon will you know, Doctor?" Julia asked.

"Several weeks, at least," Talmadge replied. "Obviously the main concern right now is loss of blood. I have stopped most of the bleeding; however, there is of course internal bleeding which I can do little about. Fortunately the bullet must have missed all the major arteries and veins, or Jim would have already bled to death."

"What about infection?" Cindy queried.

"That's my biggest worry. With wounds as serious as these, particularly abdominal wounds, the chance of infection and subsequent blood poisoning is quite high. If either sets in Jim will have quite the struggle to survive."

"What you're saying is my dad has little chance of pulling through," Charlie said.

"I'm saying he has a less than 50-50 chance, that's true," Talmadge replied. "However, let's look at the positives. Your dad's a strong man who has a powerful will to live. The chest wound, while serious, should be survivable unless infection sets in. If what I believe is true, and by some miracle the bullet which went through his abdomen only struck the liver, then Jim's chances of survival are far greater than for most gut-shot victims. Perhaps most importantly, your dad has a strong faith in God. That faith may very well be the difference between his living and dying. I've done everything I can for him from a medical standpoint. I urge all of you to pray for Jim's recovery. That's the best possible medicine."

"We'll do that, Doctor," Julia assured him.

"We certainly will," Cindy agreed. "Julia, I'll stop by St. Cecelia's and let Father Biron know what's happened, so your parish family can pray for Jim. I'll tell Reverend Howell at our church too, so our members will also pray for him."

"That's the Catholics and Methodists praying for him," Doctor Talmadge smiled. "Add in my good Baptist prayers, and Jim is in the best possible hands."

Talmadge hesitated for a moment, then continued.

"One other concern is that Jim will need someone with him round the clock for the next three weeks, at least. That will be a great strain on my two nurses, especially since I have other patients who also need attention."

"Doctor, obviously I'll be staying with Jim. I can help care for him, which will take some of the burden off your staff," Julia stated.

"But you know little about nursing," Talmadge protested.

"I know a good deal more than you realize," Julia explained. "My father was a frontier physician, and I was his assistant. I know nearly as much about gunshot or knife wounds, broken bones, and many other injuries as most doctors, meaning no disrespect. In fact, I first met Jim after he'd been badly injured by a gang of outlaws. I nursed him back to health. So you see, I'm perfectly capable of tending to my husband."

"I'll also help," Cindy added. "I'm positive Michele Tremblay will want to give a hand too, as well as Brianna. Maria Justus is another, and I'm certain plenty other of San Leanna's women also."

"Even some of the menfolk will pitch in," Charlie added. "Doc, you'll have all the help you'll need."

Talmadge rubbed his jaw thoughtfully.

"Yes, that might work," he conceded. "As long as all of you are willing to follow my orders, or those of my nurses. My wife Elmira will also be assisting as needed."

"Of course we'll do that," Cindy assured him.

"Then I'm willing to let you try," Talmadge agreed.

"Can we see Jim yet?" Julia pleaded.

"In a little while," Talmadge promised. "I'd prefer to give him a little more time to stabilize. I'll be checking his wounds again shortly to make sure the bleeding has indeed slowed or perhaps even stopped. Once I've finished you can stay with him as long as you'd like. However, I do have to warn you he probably won't realize you're there."

"He'll know," Julia responded. "He may not be able to tell us, but he'll know."

The door opened and Smoky hurried into the room.

"Got here as fast as I could. How's Jim?" he burst out.

"He's still alive, and has a chance," Talmadge answered him.

"Thank God!" Smoky exclaimed. "Any word on Foley, the man who shot him? Has he been tracked down?"

"Not as far as we know," Cindy answered. "Unless something's happened in the past few minutes, Foley's still on the loose. I'm glad you're here. The adjutant general asked me to have you report to him once you arrived. He's waiting at his office."

"Adjutant General King wants to see me?" Smoky repeated, clearly puzzled. "Are you certain?"

"Positive," Cindy confirmed. "He stopped by to see how Jim was doing, and specifically mentioned you were to report to him immediately upon your arrival. He knew you'd come here before you did anything else, and asked once you checked on Jim for you to go straight to his office."

"Reckon I'd better head on over there and see what he wants then," Smoky said. "Soon as I'm done with the adjutant I'll come right back here. And Julia, Charlie, don't worry. Jim's too ornery a cuss to let a mere couple of bullets kill him. It'd take a lot more than that to finish him off. He'll be good as new in a few weeks. As he'd say, I'd bet a hat on it."

"I appreciate that, Smoky," Julia replied.

50

"Before you leave, Uncle Smoky, are you goin' after Foley?" Charlie questioned.

"Sure am," Smoky replied. "Soon as I'm done with Adjutant King, I'll stop back here to say adios to your dad, then get on the trail."

"I'm goin' with you," Charlie flatly stated.

"No, you sure ain't," Smoky replied, with equal determination. "Your place is here with your ma and pa. They need you more'n ever right now. Besides, you're too young and inexperienced to take after a man like Tom Foley. He's been a Ranger for years and knows all the tricks of the trade, both from a lawman's and outlaw's standpoint. All you'd do if I let you go after Foley with me would be get in the way and get yourself killed . . . probably both of us, for that matter."

"You can't stop me," Charlie objected. "I'm goin' after Foley no matter what."

"You try that and I'll have you tossed in jail for interferin' with the law," Smoky snapped. "And if somehow you did manage to find Foley and kill him I'd have to arrest you for murder."

Smoky's voice softened.

"Listen, son, I know how you feel. Jim's your dad, and he's been my best friend for years. Heck, he's saved my life more'n once. There ain't nothin' I wouldn't do for him, or him for me. Right now I'm doin' this for him. You stay here with your folks, Charlie. The Rangers'll take care of that turncoat Foley."

"Listen to Smoky, Charlie," Cindy urged. "You know he's telling you the truth."

Charlie's face became downcast as he turned to his mother.

"Mom, you know that I need to do this. I won't rest until the man who shot Dad and murdered Captain Trumbull hangs, but what do you want me to do? I'll stay here if you say I should."

"Charlie, I truly wish I could tell you to go after the man who shot your father, but I just can't. Not yet, anyway. I need you here with me until we see whether or not he pulls through. Besides, as Smoky says you're still too young to try and capture someone like Tom Foley. Please think about what could happen if you did find him. I might very well be losing your father. I couldn't bear it if anything happened to you too."

Charlie's shoulders drooped as he heaved a great sigh.

"All right, Mom. I can't fight all of you," he conceded, crestfallen.

Smoky slapped the youngster on his back.

"You made the right decision, Charlie. Don't worry, I'll save a piece of Foley for you."

"Just put a couple of slugs through his belly for me, that's all I ask," Charlie replied. "I want him to die real slow. He needs to suffer just like my dad's sufferin'."

"He'll suffer even more with the humiliation of a trial, then a public hanging," Cindy pointed out.

"I know this is something you don't want to hear right now, Charlie, but let justice take its course."

"That's good advice," Doctor Talmadge agreed. "Now I'd better get back to my patient."

"And I'd better not keep Adjutant King waitin' any longer," Smoky noted. "I'll be back soon as I can. Tell Jim he's buyin' the drinks."

A few moments later Smoky was placing his borrowed horse in a carriage shed behind the Texas State Capitol. He unsaddled the gelding, filled a bucket with water for him, and tossed some hay to the weary mount. That done, he headed for a side door to the capitol building, where a lone guard waited for him. Since it was now well after dark, the building was empty save for a few watchmen and the Adjutant General.

"Howdy, Jake," Smoky greeted the sentry.

"Howdy, Smoky. Adjutant King's waiting for you in his office."

"Muchas gracias."

Smoky hurried down a long, dimly lit corridor until he came to the adjutant's office. The heavy oak door, with "W.H. King, Adjutant General" lettered in gold leaf on its frosted window, was partially ajar. Smoky knocked on the frame, then entered the walnut paneled chamber.

King was behind his desk, studying a map of Texas. He glanced up at Smoky's approach, then stood and offered his hand.

"Corporal McCue, I'm pleased you were so prompt in getting here," he stated. "Do you have any further word on Lieutenant Blawcyzk's condition? I was certain you'd stop to check on him first."

"You're right, sir," Smoky admitted, with a rueful smile. "Jim's still alive, but Doc Talmadge sure isn't makin' any promises. Jim's not gonna give up without a fight, though."

"Neither is Doctor Talmadge," King smiled.

"Boy howdy, that's for certain," Smoky agreed. "What about Tom Foley? Any sign of him yet?"

King shook his head.

"I'm afraid not," he replied. "He was tracked to the rail yards, but then the trail disappeared. Several railroad men recall seeing him, but none of them saw him get on a train, so as best we can figure he must have jumped a freight. He's probably miles from Austin by now, in which direction, we have no idea."

"How about his horse? Any sign of it?" Smoky questioned.

"No," King answered. "He must have taken it onto a box car with him. We've got the railroad checking all points, of course, but most likely Foley will get off at a whistle stop or water tank, sometime in the middle of the night. It's unlikely he'd be stupid enough to let someone see him leave whatever train he's on."

"So he's got a good start on us, and we have no

clue as to where he's headed," Smoky observed. "Sir, with all due respect, I'd like to know why you called me here when I could have already started on Foley's trail."

"That's exactly why I summoned you here, Corporal. I have another plan in mind."

"What do you mean, sir?"

"I'm keeping you here in Austin, for the time being at least."

"You can't mean that!" Smoky exploded. "Jim Blawcyzk is my riding pard and best friend. I won't rest easy until Foley is in custody or dead."

"Neither will I," King replied. "Neither will I. However, right now I feel you can be more valuable to the Rangers, and the search for Tom Foley, right here at Ranger Headquarters."

"You'd better explain that, sir."

"Of course." King gestured to the coffee pot on the stove in the corner. "Why don't you get a cup of coffee and take a seat? Have a smoke if you wish."

"All right," Smoky reluctantly agreed. He poured himself a cup of the thick black brew, then rolled and lit a quirly, while King did the same. Smoky settled onto a leather chair, and King sat behind his desk. He leaned forward, dark eyes fixed on Smoky with a steady gaze.

"Corporal, even if you started after Tom Foley tonight, you wouldn't make much progress. It's getting on toward midnight, so you couldn't possibly do any trailing until sunup. Also, look at yourself. Do you realize just how exhausted you are?"

"That doesn't matter," Smoky protested.

"Yes it does," King insisted. "You would need to be at one hundred percent to try and locate Foley. He's been a Ranger for a long time, as you know, so he won't be easy to find. Plus don't forget he's already killed Captain Trumbull and gunned down Jim Blawcyzk. He'd have no compunction about killing again, particularly if he were cornered."

King paused, took a long drag on his cigarette, then continued.

"There are several men who will be trailing Foley. In addition, I've sent wires to all Ranger company commanders in the field telling them to be on the lookout for Foley. Naturally, all local law enforcement personnel will also be notified."

"So where does that leave me?" Smoky demanded.

"As I've already said, I want you here, at least for the time being. I'm appointing Jim Huggins temporary captain, to take charge in Captain Trumbull's place until a permanent replacement is chosen. Huggins has been notified and will arrive here sometime tomorrow. You'll be working directly with him."

"Sergeant Huggins would be a good choice to

hold that position permanently himself," Smoky noted.

"That may well turn out to be the case," King answered. "Also you'll be promoted to Sergeant, effective immediately."

"Thank you, sir. I appreciate that."

"You deserve it, Sergeant McCue," King grinned. "As for what you'll be doing, we need to investigate why Tom Foley murdered Hank Trumbull in cold blood. It must have been pre-meditated, since he shot Trumbull three times in the back. I want you to go through all the records you can find which Trumbull had on Foley. There should be something in there which will give us an idea why Foley felt he had to kill Trumbull."

"And Jim," Smoky reminded him.

"And Jim, although I am almost certain Jim just happened to be in the wrong place at the wrong time. He surprised Foley, who had no choice but to shoot Blawcyzk or be shot himself."

"And if Foley'd succeeded in killing Jim there would have been no one to identify him as Captain Trumbull's killer," Smoky pointed out.

"That's correct. Now, in addition to looking for Foley's motive, you'll also be checking into his background . . . habits, friends, relatives, places where he's been assigned, where he liked to travel when off duty, things like that. With any luck, you'll find something which will give us a hint where Foley has gone. Once you figure that out, then you can go after him," King concluded.

"I understand, sir. Much as I'd like to get right after Foley, your plan makes sense. It'll make for less of a wild goose chase since as you said, Foley will be real good at coverin' his tracks. I'll get started going through those files as soon as Sergeant, I mean Captain, Huggins arrives."

"There's no need to wait for him. You can begin working your way through those records first thing in the morning."

King stretched and yawned.

"It's been a long, hard day, and tomorrow promises to be even longer and harder. In addition to my usual duties and now this case, I have to make the arrangements for Hank Trumbull's funeral services. I suggest we both get whatever rest we can for what's left of the night. Why don't you meet me at Ranger Headquarters at eight tomorrow morning? You can start right in on digging through the captain's papers then."

"All right," Smoky agreed. "Only I'm heading back to Doc Talmadge's first, to see how Jim's doing. I'd imagine Julia and Charlie will stay the night there. Mebbe he'll have a bed for my wife, too. I'll bunk at the Headquarters barracks."

"I'll ride along with you, since that's the same thing I was planning on," King answered as he came from behind his desk. "Perhaps with any luck at all Doctor Talmadge will have some good news for us, then we'll all be able to sleep better.

Chapter Five

Captain Hank Trumbull's funeral was held two days later at the Antioch Baptist Church, with full Masonic rites. The captain, as were many of the Rangers, had been a Mason for most of his adult life. The sanctuary was filled to overflowing by fellow lawmen, politicians, including even the Governor and Lieutenant Governor, friends, and many ordinary citizens who wanted to bid the captain farewell. Charlie Blawcyzk was also in attendance, interrupting his vigil at his gravely wounded father's bedside to pay his family's respects. After the service Captain Trumbull was laid to rest in the Gates of Heaven Cemetery, next to his beloved wife Maisie and their daughter.

The mood at the funeral was of course somber, mixed with an angry impatience from the Rangers in attendance. That anger came near the boiling point after Trumbull had been buried and the Rangers repaired to the Silver Star Saloon for drinks. The men vented their frustration on Adjutant General King and the man appointed to take the late captain's place, Jim Huggins.

"Captain Huggins, just what the devil are you doing about runnin' Tom Foley to ground?" Dade French demanded. "Hank Trumbull, as fine a man as ever rode for the Rangers, is lyin' in his grave, and Jim Blawcyzk's layin' in a bed with a bullet in his chest and a .45 caliber hole through his guts, most likely dyin'. Meantime while Foley's runnin' loose you've only got a few men searchin' for him. The rest of us are either stuck here in Austin or on other assignments."

"Yeah, and those who aren't have been ordered to return to their companies as fast as possible," Vince McMahon added. "Seems to me we should all be out lookin' for Foley."

The others present grumbled their assent.

Huggins took a swallow of his beer before framing his reply.

"Listen to me, all of you," he began. "You know full well I can't have every man in the Rangers searchin' blindly for Tom Foley. He knows just about every inch of the state, and I'm betting has friends willing to help him. He won't be easy to find."

"He won't be found at all if you don't send anyone after him," French muttered. "Why's Smoky McCue not leadin' the hunt? He's Jim Blawcyzk's best friend."

"Let me answer that, Captain," Adjutant General King said before Huggins could respond. "Smoky McCue *is* leading the search for Tom Foley, working directly under my orders. As Captain Huggins has said, calling in the entire Ranger force to have them look for one man is impossible. First, it would be a wild goose chase without some direction in which to begin searching. Second, we still have our duty to enforce the laws of this state and protect her citizens. Outlaws aren't going to stop their depredations just so we can concentrate all our resources on finding one man. We will be conducting a thorough, methodical search for Foley. Rest assured, I want him captured every bit as all of you. Hank Trumbull was my friend, and I will not rest until his killer is behind bars. However, we do have to face the reality that we may very well have a long quest ahead of us before our quarry is found."

"I think General King speaks for all of us," Captain Huggins concluded. "If you have no objections, sir, I'd like to explain a bit more to the men how we'll be handling this search."

"Of course, Captain," King agreed.

"Men, the first thing we need to find out is why Tom Foley suddenly went renegade, seemingly without reason, and murdered Captain Trumbull. Sergeant McCue and I are going through all of the files on Foley, hoping to find some hint as to what made him go bad. We'll also be looking for anything at all which could give us some idea where he headed. We'll be checking Foley's personnel records, ascertaining who his friends and associates were, any past relationships, women in his life, his financial status . . . in short everything about the man. Somewhere in Foley's files or Captain Trumbull's records we'll turn up something that will lead us to him. I have every confidence in that."

"Or as Jim Blawcyzk would say, bet a hat on it," Smoky broke in, to chuckles from the assembled Rangers.

"That's right," Huggins grinned. "In addition, we will spare every Ranger we possibly can to look for Foley. All county and local law enforcement personnel have been notified. As you are aware, there's been a thousand dollar reward posted for the apprehension of Tom Foley. That will certainly attract some bounty hunters, which will mean more men searching for him. We're spreading a noose for Foley, and sooner or later it will tighten around his neck. There's not a rock in Texas he can hide under which we won't turn over, sooner or later."

"You think Foley intended to also shoot down Jim?" Duffy McGlynn questioned.

"We're almost positive he didn't," Huggins explained. "Jim had already left Headquarters, then returned for some reason. He stumbled onto Foley just after he'd shot the captain, so Foley had no choice but to gun Jim and kill him. Fortunately, he didn't quite succeed."

"At least we hope not," French stated.

"You know Jim Blawcyzk as well as I do, Dade," Huggins responded. "He's not gonna give up without a fight. I don't think two bullets are enough to kill him."

"Not even with one through his guts?" French insisted.

"Not even with one through his guts," Huggins reassured him. "Besides, he told Smoky he knew Trumbull was shot, so you know Jim's not gonna quit, not until he knows Foley will pay for what he did. Now it's high time we all got back to work. That'll be the best way to show our respect for Captain Trumbull, and the way he'd want it. Finish your drinks, then those of you who have to head back to your companies take the rest of the day off. Get a good night's sleep and ride out first thing in the morning. Same goes for the men stationed in Austin. You have the rest of the day for yourselves, but no more drinkin'. I want every one of you fit for work tomorrow."

"Beggin' your pardon, Cap'n, but I'd just as soon get back to plowin' through those files," Smoky requested.

"Good, because that's exactly what I'm going to do," Huggins replied.

"Just a few more words," Adjutant King called. "Men, I know all of you feel Captain Trumbull's loss deep inside. The Texas Rangers will never be the same without him. He inspired a lot of good men to do their best, and go above and beyond what they thought they could do. Before we leave, let's lift our glasses in a toast to Captain Hank Trumbull."

Silently, the Rangers raised their drinks.

"To Captain Hank Trumbull!" King declared.

"To Captain Hank Trumbull!" the men shouted in response.

Charlie Blawcyzk didn't go to the cemetery for Captain Trumbull's burial, but hurried back to Doctor Talmadge's hospital as soon as the church service concluded. Julia was at Jim's bedside, holding his hand. Charlie gently kissed her on the cheek.

"Dad still doing okay, Mom?" he asked.

"He's about the same, which Doctor Talmadge assures me is good news. He says not to expect any changes for the better quite yet," Julia answered.

Jim was covered to his chin, freshly changed bandages over his wounds. His breathing was shallow but regular, his flesh tone almost the pallor of death. However, there was no sign of fever and he was resting quietly.

"How was the service for Captain Trumbull?" Julia inquired.

"It was real crowded, as you'd expect," Charlie replied. "The preacher did a fine job with his sermon, and thank goodness the eulogies weren't too long. The choir's singing was also real pretty. All in all, I'd guess if you have to have a funeral the Captain's was as much as you could ask for."

"I wish I could have been there for him, but I just couldn't leave your father," Julia said.

"I know, Mom. Captain Trumbull would have understood. In fact, he would have wanted you to stay with Dad."

Charlie looked more closely at his mother, who was clearly at the point of exhaustion.

"Mom, have you slept at all?" he asked.

"I've catnapped a bit," Julia said.

"How about eating? Have you tried even a bite?"

"I'm not really hungry, Charlie."

"You have to eat, Mom," Charlie answered. "You need to keep up your strength. You won't do yourself or Dad any good if you get sick."

"I know that," Julia answered, a bit more harshly than she intended, "but I just can't bring myself to eat. I really don't have much of an appetite."

"You've gotta take some nourishment," Charlie insisted. "Tell you what. I have to care for the horses sometime today. Now's as good a time as any. I'll do that, then swing by that restaurant down the street and pick up something for both of us. Anything in particular you might like?"

"I'm not certain, perhaps some soup, nothing too heavy."

"That's a start," Charlie said. "How about some

stew if they have any? It would be a bit more filling than soup."

"All right," Julia agreed. "You'd also better stop and get some peppermints for Sam and Sizzle on your way. Your dad would be really upset if he found out his horses weren't getting their treats."

She managed a slight smile.

"Boy howdy, that's for certain," Charlie grinned in return. "I'd bet my hat on it."

"Not you too," Julia moaned. "It's bad enough I have to listen to your father say that all the time. Now you've started."

"Sorry, Mom. Didn't even realize I'd said it. Is there anything you need before I go?"

"I don't think so."

"All right. I'll be back quick as I can."

Charlie kissed her again, touched Jim's shoulder, and then headed off for the Ranger stables.

He first stopped at a general store where he purchased a small sack of peppermints. Once he'd obtained those, he continued to Ranger Headquarters, where Sam and Sizzle, along with his own horse, Ted, were temporarily stabled. Charlie had to resist the temptation to go inside the Headquarters building to see if there was any further news on the hunt for Tom Foley. Instead, he turned into the barn, where the horses nickered an eager greeting to him.

"Howdy guys," Charlie called. "Got some candies right here for you." He gave each horse a peppermint, then got down their brushes from a wall shelf. He first groomed Ted thoroughly, then turned his attention to his father's paints.

Sam nuzzled Charlie impatiently as the youngster rubbed him down, whickering questioningly. Because Sam had known Charlie since the boy had been born—in fact when Charlie was only six months old Jim had placed him on Sam's back for his first ride—Charlie was the only person besides Jim whom Sam fully trusted, and allowed to handle him without hesitation. The big sour-tempered paint had also over the years reached a truce with Jim's wife, Julia. From the adjacent stall, Sizzle added his own puzzled whinny.

"I know, I know, you both miss Dad somethin' fierce," Charlie sympathized, patting Sam's neck and rubbing Sizzle's nose. "Look at it this way. You're both gonna have a chance to relax and take a nice long rest. In a few weeks Dad'll be up and around, and then he'll run the legs off you both trackin' down outlaws again, so enjoy the time off while you've got it."

Charlie spent over an hour brushing the three horses, lost in thought.

"I'll be back in the morning to check on you again," he promised them, with a last pat to Ted's shoulder. After giving each a final peppermint,

Charlie proceeded to a small restaurant he'd noticed, the Capitol Café, which was located only two blocks from Doctor Talmadge's. From the outside it appeared bright and cheery, with lace curtains in the windows and flowers on the sills. When he stepped inside, the tantalizing odors of various foods cooking set his mouth watering.

Since it was now mid-afternoon, the place wasn't crowded. Charlie walked past tables covered with red-checked cloths and took a seat at the counter. A motherly waitress noticed the worried expression on his face and smiled kindly at the boy.

"Good afternoon, son. Are you looking for something to eat?"

"I sure am," Charlie smiled in return. "Do you happen to have any stew or, if not, some soup?"

"I surely do. I make the best beef stew in the entire county, if I do say so myself. I'll bring a bowl right out for you. I've got fresh-baked bread and newly churned butter to go with it."

"That sure sounds good, ma'am," Charlie replied. "But I don't want to eat it here. I'd like two orders to take with me, if I might. I'll be sure and bring back your dishes and silverware."

"That would be all right long as you do, and as long as you stop calling me ma'am. My name's Ruby."

"All right . . . Ruby. Mine's Charlie. I'll return

your things soon as my mom and I are done eatin'."

"Your mom?"

"Yeah. She's at Doc Talmadge's, keepin' watch over my dad. She's so worried about him she hasn't eaten for some time, but I finally talked her into trying to, I hope. I'm worried enough about him myself, and sure don't want to have to worry about her too."

"My stew should convince her to eat all right," Ruby assured him. "What's wrong with your dad, if you don't mind my asking? Is he very ill?"

"No. My Dad's a Texas Ranger," Charlie explained. "He was shot by the same man who killed Captain Trumbull."

"Your dad's Jim Blawcyzk? I should have known," Ruby exclaimed. "You're the spitting image of him."

"You know my dad?" Charlie questioned.

"Sure do. He eats here quite often. That man sure loves his food, especially his sweets. It made me just sick to hear about him and Captain Trumbull. How's he doin'?"

"That's my dad all right," Charlie grinned. "And so far he's holdin' his own. He's pretty tough, so he won't give up easy."

"I'll say a prayer for him," Ruby promised.

"Thank you. He'd appreciate that," Charlie answered.

"Everyone needs prayers one time or another,"

Ruby replied. "Now I'd better get your food. You don't want to keep your mom waiting."

"Much obliged."

Ruby disappeared into the kitchen, but soon returned with a covered tray which she placed in front of Charlie.

"Here you go, son. There's two bowls of stew, bread and butter, and I added a couple slices of apple pie. Would you like a pot of coffee to take along?"

"No thanks, that won't be necessary," Charlie replied. "Doc Talmadge's wife has kept a pot warm for us, so this will be fine. How much do I owe you?"

"Not a thing, it's on the house," Ruby answered.

"I can't let you do that," Charlie protested.

"I won't take your money," Ruby retorted. "You just make sure your mom eats. Once I hear she's doing that, it will be payment a-plenty. Don't worry about hurrying the dishes back here, either. Whenever you get the chance is soon enough."

"All right," Charlie reluctantly conceded. "Muchas gracias. I've got to come this way again tomorrow to check on our horses, so I'll bring the plates back then. Adios."

"Adios to you also, and don't fret. Your dad is gonna be up and around before you know it, Charlie."

"Thanks again for your kindness, Ruby. See you soon."

70

● ● ●

Charlie returned to find his mother still at his father's bedside, continuing to hold Jim's hand.

"Sorry, Mom. I took a little longer than planned, but I've brought you some nice hot stew and bread and butter to go with it. There's even some apple pie. It turns out the lady who owns that restaurant knows Dad. She said he eats there quite a bit when he's in Austin."

"It sure smells delicious, Charlie," Julia admitted. "Perhaps I am a bit hungry after all."

"All right, then."

Charlie uncovered the tray and placed a bowl of stew, along with some bread and butter, on the bedside table.

"You start eating, Mom. I'll go get some coffee. Be right back."

Charlie left Jim's room, returning a few minutes later with a coffee pot and two mugs. Accompanying him were Doctor Talmadge and his wife, Elmira.

"Charlie tells me you're finally going to take some nourishment, Julia. I'm certainly glad of that," the doctor said. "I was getting worried about you."

"My stomach was so upset I don't think I could have kept anything down until now," Julia answered.

"You know these men, always more worried about us than they need be," Elmira answered, with a smile for her husband. "We're a lot stronger than they realize. My, that stew does smell delicious."

"It's really tasty, perhaps even better than what I make," Julia admitted.

"Then as long as you don't need us for the moment, we'll leave you and Charlie to have your meal in peace," Elmira said. "Calvin, you'd better eat your own dinner before your afternoon patients arrive. I've got some roast beef sandwiches ready for you."

"All right, dear," Talmadge complied. "Julia, Charlie, I'll be back to check on Jim and change his bandages in a couple of hours. If you need me in the meantime, just holler."

"We'll do that, Doctor," Julia assured him.

Once the Talmadges had departed, Charlie and Julia fell to their meal, eating mostly in silence. When his mother had finished her stew, Charlie passed her one of the slices of apple pie. As he did, Jim moaned softly and his nostrils twitched.

"Mom, look. I think Dad realizes we've got some pie here," Charlie exclaimed.

"I believe you might be right, Charlie," Julia agreed. "Perhaps that's a good sign."

"I'm positive it is, Mom. Wish he could have some right now. You'll have to eat it for him."

"No, Charlie, you have this pie. I'm full," Julia said, passing the slice back to him. "Besides, I know how much you enjoy your sweets, just like your father does."

"I'm not gonna argue with you, Mom, that's for certain," Charlie answered. He polished off his piece of pie, then Julia's.

Once they had finished their meal, they remained with Jim, sitting quietly and taking turns holding his hand or putting wet cloths on his forehead.

"Mom," Charlie finally said, "I know how you feel about me leaving and taking off after the skunk who shot Dad, but I just can't stay here any longer doin' nothing. I've got to try and find Tom Foley."

"Charlie, you promised me you wouldn't," Julia objected.

"I know, but I'm asking you not to hold me to that promise," Charlie pleaded. "Please try and understand."

"I do understand," Julia replied, "However, you need to take my feelings into consideration. Look at your father, lying there with two bullet holes in him. Do you know what it would do to me if the same thing happened to you? I can't bear the thought of losing you, too."

"Mom, you wait and see, Dad's gonna be all right, and I promise I won't let anything happen to me. Don't forget, Dad's been helping me train to be a Ranger for years. I know what I'm doin'."

"But you can't just take off like this, Charlie. What would your father say?"

"That's right, Mom. What would he say?" Charlie rejoined.

Julia hesitated while tears welled in her eyes.

"He'd tell you to go after Foley," she reluctantly conceded. "And I have to admit deep down inside, this nagging voice keeps telling me to let you do just that, much as I despise myself for it."

"Then you'll let me go?"

"I couldn't stop you in any event, could I?" Julia challenged.

"No, Mom, I guess you couldn't," Charlie ruefully admitted.

"May I ask if you'll do me one favor?"

"Anything, Mom. What is it?"

"Wait until morning, then stop at Ranger Headquarters and ask Captain Huggins for his advice. Perhaps you can convince him to let you work with the Rangers, even if not in an official capacity. The last thing you would need to do is get in trouble with the law. You can't take it into your own hands. That would go against everything your father has ever stood for, every lesson he's ever taught you. You wouldn't do that to him, would you?"

"Of course I wouldn't, Mom. Thanks for bringing me back to my senses. You're right, I could never forgive myself if I did anything to make Dad ashamed of me. I'll do what you ask and go see Captain Huggins first thing tomorrow."

"If you will, that would ease my mind considerably," Julia said. "If you can somehow talk the captain into allowing you to assist the Rangers, then I won't stand in your way."

"I'd never want to hurt you, Mom. You know that," Charlie answered, squeezing her hand. "It's just what I have to do."

"I know, Charlie. Now I realize it's still early, but you had better get some rest. You'll need it if Captain Huggins agrees to your plan, and you haven't slept much more than I have."

"All right, Mom. What about you, though?"

"I'll sleep here in this chair as I've been doing. You use the bed in the next room Doctor Talmadge has set aside for us."

"Okay, but you call me if anything changes or you need something. Wake me up when Doc Talmadge comes to check on Dad again, too."

"I'll do that," Julia promised. "Good night, Charlie."

"Good night, Mom."

Charlie kissed his mother, squeezed his father's shoulder, then headed for bed. He said his evening prayers and quickly undressed. More tired than he'd realized from the past few days' events, he was asleep almost as soon as his head hit the pillow. Despite her assurances, Julia didn't wake him when Doctor Talmadge made his last check on Jim for the day, allowing the boy to sleep through the rest of the afternoon, straight through to dawn.

Captain Jim Huggins looked up when a soft knock came at his office door just after seven o'clock the next morning. He was a bit startled to see Charlie standing there.

"Howdy, Charlie. Come on in, son."

"Thank you, Captain," Charlie replied, stepping into the cramped room.

"What brings you by so early?" Huggins asked. "Nothing's happened to your dad, has it?"

"No sir, he's still the same, unconscious but resting as comfortably as he can. Doctor Talmadge was with him when I left. The doc says there's still no sign of infection, which is a good thing. Other than that, all we can do is wait and pray."

"We're all doing that," Huggins assured the boy. "Is that why you stopped by, to let us know how your dad's doing, or is there another reason?"

"There is. I came by to talk to you, sir."

"All right, take a seat and tell me what's on your mind, Charlie."

Charlie sat in a corner chair and pulled off his Stetson, fidgeting with the hat and twisting it nervously in his hands.

"Captain Huggins, I can't sit idly by any longer while Tom Foley is still on the loose," he began.

"I want to help track him down, and the only way I can do that legally is by joining the Rangers. I came to ask you to sign me up."

Huggins leaned back in his chair, studying the earnest young man before him, noticing the determined set of his jaw, the glittering icy blue eyes so much like Jim's. There was something in those eyes he'd never seen in Jim's, something which sent a chill up his spine. He thought carefully before framing his reply.

"Charlie, as much as I'd like to sign you on as a Texas Ranger, I don't believe it's a good idea, especially in this case. Obviously you would be too emotionally involved to be assigned to the hunt for Tom Foley. After all, he gunned down your father. There's no chance you could conduct yourself professionally and objectively under these circumstances."

"Begging your pardon, but you're wrong, Captain," Charlie protested. "I've wanted to join the Rangers as long as I can remember, ever since I was a little kid. My dad's given me plenty of lessons on how to handle myself. In fact, he told me just a couple of months ago there's nothing more he could teach me. He said all I could do now is keep practicing until I actually am a Ranger, then experience will teach me more after that. Please don't turn me down."

"It's not that simple, son," Huggins answered. "First of all, how old are you?"

"I'll turn eighteen come next May," Charlie replied.

"That's another problem, you're not old enough. You have to be at least eighteen to be eligible for the Rangers," Huggins pointed out.

"That's not necessarily true, sir," Charlie objected. "There've been Rangers as young as sixteen, even fourteen."

"You're correct, Charlie, there certainly have been. However, that's no longer the case. It was back in the old days before the War, when the Rangers were a volunteer force, that boys as young as fourteen were allowed to serve."

"Couldn't you make an exception for me?"

"I honestly don't know. Don't forget, I was just made captain when Hank Trumbull was killed, and it's a temporary appointment. As soon as a permanent replacement can be found, I'm going right back into the field. I'm not certain what the regulations would say in a case like this."

Huggins looked up when another knock came at his door. Adjutant General King stepped into the office.

"Jim, am I interrupting?" King asked.

"Not at all, General. This is Jim Blawcyzk's son, Charlie."

"Ah yes, Charlie. I recall seeing you at Captain Trumbull's funeral. How's your dad doing, son? I was heading over to see him once I took care of some paperwork that can't wait."

King and Charlie shook hands.

"His condition hasn't changed, sir. He's still unconscious but not uncomfortable. Doc Talmadge says it will probably be a few days at least before we know anything one way or the other."

"General, Charlie came by to ask if he could join the Rangers, so he can go after Tom Foley legally," Huggins stated. "Perhaps you can help explain to him why it's just not possible. I've already told him that he's too emotionally involved for us to even think about allowing him to take part in the search for Foley. In addition, he's not old enough."

"Captain Huggins is right on all counts," King agreed. "Don't worry, son. We have plenty of men looking for Foley. He won't be on the loose for long."

"General, Captain, you don't understand. I have to do this. I just can't keep sittin' in that hospital room, watchin' my dad lyin' there, not knowin' if he'll live or die. Please, can't you find some way to let me become a Ranger right now, rather'n next year?"

"Charlie, even if we did manage to bend the rules and sign you on, what about your mother? How would she feel about that?" King asked.

"My mom and I had a long talk about this last night," Charlie explained. "She's not real happy about the idea, but she understands my feelin's.

In fact, now that she understands how determined I am to go after the man who shot my dad, she told me to come here and see Captain Huggins. She said if you allowed me to join the Rangers she wouldn't stand in my way. It doesn't matter, because if you don't, I'm goin' after Foley anyway, despite how Mom feels or even what my dad might think."

King looked at the youngster, struck by the resemblance between Charlie and his father. The boy had the same blonde hair and clear blue eyes. He even wore his gun on his left hip, just like his dad. King stroked his jaw thoughtfully. The determination reflected in those chilling eyes convinced the adjutant there was no possibility of dissuading Charlie from taking up the chase. It would be better to have him in the Rangers where he could be watched and guided, rather than out on his own, taking the law into his own hands.

"Jim, perhaps there is a way Charlie can help out," he told Huggins.

"How's that, sir?" Huggins asked.

"Please, General . . . I'll do anything you say," Charlie interjected.

"Hold on just a minute, son," King answered. To Huggins he continued, "Jim, has Sergeant McCue come up with anything in Foley's records or Captain Trumbull's files yet?"

"Not that I've heard of," Huggins replied. "He's still plowing through them."

"Then that's our answer. Charlie, would you be willing to help Sergeant McCue search through those files? He's looking for anything which would tell us why Foley murdered Captain Trumbull, or give us an idea where he might have headed."

"Of course I would," Charlie exclaimed. "Anything's better'n just sittin' around. Will that mean I'll be a Texas Ranger?"

"I guess it will," King answered. "I'll have the necessary papers drawn up, then Captain Huggins will swear you in. We'll work out the problem with your age, so don't worry about that. Just remember, as a Ranger you have to follow orders. There will be no going after Tom Foley on your own. Is that understood?"

"Perfectly, sir. I'll be a good Ranger, you wait and see."

"I'm sure you will, Charlie. One thing I know I don't have to worry about is you're havin' a good horse. Your dad would never let you ride a crow-bait mount. I'm bettin' you can ride like him, too."

King looked the youngster over once again, then chuckled.

"Something strike you as funny, General?" Huggins questioned.

"Yes, something that Jim would appreciate," King answered. "Charlie looks so much like his dad, I can't resist saying he's a chip off the old Blawcyzk."

"No!" Huggins groaned. "Actually, sir, I wish you had resisted."

"I couldn't help myself," King retorted. "What'd you think of that, Charlie?"

"I think my dad would be jealous he didn't come up with it first, sir," Charlie answered.

"There is one other problem now though, General," Huggins said.

"What's that, Jim?"

"That nickname's gonna stick to Charlie like glue," he explained, adding, "You might as well get used to it, Charlie. From now on every Ranger's gonna be callin' you Chip. I know I sure will."

"They can call me anything they want, long as I'm a Ranger," Charlie answered. "How soon can I get started?"

"Whoa, not quite so fast," King chuckled. "Why don't you go back and tell your mom what we've decided and spend a bit more time with your dad? Have dinner, then come back. By then I'll have the paperwork all ready. Captain Huggins will swear you in, then take you to Sergeant McCue."

"That's if McCue will have him," Huggins chuckled.

"Uncle Smoky won't say no, you can bet a hat on that," Charlie said.

"Chip, you'll have to remember not to call Sergeant McCue Uncle Smoky," Huggins warned him. "Also, would you please try not to say 'bet a hat' either? Leave that for your dad."

"I'll remember, leastwise about Uncle Smoky," Charlie assured him. "Not too sure about bet a hat, though. I can't help usin' that, since it reminds me of my dad."

"That's all right, son," King replied. "And Captain Huggins, I see what you mean about the nickname. You just called the boy Chip and didn't even realize it."

"I did? I'm sorry, Charlie," Huggins apologized. "I should have called you Ranger Blawcyzk."

"It's all right, Captain," Charlie said. "I'm finally a Texas Ranger."

Chapter Six

Despite her trepidation at leaving Jim, even for a short while, Julia accompanied Charlie to Ranger Headquarters for his brief swearing-in ceremony, which was little more than taking the Ranger oath and signing the enlistment papers. Even with her misgivings, Julia swelled inside with pride at seeing her son follow in his father's footsteps, something the boy had wanted since he was little more than a toddler. Her only regret was Jim could not be with her to see Charlie fulfill his lifelong dream.

Smoky McCue had also left his chore of searching through Captain Trumbull's files to watch Charlie take the Ranger oath. He had to swallow a lump in his throat at seeing the boy he'd known from an infant now grown to a young man enlisting in the Rangers and swearing to uphold and enforce the laws of Texas. Smoky was certain Jim himself couldn't have been more proud than he was at that moment.

"Congratulations, Chip. You are now officially Private Charles Edward Blawcyzk of the Texas Rangers," Adjutant King said, shaking the youngster's hand. "I know you will serve the state of Texas honorably, courageously, and well."

"Thank you, sir," Charlie answered, stepping back and touching the brim of his Stetson in a quick salute. "You can count on me."

"The same from me, Chip," Captain Huggins added.

"Thanks, Captain," Charlie answered. He turned to his mother and embraced her, kissing her on the cheek and hugging her.

"Mom, thanks for all you've done for me, and for understanding why I had to do this," he said.

"Charlie, I've always known this day would come. I've both dreaded it, and looked forward to it," Julia replied, her eyes moist. "I just wish your dad could have been here with us. He so wanted to see you become a Ranger."

"Jim will see Charlie wearing the badge, Julia," Smoky broke in. "You can be certain of that. Wanting to see his boy become a Ranger is one more reason Jim's gonna pull through."

"Thank you, Smoky," Julia answered, giving him a hug. "That means a lot."

Smoky turned to Charlie.

"Now it's my turn to say congratulations to you, Charlie," he said, giving the boy a salute. "But why's everybody callin' you Chip?"

"I'll let one of them answer your question, Uncle Smoky, I mean Sergeant McCue," Charlie responded, hastily correcting himself.

"It's a long story, and it involves General King here coming up with a pun so bad it would even make Jim groan," Captain Huggins answered. "I'll explain it on our way back to Captain Trumbull's office. Speaking of which, it's high time we all got back to work."

"You're right there," King agreed. "I've got a desk stacked with paperwork I have to get completed by tonight. Julia, I'll stop by and see Jim on my way home."

"I appreciate that," she answered. "Charlie, I'm going back to your father now. I've left him long enough."

"All right, Mom," Charlie replied. "I'll be with you tonight as soon as I can."

"I won't keep him too late, Julia," Smoky reassured her. "Cindy would have my head if I did."

Once Julia had departed, Smoky took Charlie to the room which had served as Captain Hank Trumbull's office for many years. Except for the files piled high on Trumbull's desk and scattered about, the office was exactly as Trumbull had left it the day he was killed.

"Wow! That sure is a lot of papers," Charlie exclaimed.

"I know," Smoky concurred. "That's why it's takin' me so long to try'n make heads or tails of 'em. I've found Foley's personnel file, plus some other things, and hopefully all of his assignment records and case files. I was hopin' to find something which would tell us why Foley murdered Captain Trumbull by shootin' him in the back, and then shot your dad, but so far there's nothing definite."

Smoky practically spat out the words "shootin' him in the back." If there was anyone most men hated, whether lawman or outlaw, it was a backshooter—someone who didn't have the courage to face his victim, but killed him from ambush with a bullet in the back.

"Mebbe Foley took the file you're lookin' for after he shot the captain," Charlie observed. "It was probably on the desk or in Captain Trumbull's hands. Foley grabbed the file, shoved it inside his shirt, and ran."

"That's exactly what we're beginning to think, Charlie . . . or I guess I should call you Chip," Smoky replied. "So now we're mostly lookin' for some pattern to see if we can determine where Foley might have fled, perhaps where he has friends or kin."

"There haven't been any sightings of him at all?" Charlie questioned.

"There've been plenty of them, but nothing credible," Smoky answered. "We've checked them all out, of course, but none of them have panned out. Naturally we've still got every man we can spare hunting Foley, without any luck so far. Once we have something, then we can narrow our search."

"And then can I help track him down?" Charlie questioned.

"We'll see," Smoky answered. "In the meantime, the papers on the desk are files I haven't gotten to yet. The ones on the shelf in the corner don't have anything useful, at least as far as I can tell. The others on the sofa I've gone through, and want to recheck them because they might contain some information we can use. What I'd like you to do is read over those files again, to see if you find something—anything—which I might have missed. Once you're done with those I'd like you to double-check the papers I've set aside as useless. By then I'll have gotten to more of the files I haven't read yet and will give those to you. Is that all right with you?"

"It sure is, Sergeant. I'll get started right now."

"One more thing, Char . . . Chip. This isn't the United States Army. We're not all that strict in the Rangers, so you don't need to call me Sergeant. Since you can't really call me Uncle Smoky any longer, just plain Smoky will do. Is that clear?"

"It sure is . . . Smoky," Charlie agreed.

"Good. Now get to work, Ranger."

Charlie spent the rest of that day and all of the next reading through the files Smoky had assigned him. He found a few which he set aside for further review; however, as Smoky had said, most of them contained little if any useful information.

"Boy howdy, I never knew bein' a Ranger would involve so much readin'," he complained, as he leaned back in his chair, yawned and stretched. "Dad never mentioned this."

"Your dad hates paperwork as much as you seem to," Smoky chuckled. "Then again, most of us Rangers do. Why do you think Jim Huggins is so anxious to have a permanent replacement for Hank Trumbull named? He can't stand dealing with all the paperwork and regulations a captain has to put up with. He can hardly wait to get back in the field."

"I can sure understand that," Charlie replied. "I thought I'd be on the trail by now, rather'n stuck here in Austin."

"I know it's frustrating," Smoky sympathized, "but what we're doing is every bit as important as the men out there. Don't worry, you'll have plenty of chances to spend days or weeks in the saddle, with nothing to eat but bacon, beans, and biscuits, the hard ground for a bed and your saddle for a pillow, roastin' durin' the day and freezin' your backside off at night. Enjoy this easy life while you can."

He turned and glanced at the Regulator clock ticking away the time on the wall behind him.

"Tell you what, Chip. It's past six o'clock. Let's call it a day and go check on your dad, then I'll get you and your mom some supper. Since Cindy's gonna be helping watch your dad tonight, that will give your mom a chance to get out for a bit. I know she doesn't want to leave your dad for even a minute, but she needs to take a break once in a while. We'll pick up where we left off in the morning."

"That sure sounds good, Smoky," Charlie readily agreed. "If my dad's still holding his own, I might even spend some extra time carin' for our horses later."

"That's not a bad idea," Smoky agreed. "You need some time off too, son. Let's go."

Smoky turned off the lamps and closed the office door, locking it behind them. Charlie's buckskin paint, Ted, and Smoky's steeldust, Soot, were retrieved from their stalls in the Ranger stable, then quickly saddled and bridled. It took only a few minutes for the short ride to Doctor Talmadge's small hospital. They hitched the horses to the rail out front and hurried inside.

Elmira Talmadge, the physician's wife, was in the front room when they entered. She smiled at the two Rangers.

"I'm going to tell you before you even ask, Jim seems a bit better this evening. He's also got some unexpected visitors."

"That's great news!" Charlie exclaimed. "Does that mean my dad'll be all right?"

"We just don't know yet," she replied. "But

every day that passes without a crisis is a hopeful sign."

"You mentioned visitors, Mrs. Talmadge," Smoky said. "Who are they?"

"Why don't you just go in and see for yourselves?" she answered.

"Thanks, Mrs. Talmadge. We'll do just that," Charlie said. He headed for Jim's room, Smoky right behind him.

To Charlie's surprise Ty Tremblay, his best friend, greeted him as soon as he stepped through the door.

"Howdy, pard," Ty called. " 'Bout time you showed up, although we figured you'd be along any time now."

Along with Ty were his younger sister, Brianna, as well as his parents, Mark and Michele Marie. Cindy Lou, Smoky's wife, was also present.

"Ty! You're the last person I expected to see. Hold on a minute, will you?"

Charlie crossed the room, kissed his mother's cheek, then took his father's hand.

"Mom, Mrs. Talmadge says Dad's doin' a bit better," he stated. "He looks to me like he has a bit more color."

"He does," Julia agreed. "He's also breathing a little more easily."

"That's certainly good to hear," Charlie answered.

"Charlie, I know you're surprised to see us,"

Michele Tremblay told him. "Most of the work around our place and yours is caught up, and what little is left can wait a day or two, so we decided to come into town and visit your dad. Brianna and I are also going to take our turns helping with your dad's nursing."

"You don't need to do that," Charlie said.

"We don't need to, but we want to," Brianna replied. "Don't forget, that will take some of the burden off your mother."

Charlie flushed slightly.

"I'm sorry Brianna, Mrs. Tremblay. Of course everything you're doin' is appreciated. Guess I'm just so tired I don't know what I'm sayin'."

"That's perfectly understandable, and there's no apology necessary," Michele replied. "You've been under a great deal of strain."

"Yeah, and what's this we hear about you joining the Texas Rangers?" Mark added. Like his son Ty, he was tall and lanky, standing five inches over his son's six foot height. Brianna, on the other hand, favored her mother. She was just a bit under her mother's five feet two inches tall. The entire family, though, had hair a shade of medium brown and hazel eyes. With the exception of the differences in height, their resemblance was strong.

"It's true," Charlie confirmed. "I was able to convince Adjutant General King and Captain Huggins to let me sign up."

"They even gave him a new nickname," Smoky added. "Chip."

"Chip?" Ty repeated. "How'd they come up with that?"

"Blame General King," Charlie explained. "He says I look so much like my dad I'm a chip off the old Blawcyzk, which is a real bad joke my dad would love. Anyway, the Chip part stuck."

"Well, then congratulations are in order," Brianna exclaimed, as she kissed Charlie on the cheek. Charlie blushed several shades of crimson.

"Thanks a lot, Brianna," he finally spluttered.

"You'll be a fine Ranger, Charlie," Michele assured him.

"Same goes for me," Mark added, shaking Charlie's hand.

"Thanks, all of you," Charlie answered. "What about you though, Ty? Don't you have anything to say? I figured you'd be the first one to tell me how glad you were that I made the Rangers."

To his bewilderment, Ty hadn't said a word about his appointment to the Rangers. Instead, he was standing there with a mile-wide grin on his face.

"What's there to say?" Ty replied. "It's what you've always wanted, and now you're a Ranger."

"Ty, stop tormenting Charlie," Michele ordered.

"All right, Mom. Charlie—or I guess I've gotta start callin' you Chip now—we've been in Austin since this mornin'. While you were workin', I was signin' up with the Rangers too."

"You what?" Charlie exclaimed. "But how?"

"Just walked into Headquarters, asked if they needed another man, and they signed me up," Ty answered. "My eighteenth birthday was two days ago, so I'm old enough."

"That's right, I plumb forgot about your birthday. We were gonna celebrate it at McGinty's Saloon with some of the gals from . . ." Charlie stopped short and blushed again, realizing what he'd just let slip. "Well anyway, Happy Birthday, Ty. What made you sign up with the Rangers, though? You never mentioned wantin' to do that to me."

"Thanks, Chip," Ty answered. "Far as my joinin' the Rangers, I'd had the thought in the back of my mind for some time now. I was planning on waitin' until next year when you signed up to decide for certain, however. Instead, when we got the news you had joined that made up my mind. Plus, your dad's always been real good to me and my family, and I want to help catch the hombre who gunned him down."

"I'm sure glad we're both gonna be Rangers, but I wish you'd said something sooner," Charlie said.

"I wanted to surprise you," Ty explained. "Besides, remember when we swore to be pardners forever? We sure couldn't keep that vow if you were ridin' all over Texas with the Rangers while I was back home in San Leanna."

"You sure did that," Charlie admitted. "Uncle Smoky, you knew about this, didn't you?"

"Uh-uh, you've gotta call me just plain Smoky, remember?" McCue reminded him.

"All right, Smoky. You knew," Charlie accused.

"Yep, I knew. Ty and his family swore me to secrecy, though, so I couldn't tell you. Both of you just remember there's no guarantee you'll be assigned to the same troop. You may well not be ridin' pards at all."

"We'll cross that bridge when we come to it," Charlie said. Just as he did, Doctor Talmadge entered the room.

"Hello, everyone. Listen, I hate to break up this gathering, but it's time for me to clean Jim's wounds and change his bandages," he said. "I'll be finished in about an hour. Why don't y'all take the opportunity to have a decent supper while I work on Jim? By the time you're through eating I'll have him settled for the night."

"That's a fine idea, Doctor," Cindy concurred. "Julia, take his advice."

"I'm not certain," Julia hesitated.

"Julia, have supper with your friends and son," Talmadge firmly stated. "Those are doctor's orders."

"Doctor Talmadge is right," Michele said. "You're joining us for supper."

"We won't have to go far, Mom," Charlie added. "We'll eat at the restaurant where I got you that stew. It's only a little way from here."

"If anything should happen I'll send for you immediately," Talmadge assured her.

"All right, you've convinced me," Julia reluctantly agreed.

"Good," Cindy answered. "When we return, Michele and I will take turns caring for Jim overnight so you can get a good night's rest . . . and no arguments," she concluded, when Julia started to object.

"Cindy's right," Michele added. "You'll be sleeping right in the next room, so there's no reason to worry. Let us do the nursing for one night."

"Listen to them, Julia," Mark urged.

"Yes, please do," Doctor Talmadge added. "You're on the verge of exhaustion, Julia. A full night of sleep will do wonders for you."

"I guess I can't fight all of you," Julia gave in. "You win, I'll go for supper with you."

"Now you're being reasonable," Talmadge said. "You can't help your husband if you collapse and end up in bed yourself."

"I know, Doctor," Julia admitted. "It's just that I hate leaving Jim, even for a few minutes."

"Dad'll be just fine while we're gone, Mom," Charlie said. "But we'd better head over to the café before they close."

"All right." Julia leaned over and kissed Jim.

"I'll be right back, Jim," she whispered. "Promise you won't leave me while I'm gone."

"Now I'm ready," she announced, turning from Jim's bed, her eyes moist.

"Don't hurry your supper to rush back here," Talmadge answered. "Elmira will remain with Jim until you return."

"We'll make sure Julia relaxes over a nice hot supper," Cindy promised.

"Good."

"We'd better get movin'," Smoky urged.

"All right, my impatient spouse," Cindy retorted.

A moment later, with Julia glancing back every few yards, they started the short walk to the café. At her friends' and Charlie's insistence, Julia ordered a complete dinner, including dessert. Despite her anxiety over leaving her husband, for the first time since Jim had been shot, she managed to eat a full meal.

Following supper, Charlie and Ty went to care for the horses, while the rest returned to the hospital. As Doctor Talmadge had promised, he had finished cleaning and redressing Jim's wounds and replacing the bandages. Julia settled into the chair next to his bed, the chair she'd hardly left since her arrival in Austin.

"Julia, you are not spending one more night sleeping in that chair," Cindy ordered. "That's why Michele, Brianna, and I are here. Tomorrow Maria Justus will arrive to take over from us for a few hours. Most of the other women from town will be taking turns also. Between them and Doctor Talmadge's nurses, it's not necessary for you to stay with Jim twenty-four hours a day."

"I just can't leave him," Julia objected.

"You're not leaving him," Michele pointed out. "You'll be right in the next room, within earshot. We'll call you if Jim wakes up."

"Listen to my mom, Mrs. Blawcyzk," Brianna urged. "Please get some sleep."

"Brianna's right," Cindy added. "I hate to say this, Julia, but frankly, you look awful. Why not get that sleep, then pretty yourself up a bit come morning? We've left some clean clothes for you, including a nightgown and robe. You sure don't want to have Jim come to and catch you looking a mess."

"I guess you're right," Julia finally conceded. "You promise to call me if anything changes, anything at all?"

"They promise," Mark reassured her.

"They promise," Smoky added. "So that's that."

"All right," Julia answered. "I'll see you in the morning, and I'm grateful to all of you."

"You'd do the same for us," Cindy said. "Now good night, Julia."

Julia kissed Jim once again and whispered

"Good night" to him, promising to be back at his side first thing the next morning. Once she went to the next room, she undressed, put on her nightgown, said her evening prayers, and crawled under the covers. Slumber claimed her a few moments later, and she would sleep until well after sunrise.

Chapter Seven

It was mid-morning the next day when Captain Huggins rejoined Smoky in Captain Trumbull's office. He held a Western Union yellow flimsy. Smoky was still at Trumbull's battered old desk, working on the few remaining Tom Foley files he had yet to read. As always, a quirly dangled from his lips.

"Smoky, where's Chip Blawcyzk?" Huggins asked.

"I sent him to help Ty Tremblay clean out the corrals," Smoky explained. He waved a hand at the papers stacked on a corner table. "I figured he needed a break from all this reading, plus I wanted him, just like Ty, to realize bein' a Ranger isn't all guts and glory. You know new recruits usually start with the drudge work."

"I'm sure Jim's probably told Chip that, but it won't hurt him to learn first hand," Huggins chuckled. "Let's go get both of them. I've got some news. You won't have any more files to read."

"Why? What've you got there? Word on Tom Foley's whereabouts?"

"I sure do. You'll be leaving immediately. I'll give you the details as soon as we round up Chip and Ty. There's no need for me to have to tell the story more'n once."

" 'Bout time." Smoky dropped the file he was holding and pushed back his chair. Both men headed down the hall and outside to the horse corrals.

Charlie and Ty had cleaned two corrals and were working on a third. In the sultry Texas heat, they had stripped to their waists, their sweat-soaked shirts hanging from a fencepost. Charlie was grumbling while he shoveled manure into a wheelbarrow. He dumped a shovelful into the barrow, then pushed back his Stetson and pulled the bandanna from his neck to wipe perspiration from his dripping brow.

"Chip! Ty!" Huggins called.

"Yeah, Captain?" Charlie answered.

"Get your shirts on and come with us, both of you. Right now."

"Why? Has something changed with my dad?" Charlie said.

"No, but we've got a good lead on Tom Foley."

"That's all you needed to say, Captain." Charlie dropped the shovel, grabbed his shirt, and jumped the fence.

"Let's go!"

Captain Huggins waited until everyone had poured themselves a cup of coffee—Smoky rolling and lighting a fresh cigarette—and had found a seat before sharing the information contained in that telegram.

"Men, this telegram is from Sheriff Yancey Tucker up in Comanche County," he began. "Tucker says Tom Foley was spotted up there. Unfortunately, when the deputy who recognized Foley attempted to apprehend him, Foley shot and wounded him and escaped."

"So we know where Foley was, but still don't have him in custody, and have no idea where he's headed now," Smoky said.

"Not quite so fast, Sergeant. There's more."

Huggins took a swallow of his coffee, then continued.

"Foley was traveling with a companion named Junie Blaisdell. You recognize that name?"

"Seems familiar," Smoky answered.

"It should. Blaisdell's a small-time horse thief and con artist, who's been arrested by the Rangers more'n once. He's been in and out of prison several times. It appears to me he's one of those outlaws who're always tryin' to make it big but never quite succeed."

"Let me guess," Charlie interrupted. "One of those arrests was made by Tom Foley."

"That's right," Huggins agreed, grinning. "You've got a sharp mind, Chip, just like your dad's."

"Which means Foley somehow contacted Blaisdell for help after he shot Captain Trumbull and Lieutenant Blawcyzk," Ty concluded.

"Either that or he and Blaisdell had already

come up with some scheme even before the shootings," Huggins added. "Luckily for us, Blaisdell didn't elude capture along with Foley. He's being held in the Comanche jail right now. That's where you're headed. I want you to question Blaisdell as to Foley's whereabouts or plans."

"All three of us?" Smoky questioned.

"All three of you, plus Duffy McGlynn. He just rode into town an hour ago from Cameron, where he'd been checking on another reported sighting of Foley. I told Duffy he can have two hours to rest himself and his horse, then he'll be riding with you for Comanche."

"Begging your pardon, Cap'n, but four Rangers just to question one man, then to track down one more?" Smoky asked.

"That's right. I'm not taking any chances of letting Foley slip through our fingers," Huggins confirmed. "He's already shot down two of the best Rangers on the force. Foley's smart, dangerous and desperate, plus since he's been a Ranger for years, he knows our methods and how to use them to his advantage."

He paused, then continued.

"Listen Smoke, you're the only really experienced man I've got available right now, what with the trouble down along the Border and the problems we're still havin' in parts of the Panhandle. I can't call in anyone else to give you a hand. Sure, Duffy's been a Ranger for a few years now, but he's still young, and most of what he's done has been with a troop, not trackin' or huntin' down a man single-handed. I don't need to tell you that Chip and Ty are raw recruits. I sure can't send them after Foley on their own. In fact, I've still got misgivin's over lettin' Chip ride with you. Obviously he's too emotionally tied to this case, what with his dad's bein' shot."

When Charlie began to object, Huggins cut him short.

"Hear me out, Chip. The only reason I'm allowing you to go with Smoky is I know there's no way I could stop you, short of tossing you in jail for your own good. Besides, I have to admit if I were in your boots I'd feel the same way. Your dad and I have been friends since way back. We've ridden together, fought together, and had a lot of fun together. Heck, I wish I could be ridin' with you, but I'm chained to this blasted office until a permanent replacement for Hank Trumbull is chosen. Pay attention to me, Chip. You're to follow Sergeant McCue's every order without hesitation and without question. If I hear back from him or anyone else that you haven't obeyed his orders to the letter, I'll personally make sure you are drummed out of the Texas Rangers permanently. The same goes for you, Ty. Is that clear?"

"It sure is, Captain," Charlie agreed. "I won't

do anything to disgrace the Rangers or embarrass my dad."

"That also goes for me, Captain Huggins," Ty added.

"Fine, as long as everything is understood. You've got a long, hard ride ahead of you, so get your horses ready and make sure you have plenty of supplies. Be ready to go in two hours, which will also give you time to visit your dad before you leave, Chip. Any other questions?"

The three men shook their heads negatively.

"All right, there's just one more thing," Huggins said.

"What's that, Cap'n?" Smoky responded.

"You'll do whatever is necessary to convince Blaisdell to tell you what Foley is planning or where he's heading," Huggins answered.

"Whatever?" Smoky repeated.

"Whatever it takes," Huggins reiterated. "My only other order is you are not to return until you capture Tom Foley . . . or kill him."

Once Charlie had readied Ted for the long trail ahead, he went to Doctor Talmadge's hospital.

"Go right in, Charlie," Elmira Talmadge told him. "I'm sure your mother will be happy to see you here a bit earlier than you planned."

"Thanks, Mrs. Talmadge," Charlie answered. He went into his father's room and stopped dead in his tracks.

"Mary Jane! What are you doing here?" he asked, shocked at seeing the girl he was sweet on there in Jim's room. Mary Jane Jarratt was just entering the full bloom of young womanhood. She had auburn hair the color of deep copper, green eyes which complemented that hair perfectly, and a peaches and cream complexion. The gentle curves of her bosom and hips nicely filled the blue gingham dress she wore. Her mother, Bethea, was also there, sitting next to Julia.

"I'm very happy to see you also, Charlie," Mary Jane responded, smiling.

"That's not . . . Mary Jane, you know I'm happy to see you," Charlie spluttered. "It's just so unexpected, that's all."

"Mary Jane and I are here for our turn helping care for your father," Bethea explained.

"Oh, I see. Thank you, Mrs. Jarratt," Charlie replied, still unnerved.

"Charlie, why are you here so early in the day?" Julia asked. "I didn't expect you until this evening."

"Mom, I'm sorry," Charlie answered. "I was so surprised to see Mary Jane, I forgot to kiss you."

He promptly remedied that oversight, kissing his mother on the cheek.

"How's Dad doing?"

"He's pretty much the same, basically holding his own, which Doctor Talmadge assures me is all we can expect at this point," Julia explained.

"But you still haven't answered my question."

"Tom Foley was spotted up in Comanche," Charlie answered. "He was involved in a shootout with a deputy there. Foley got away, but his pardner was captured and is being held in the Comanche jail. Ty and I, along with Smoky and another Ranger named Duffy McGlynn, who I don't believe you know, are heading to Comanche. We're leaving in less than an hour. I came by to see you and Dad before we ride out."

"Oh, I see," Julia said, chagrined. Distress was plain in her expression.

"Mom, it'll be all right, I promise you," Charlie tried to reassure her. "Captain Huggins made me swear I'd follow Smoky's orders or he'd have me thrown out of the Rangers. You know I'd never let that happen, plus I'm not gonna let anything happen to me before I can see Dad and talk with him again. I won't do anything foolish."

"You're still going after a dangerous man, one who even fooled your father," Julia murmured.

"All the more reason for me to be careful," Charlie answered. "Mom, we already had this discussion. You know why I have to do this."

"Yes, I do, and I want you to," Julia conceded. "I do have one request, however."

"You just say what it is, Mom."

"Try not to let worry about me or your father distract you. That could get you hurt, or worse. Promise me you'll concentrate on the task at hand. I'm also going to ask when or if you come across Tom Foley you don't let your emotions get the better of you. Please do your job as your father has trained you to do it."

"You have my word on that, bet a hat on it," Charlie replied.

"You said it again, Charlie."

"Said what again, Mom?"

"Bet a hat, just like Jim would say."

"I didn't even realize it. I'm sorry, Mom."

"Don't be. It reminds me even more how much you're like him."

Charlie glanced at Mary Jane.

"Mom, Mrs. Jarratt, would you mind if I spent a few minutes alone with Mary Jane?"

"Not at all," Julia answered.

"Of course not," Bethea agreed. "You youngsters should have a few private moments before you have to leave, Charlie."

"Thanks, both of you," Charlie replied.

"You haven't asked me if I want to spend a few minutes alone with you, Charles Edward Blawcyzk," Mary Jane pointed out.

"I'm asking you now," Charlie responded.

"I suppose I must," Mary Jane pouted.

"Good. Doctor Talmadge has a garden out back, where we won't be disturbed," Charlie smiled. He took Mary Jane's hand and led her outside. They found a bench in a shady corner and settled there.

"Mary Jane, I'm sorry I have to leave you, but you know I've gotta find the man who gunned down my dad," Charlie said. "I don't know when I'll be back."

"Or if you'll ever be back," Mary Jane pointed out. "You might get killed, Charlie."

"There's no denyin' that," Charlie admitted. "Just as I might get killed fallin' off a horse, or gettin' trampled movin' cattle, or drown while swimmin' in the river."

"You fall off a horse? That'd be the day," Mary Jane scoffed. "You ride as well as your father. Besides, horses and cows aren't deliberately trying to put a bullet in you."

"I reckon that's so," Charlie conceded.

"It's so, and you know it," Mary Jane retorted. "However, I also know you've always wanted to be a Texas Ranger, and there's nothing I can do or say which will hold you in San Leanna. All I ask is you be careful. I'll never forgive you if you get yourself killed and come back to me dead."

Charlie tried but failed to keep from laughing.

"You know what you just said, Mary Jane?"

Mary Jane was also chuckling.

"I guess it was pretty silly, wasn't it?"

"That's all right." Charlie paused, then sighed.

"Mary Jane, I don't have the right to ask you to wait for me unless you want to. I know there are plenty of other boys whose heads you've turned.

I can't blame them, since you're the prettiest girl in San Leanna, in fact probably all of Texas."

"Only probably?" she teased.

"All right, definitely. Absolutely, positively, definitely you are the prettiest girl in the entire Lone Star State," Charlie replied.

"That's better," Mary Jane smiled, the smile which always sent a thrill through Charlie.

"Now, as far as whether or not I'll wait for you, does this answer your question?"

Mary Jane wrapped her arms around Charlie and pulled him to her, placing her lips to his for a long, lingering kiss.

"I . . . I reckon it does," Charlie gasped, once she turned him loose.

"Good. So make sure you're faithful to me also, no matter how many pretty girls you might meet," Mary Jane ordered.

"That's a promise," Charlie answered. "Now I reckon we'd best head back inside. I need to spend some time with my dad before I leave."

He kissed Mary Jane again, reluctant to end this moment. She finally had to push him away.

"We'd better go right now," she said.

"I guess so," Charlie answered.

They returned to find Bethea had gone to the nearby store to purchase a few necessities for Julia.

"I'll catch up with my mother while you sit

with your mom and dad," Mary Jane told Charlie. "Just remember, be careful."

"I will be," Charlie assured her yet again.

Once Mary Jane departed, Charlie sat next to his father, taking Jim's hand.

"Dad, Mom's gonna be here with you while Smoky and I go after the hombre who did this to you. We won't be back until we track him down. I just don't want you to worry about me. I'll remember everything you taught me, and don't fret, I'll make every shot count. I'm gonna be a good Ranger, Dad. You can bet your hat on it."

Jim shifted slightly and sighed.

"Mom, did you see that?" Charlie exclaimed.

"I surely did, Charlie. I think it means even your father is tired of 'bet a hat'."

"Nah, Mom, that's not it. Dad's getting better, sure as shootin'."

"I certainly hope you're right, Charlie."

"We'll both just keep prayin' I am," Charlie answered.

"Dad," he continued, "When I'm done with this job, and you're all healed up, mebbe we'll be able to ride together. That'd be real fine. Meantime you just rest and get better as fast as you can. You're too ornery to let just a couple of slugs kill you, so I'll be countin' on seein' you back at the ranch real soon, you hear me? Besides, Sam and Sizzle are missin' you something fierce, and

I can't take them with me. Dunno who's gonna handle Sam."

"Don't worry about those horses," Julia broke in, "I'll take care of them, being as Sam will at least tolerate me handling him."

"You will, Mom? That's a big load off my mind," Charlie said.

"It will give me something to do when I have to leave this room, and it would make Jim happy," Julia answered.

"See, Dad? Everything's all set," Charlie stated. He remained alongside Jim's bed, holding his hand, until a soft knock came at the door.

"Charlie? It's time to go," Smoky called.

"All right, Sergeant. Just a minute," Charlie answered. He kissed his father's cheek, then embraced his mother. Charlie's eyes were moist, while tears trickled down Julia's cheeks.

"Charlie, write me whenever you get the chance," she whispered. "Take a bath as often as you can, and wash your socks and underwear."

"I will, Mom," Charlie promised, blushing slightly.

"I won't let anything happen to your boy. I promise you that, Julia," Smoky said, hugging her.

"I know you won't," Julia replied. "Take care of yourself, too."

"Always do," Smoky chuckled.

"Sergeant, we'd better leave now," Charlie gritted, his voice husky with emotion.

"I believe you're right, son," Smoky agreed.

He gave Julia one more reassuring hug, then Charlie kissed her once more. Julia followed them to the front porch, waiting as they joined Ty and Duffy, then mounted their horses. She stood watching and waving until they rode out of sight.

The quartet of Rangers rode until well after sunset, wanting to put as much distance between themselves and Austin as possible. Comanche was a trip of about one hundred fifty miles, normally a five, or at best four, day journey by horseback. With luck, Smoky and his companions would make it in three. The sergeant had observed the three younger men as they traveled, pleased to see that at least all were well mounted.

Smoky was riding his long time mount, Soot, a steeldust gelding. The dark gray had served Smoky admirably over many years, and the Ranger was not looking forward to the day fast approaching when he would have to retire Soot.

Charlie likewise was on an aging horse, Ted, his buckskin paint. Jim had given the gentle gelding to his son when Charlie was barely out of diapers. While Ted was getting a bit on in years, he was in better shape than most horses half his age, thanks to Charlie's fine care. Smoky wasn't worried about the untested paint facing his first gun battle, either. Jim and Charlie would have been sure to train Ted to face the sounds and smells of a gunfight.

Duffy McGlynn rode a big-boned, blaze-faced bay gelding named Cactus. He'd owned the horse since before joining the Texas Rangers, and over the past few years the big bay had proved a steady, dependable mount. In fact, Jim Blawcyzk had "borrowed" the horse when he'd escaped jail in Quitaque, where he'd been falsely accused of murder. It was this chance encounter which had given Duffy the opportunity to join the Rangers.

Ty Tremblay's horse was the only question in Smoky's mind. It was a blocky palomino gelding with a star on his forehead, whose hide shone like molten gold in the sun. Bandit, as Ty had named the horse, was a quarter horse mustang cross, compact but heavily muscled. Smoky was positive that Bandit had plenty of staying power, and was tough enough to handle a long trek on little feed and water. His only worry was how the horse would react to its first taste of gunfire.

With only a waxing crescent moon to guide them once the sun had set, Smoky had chosen to camp for the night alongside a small stream. After caring for their horses, the men ate a quick supper of bacon, biscuits, and beans, then pulled off their hats, boots, and gunbelts and rolled into their blankets.

Smoky lay on his back, smoking a final cigarette and gazing up at the stars, his mind

114

drifting. Duffy, the burly blonde cowboy with the mischievous streak, whose light brown eyes always seemed to hold a glint of merriment, was propped against his saddle, also smoking. The lanky Ty was already asleep, snoring softly, while Charlie was murmuring his evening prayers.

Just like his dad, Smoky thought. *Sure do miss him. Things are changin' fast. Dunno how much longer men like me'n Jim Blawcyzk are gonna be of much use. We're kinda too stuck in our ways, too old-fashioned. Jim hates ridin' the train, and I'm not overly fond of it, but the railroads' tracks are spreadin' like spider webs all over the state. Won't be long before we use them almost exclusively, rather'n our horses. Heck, I saw one of those hot air balloons at a county fair a while back. Wouldn't surprise me one bit if we're flyin' around like the birds in a few years. Every time I pick up a newspaper it seems there's some new invention comin' along.*

Smoky sighed and took another drag on his quirly. His jet black hair was frosted with gray at the tips and gave the illusion of a puff of smoke—hence his nickname. It was gradually turning more gray than black, and his pencil-thin mustache had faded from black to salt and pepper. While he was reluctant to admit it, Smoky had to concede there was just the beginning of a slight paunch starting to thicken his middle.

Mebbe it's time for me and Jim to hang up

our hats and guns, put our saddles on the fence, stop chasin' outlaws and dodgin' bullets and let some younger men take over, he mused, once again glancing at his three young partners. *Look at Duffy. He's only twenty-two, but already a Ranger for four years now. Charlie's gonna be as good a Ranger as his dad, mebbe better, and Ty's also gonna be a man to ride the river with. All youngsters. Charlie and Ty need a bit of fillin' out, but I'm happier to have 'em sidin' me than plenty of men I've ridden with. Then again, a lot of my old compadres are gone, some retired, some so crippled up they'll never ride again, and quite a few dead.*

Smoky sighed again.

Tom Justus isn't gonna run for sheriff again, or so he says. Mebbe I should try for his job. It'd be a lot easier 'n Rangerin', that's for certain. I could be home with Cindy every night, sittin' in my rocker on the front porch and takin' it easy. Most of my law enforcin' would be tossin' an occasional drunk in jail for the night and lettin' him sober up. Yep, perhaps it's time to step aside and let the younger generation take over. Lord knows they'll be a whole bunch smarter, and'll do a lot more crime solvin' with their brains, rather 'n their fists and guns.

Smoky took a last pull on his smoke, crushed out the butt, and tossed it away. He rolled onto his side and pulled the blankets to his chin.

Despite his efforts to convince himself otherwise, he knew the truth was he could never quit the Texas Rangers. Just like Jim Blawcyzk, he'd ride for the silver star on silver circle until old age, or more likely an outlaw's bullet, claimed him.

Late in the afternoon three and a half days after leaving Austin, the four tired men rode their exhausted horses into the town of Comanche.

"Pretty pleasant lookin' place," Smoky noted, observing a large grove of oaks from which the town extended outward. Beside the oaks was the town square, on the southwest corner of which was a venerable old courthouse. Next to the building was a hand dug well.

"We'll check in with the sheriff first, then put up our horses and find rooms for ourselves for the night."

"What about questioning Junie Blaisdell?" Charlie asked.

"Plenty of time for that," Smoky answered as they reined up next to the well. "We're not goin' any further tonight. Besides, we need rest, and more important so do our broncs. No matter what we learn from Blaisdell, we've got a lot more travelin' ahead, so we can't wear out our mounts."

After allowing their horses a short drink from the trough next to the well, they crossed the street, dismounted, and tethered the mounts to the tooth-scarred rail in front of the Comanche County Sheriff's Office. A few of the passersby gave them a quick once-over, but since they wore nothing which would mark them as Texas Rangers, most didn't give them a second glance, assuming they were just more drifting cowpunchers looking for work on one of the surrounding ranches. They ducked under the rail and climbed the steps to the office. Smoky pushed open the door and stepped inside, the others trailing.

There were two desks behind the railing separating the entry from the rest of the office. Behind the nearest was a man reading a week-old newspaper. He put down the paper and looked up when they entered, revealing a sheriff's badge pinned to his cowhide vest.

"Can I help you gentlemen?" he inquired.

"You sure can," Smoky answered. "I'm Sergeant Smoky McCue of the Texas Rangers. These are Rangers Duffy McGlynn, Charles Blawcyzk, better known as Chip, and Tyler Tremblay."

Smoky reached into his vest pocket and pulled out his badge, holding it up for the sheriff to see.

"Well, howdy," the local lawman exclaimed, coming to his feet. "I'm Yancey Tucker, the Comanche County Sheriff. Been expectin' you boys, but didn't figure on seein' you for a couple more days."

Tucker was in his late forties, dark haired and dark eyed, with a huge brushy mustache drooping over his upper lip. A good sized gut pushed out his gunbelt, from which hung a holster holding an old but serviceable Navy Colt. Despite that belly, the sheriff exuded an aura of toughness, and Smoky would bet anyone who made the mistake of tangling with Tucker most likely would come out on the losing end.

"We pushed pretty hard," Smoky explained. "We wanted to get here as quickly as possible. I assume you've still got Blaisdell in custody?"

"Locked up tight and waitin' for you," Tucker replied. "You want to question him right now?"

"I'd like to see him for a minute is all," Smoky answered. "After that, we'll need to put up our horses and find a place to spend the night. Once that's done and we have a good supper under our belts, we'll return to question him. Also, we'll need to talk with your deputy who tangled with Foley and Blaisdell, if that's possible."

"I understand," Tucker responded. "Ben Drake's the man who ran across those two renegades. He was shot up pretty bad, but he's back to work, watching the office and cells while I cover his rounds at night. By the time you return he'll be here, so you can talk to him then. Will that do?"

"That'll be fine," Smoky said.

"Good. Let me take you to see Blaisdell."

Tucker lifted a ring of keys from a wall peg.

"Duffy, you and Ty wait here. Chip, come with me," Smoky ordered.

"Sure thing, Smoke," Duffy mumbled. He and Ty took seats on a battered rung-back bench, Duffy pulling out the makings to build a quirly.

"Blaisdell's right back here," Tucker stated, opening the swinging gate in the railing. "Follow me."

As he led Smoky and Charlie down the corridor leading to the cells, he gave the younger man a sideways glimpse.

"Your name's Blawcyzk, huh?" he questioned.

"That's right," Charlie confirmed.

"Any kin to the Ranger who got shot the same time Captain Trumbull was killed?"

"I'm his son," Charlie answered.

Tucker halted and gave out a low whistle.

"That was your dad? I figure you've got a real reason for seein' Blaisdell then."

"Not as much as one for findin' Tom Foley," Charlie responded.

"I reckon not," Tucker agreed. "I'm sure sorry about your dad, even though I never met him. How's he doin'?"

"He was still hangin' on when we left Austin," Charlie said. "I guess if you haven't received any word from Captain Huggins then he still is."

"No, I sure haven't," Tucker said. "So I figure that's good news."

He unlocked the heavy oak door leading to the cells and swung it open.

"Blaisdell," he called, "Got a couple of visitors here for you."

"I'm not expectin' anyone," a voice called back from the nearest cell. "Who've you got there, Sheriff?"

"Pair of Texas Rangers who want to talk with you," Tucker replied. He stepped up to the cell, unlocked the door, then motioned Smoky and Charlie inside.

Junie Blaisdell was lying on the bunk, a man in his early forties, slim and swarthy, his black hair slicked back. Eyes so brown as to appear black were set under heavy eyebrows. They seemed to dart in almost constant motion.

"I've got nothing to say to the Rangers," he sneered.

"Mebbe not, but you'd better find something to say, and darn quick," Smoky half snarled. "Listen, Blaisdell, we don't have any particular use for you. We're after Tom Foley. Since you were the last person seen with him, you'd better tell us where he went, unless you feel like being charged as an accessory to Hank Trumbull's murder. I guarantee you'll swing if you are."

"I had nothin' to do with that," Blaisdell snapped.

"Mebbe not, but if you're helpin' Foley, it's the same as if you pulled the trigger yourself,"

Smoky replied. "Don't worry, you don't have to talk right now. We've had a long hard ride from Austin, so we're gonna take care of our horses and grab some chuck. Once that's done we'll be back, and by then you'd better be ready to tell us everything we want to know."

"And if I don't?" Blaisdell retorted.

"If you don't . . . Chip, c'mere," Smoky ordered Charlie, who stood just outside the cell door.

"Blaisdell, this here is Chip Blawcyzk. In case you don't recognize the name, his dad's Lieutenant Jim Blawcyzk, the man your pardner gunned down along with Hank Trumbull. Chip'd like nothing better than to be left alone in this cell with you for about ten minutes. You might want to think about that."

Blaisdell looked at Charlie, shuddering at the cold fury glowing in the depths of the young Ranger's icy blue eyes.

"You wouldn't do it," Blaisdell protested, a slight quaver in his voice.

"You want to chance that?" Smoky responded. "We'll be back in two hours, mister, and you'd better be ready to spill your guts. C'mon, Chip."

They stepped out of the cell, waiting while Tucker locked it.

"You gonna want to take Blaisdell with you?" he asked, "After all, I've still got charges pending against him here for assault and attempted murder of my deputy. I'm holdin' him for the circuit judge, who'll be here in ten days or so."

"That depends on how cooperative your prisoner is, Sheriff," Smoky answered, looking directly at Blaisdell. "If he won't provide the information we want, he might have to come with us. One of those oaks or cottonwoods along the trail could come in mighty handy."

"I see what you mean," Tucker said, a wide grin splitting his face. "Well, let's go. I'll introduce you to Luke at the livery stable and Jessie at the hotel. Once you and your horses are settled, I'll be ready for supper myself. Don't worry, Blaisdell, I'll bring back somethin' for you. After all, it might be your last meal."

Tucker laughed harshly.

After arranging for stalls for the horses, rooms for themselves, and eating a hearty meal, Sheriff Tucker accompanied the Rangers back to his office. As he'd promised, Deputy Ben Drake was waiting for them. The deputy had his right arm in a sling, while a walnut cane was alongside his desk.

"Don't bother to get up, Ben," Tucker ordered. "These are Rangers McCue, Blawcyzk, McGlynn, and Tremblay. Rangers, Ben Drake."

"Glad to meet you, Deputy," Smoky said. "Sure wish it was under better circumstances. How are you doin'?"

"Not too badly, considerin'," Drake replied.

"Won't be usin' my arm for a spell, and ain't movin' very fast after takin' three slugs. Besides my arm and leg, Foley put one in my ribs, too."

"You're darn lucky he didn't kill you," Ty said.

"Boy howdy, don't I know it," Drake agreed.

"Ben, I've just got a couple of questions for you," Smoky said. "Did you notice which way Foley headed after he plugged you?"

"Sorry, Ranger, I sure didn't," Drake answered. "I was too busy keepin' Blaisdell pinned down. Couldn't watch him and Foley too. Mainly I was tryin' to get Blaisdell rounded up before I passed out. Knew I didn't have a chance to catch Foley by then."

"I understand," Smoky said. "You didn't hear Foley say anything about where he was headed, mebbe shout to Blaisdell where to meet him if he got away from you?"

"I sure didn't," Drake said. "Only thing I heard was gunfire, and the only thing I felt was Foley's slugs tearin' into me."

"Nobody in town heard Foley mention where he might be goin' next either," Tucker added. "'Course, we figure he wasn't in town more'n an hour or so before he tangled with Ben here."

"All right, then I guess it's time we talked with Blaisdell," Smoky answered. "Give me your keys, Sheriff."

"You don't want me to come with you?"

"It'd be best if you don't. Stay here and keep an eye on things."

"Suit yourself," Tucker shrugged. He took the keys off their peg and handed them to Smoky.

"Thanks."

Smoky and the others headed down the corridor to Blaisdell's cell. The prisoner was still lying on his bunk.

"You ready to talk, Blaisdell?" Smoky asked.

"I've already told you I've got nothin' to say to you," Blaisdell growled.

"We'll have to see about that," Smoky replied, unlocking the cell door.

"You and Ty stay out here, Duffy," he ordered. "Chip and I'll question Blaisdell."

Smoky stepped inside the cell, grabbed Blaisdell by his shirtfront, and yanked him to his feet.

"I'm not gonna waste much time on the likes of you, Blaisdell," he said. "I've just got one question. Where's Tom Foley gone?"

"You can go to blazes, lawman!" Blaisdell retorted. "I want my supper. Where is it?"

"I've already warned you," Smoky replied, his voice calm but menacing. "Far as your supper, that can wait. You've got one last chance. Where's Foley?"

"I've got no idea."

"All right. Chip, he's yours."

"Thanks, Sergeant. Step outta the cell and lock the door, will you?"

"Sure."

Smoky exited the cell, locking it behind him. Charlie glared at Blaisdell.

"Your pardner gunned down my dad," Charlie stated, "My dad, who thought Tom Foley was his friend, a man he'd ridden with and fought alongside. Now, are you gonna tell me where he went?"

"I don't know what you're talkin' about, Ranger," Blaisdell answered, his voice cracking.

Charlie slapped him sharply across his face.

"Are you positive about that?"

"I told you, I don't know where Tom Foley went, and I had nothing to do with Trumbull's murder, or your father's being shot."

"You know where Foley's gone, and you will tell me," Charlie snapped. He sank a fist deep into Blaisdell's belly. When the outlaw folded over his fist, Charlie shoved him back against the cell door.

"Where's Foley?" Charlie demanded.

"I dunno," Blaisdell insisted.

Charlie drove a knee into his groin. Blaisdell jackknifed to the rock floor, retching. Charlie dragged him to his feet and once again shoved him against the cell door.

"I said, where's Foley?"

"I, I dunno," Blaisdell repeated, cringing.

126

"I'm done wastin' time," Charlie snarled. "Duffy, grab his arms."

"With pleasure, Chip."

McGlynn reached through the bars and grasped Blaisdell's arms, pulling them outside the cell and twisting them behind Blaisdell's back, pinning him to the bars.

"You gonna tell us where your pardner's gone?" Charlie asked one last time.

Blaisdell swallowed hard, seeing death in those ice-cold blue eyes. His voice was barely a squeak when he answered.

"I . . . I can't tell you, Ranger."

Wordlessly, Charlie sank several more punches into Blaisdell's gut, following them with two to his groin. Blaisdell hung there, gasping for breath, his knees buckling. Only Duffy's firm grasp kept him from dropping to the floor.

"He ain't gonna talk, Chip," Smoky said, "Guess we're gonna have to take him along. You've got plenty of rope on your saddle, haven't you?"

"Got a brand new one that needs stretchin'," Charlie answered. He drove yet another punch to the pit of Blaisdell's stomach.

"Let's get him outta here."

"No, no," Blaisdell choked out. "I'll talk. I'll . . . tell you whatever you want to know."

"We've got only one question, Blaisdell, and you know what it is," Smoky challenged.

"Yeah . . . Yeah. Foley's headed for Mex . . . Mexico."

"Narrow it down. Where in Mexico?"

"Little town called Zaragoza, some miles southwest of . . . Piedras Negras."

"Why's he headed there?" Smoky demanded.

"I dunno for certain," Blaisdell responded. "I know he's got friends there."

"Why'd he meet up with you, and why'd he ride clear up here, the complete opposite direction from where he's headed?"

"He contacted me up in Fort Worth and said I could help him with some kind of deal that'd make both of us a lot of money," Blaisdell explained. "Wanted to meet me here, figurin' you Rangers'd be scouring the border country for him, since that was the territory he knows, where he spent most of his time. He thought ridin' north first might throw you off his trail."

"So now he's headed straight for Mexico? You'd better not be lyin' to us, Blaisdell," Smoky said.

"I'm not, except Tom's not goin' directly to Zaragoza. He's planning on swingin' by the Bar 7 Ranch on the way. It's a big spread on the upper Frio River. Tom worked there before he joined the Rangers, and stayed in touch with the owners. He said they were still friends, and that they might help him."

"All right, you've done yourself a favor,"

Smoky stated. "What about this 'big deal'? Foley didn't give you a hint as to what it was?"

"Not a clue, I swear it," Blaisdell whined. "I've told you everything I know, Ranger. Can't help you more'n that."

"Okay, Duffy, let him go," Smoky ordered. When McGlynn released Blaisdell's arms he dropped to the floor, doubled up and whimpering. Charlie drew back his foot for a kick to Blaisdell's middle.

"He's had enough, Chip," Smoky ordered. "Enough!" he repeated, when Charlie hesitated. "Let's get outta here."

Smoky unlocked the door.

When they returned to the front office, Sheriff Tucker looked at them quizzically.

"Did he talk?"

"He sure did," Smoky answered. "We'll be ridin' for Mexico first thing in the morning."

"Mexico, huh?"

"Yeah, Mexico." Smoky left unsaid what they were both thinking, that Rangers had no authority below the Rio Grande.

"Good luck then. Guess I'd better feed Blaisdell if you're through with him."

"I doubt he's gonna be very hungry tonight," Charlie said.

"Oh?" Tucker began, then stopped, seeing the grim expression in the young Ranger's eyes.

"Yeah, it seems your prisoner suddenly

developed a real bad bellyache," Ty chimed in. "Dunno how it happened."

"I'm sure you don't," Tucker answered. "Well as I said, good luck. That goes for all of you."

"Thanks, Yancey," Smoky replied. "We'll stop by in the morning before we leave, long as you're awake."

"I'll be here," Tucker promised.

"Fine. Good night then. We'll see you manana."

"Good night, men."

Chapter Eight

Julia was in her usual place alongside Jim when Elmira Talmadge knocked softly on the open door.

"Julia," she called. "There is a visitor here to see you and Jim."

"Who is it?" Julia asked.

"The pastor from your church has returned."

"Father Biron? Send him right in."

"I'm already in, Julia," Father Robert Biron smiled, as he stepped into the room. The long-time pastor of Saint Cecelia's Roman Catholic Church was middle-aged, stocky, and balding. A pleasant smile creased his face.

"Father, I didn't expect to see you back so soon," Julia replied.

"I didn't think I'd be able to return this quickly either; however, things are quiet at the church right now so I was able to get away. Truthfully, I also wanted to visit a few friends, so this way I can kill two birds with one stone, so to speak. I'll be in town for a couple of days. Father Kosmowski is taking care of things back home until I return."

"I don't care what brought you to Austin again, I'm just happy you were able to visit Jim once more."

"So am I," the pastor replied. "How is he doing?"

Julia hesitated before responding. Her eyes shone brightly with worry, and her voice quivered slightly when she spoke.

"I'm not certain. He seems a bit uneasy today, more restless than he has been. Doctor Talmadge isn't sure if Jim's getting nearer to coming out of his coma or if some other problem may be developing."

"If it's the Lord's will, Jim shall recover, and if in fact something is going on, I'm certain it's just a minor setback," Father Biron attempted to comfort Jim's distraught wife. "I'll pray that's all it is."

"Thank you, Father," Julia answered. "You and Father Kosmowski, the sisters, and all of the parishioners have helped keep me strong with your prayers and support."

"You know your friends are always there for you and your family, Julia," Father Biron reminded her. "When we got word that Charlie and Ty had joined the Rangers we added their safety to our intentions also."

"That means more than you'll ever know, Father," Julia said. "Thank everyone for me when you get back to San Leanna."

"Of course. Now I'd like to stay with Jim for a few minutes. He's already had Extreme Unction administered, so there's no reason to repeat the sacrament, but I'll say some prayers and bless him again."

The pastor stood alongside Jim's bed, praying softly. When he concluded, he made the Sign of the Cross over the gravely wounded Ranger.

"Julia, I had a thought while praying," he said. "Have you ever visited Saint Mary's Church here in Austin? It's quite beautiful, even though it is still a work in progress."*

"No Father, I haven't," Julia admitted.

"It's only a few blocks from here. Why don't you accompany me on a short visit there? I'll introduce you to Father O'Connor. He and I went through seminary together, and we've been good friends since. I'm positive he'll make it his business to visit you and Jim as often as possible until Jim's recovered and strong enough to travel home to finish recuperating."

"I'd love to, but I'm not sure if I should leave Jim," Julia replied.

"Of course you can leave Jim for a little while," Father Biron responded. "He's in the best of hands under Doctor Talmadge's care, and we won't be all that long. A visit to the church is certain to comfort you and bring peace to your soul. In addition, you'll be able to light some candles for Jim and Charlie."

The last argument hit home.

"All right, Father, you've convinced me," Julia

---

* For more information on the history of St. Mary's Church in Austin, see page 359.

answered. "Just let me tidy up a little, and get a veil to cover my head."

"Splendid," Father Biron answered. "You won't regret your decision. While you're freshening up, I'll let Doctor Talmadge know what we're doing."

"Thank you, Father. It won't take me long to get ready," Julia promised, kissing Jim and telling him she would return soon.

True to her word, fifteen minutes later Julia met the pastor on the front porch. She had changed into a blue cotton dress, while a white lace veil covered her dark hair.

"I told you I wouldn't be long, Father," she smiled.

"And you weren't," Father Biron agreed, glancing up at the brilliant blue and cloudless sky. The temperature was unusually cool, with low humidity, and a refreshing breeze from the northwest.

"It's a lovely day for a walk," he concluded. "Shall we start?"

"Lead the way, Father."

A short while later they reached Saint Mary's and went inside. Julia would spend over an hour there, lighting several candles, asking the Blessed Virgin's intercession for Jim's recovery and Charlie's and Ty's safety. As Father Biron had promised, after the visit and meeting Father David O'Connor, she left the church refreshed in both mind and spirit.

• • •

When Julia returned, she found Doctor Talmadge and Nancy, one of his nurses, working on Jim. They had pulled back his covers and were changing his bandages. Sweat glistened on his brow and dampened his hair, with rivulets of perspiration running down his chest.

"Doctor, what's happened? Is anything wrong?" Julia cried.

"I'm not certain," Talmadge admitted. "Jim's running a fever, which is not unexpected. In fact, I'm a bit surprised it took this long."

"Does that mean he's developed an infection?" Julia asked.

"Most likely," Talmadge answered. "Truthfully, with wounds as severe as Jim's, and the trauma to his internal organs, I've been waiting for this to happen. Julia, this is not necessarily a bad thing. A fever is nature's way of helping the body fight off illness or infection. We just have to make sure Jim's temperature doesn't rise so high it leads to convulsions. A seizure, especially considering his weakened state, might very well prove fatal."

"Which means Jim's taken a turn for the worse," Julia said.

"For the moment," Talmadge conceded. "However, this fever could prove beneficial in the long run. You're well aware that your husband has been merely lying in a comatose state since he was shot, showing no change in his condition

135

one way or the other. Although I didn't want to tell you this, he could not have survived much longer without some sign of improvement. I've been expecting a crisis for the past several days, and this fever is it. If we can get Jim through the next few days, then I would say his chances of survival are good. If we cannot control the fever or the infection overwhelms his body . . ."

"Jim will die."

"Yes, in that case Jim will die. However, I strongly believe he will pull through. Jim has a strong desire to live, a powerful faith in God, and the support of his family and friends. All those are very important, at this point at least as important as whatever I can do, perhaps more so."

"Don't worry, Julia, Jim will be fine once he fights off this fever," Nancy tried to reassure her.

"I wish I had your confidence," Julia answered.

"Julia, I know this may sound a bit harsh, but please believe me, it is not intended that way," Talmadge said. "Jim couldn't have kept lingering the way he was in any event. At least now we'll know, within a few days at most, whether or not he will indeed recover."

"I understand, Doctor," Julia answered, her voice dull. "What needs to be done now?"

"We have to let the fever run its course, but not let Jim's temperature climb too high," Talmadge explained. "To that end, someone will need to keep cool, wet cloths on his forehead, and perhaps his chest, depending on how high his temperature rises. Jim will also need to have perspiration wiped off him as necessary. We'll also need to continue giving him as many sips of water as he'll take. In addition, his sheets will need to be changed often."

"I'll handle it," Julia said. "I'll just need a supply of cloths and cold water."

"I'll be here to do that," Nancy stated.

"You can't neglect your other patients to be with my husband constantly," Julia pointed out. "I will be. Please, Doctor Talmadge, let me do this."

"Are you certain?" Talmadge asked.

"Of course I'm certain," Julia insisted. "I've been here all along, haven't I?"

"Yes, you have," Talmadge agreed. "All right, as long as you'll agree to let my nurses assist you, then I'll grant your request. However, that's only for keeping Jim cool. Nancy or Juanita will change the sheets. Agreed?"

"Agreed, Doctor."

"Fine. I'll be checking on Jim every three hours, more frequently if I can, or if I feel it's necessary. Nancy will show you where I keep the clean cloths. She'll bring you a supply of those and a bucket full of cold water. You can pump more water at the kitchen sink when you need it."

Talmadge gazed at Julia, his eyes reflecting his innate kindness.

"Julia, I know this is not what you wanted, but it had to happen. With all of us working together, and Jim's stubbornness, in a few days I fully expect the fever to subside and Jim to come out of his coma. While you're working on him, keep talking to him as I know you have been. He may not show it, but he could well be aware you're with him, helping him with his fight to live. That could be the best medicine of all."

"Of course I'll keep talking to Jim," Julia agreed. "I know that somehow he senses my presence."

"No doubt it comforts you also, Julia," Nancy observed.

"Yes, it does," Julia confirmed.

"Then everything is settled," Talmadge said. "Julia, you know to call if you need anything. Nancy will relieve you for a time later this evening, just enough so you can eat supper. I'll look in on Jim before then."

"Thank you, Doctor, for everything."

Julia left Jim's side only once that evening, to clean up a bit and have a quick supper. About ten o'clock Juanita, Doctor Talmadge's second nurse, knocked gently on the door to Jim's room.

"Mrs. Blawcyzk, are you awake?" she softly called.

"Yes, Juanita, I am," Julia answered.

"I've brought you some tea if you'd like."

Juanita entered, carrying a tray holding a teapot, cup and saucer, along with a spoon, pitcher of milk, and sugar bowl.

"That would be lovely. Thank you."

"I'll set it right here."

Juanita placed the tray on a side table, then poured a cup of tea for Julia.

"Milk or sugar in your tea?"

"Just a bit of sugar, thank you. Would you like some also?" Julia asked.

"I would love to take a few minutes with a cup of tea, but I still have three other patients to look in on," Juanita explained, as she put a half-spoonful of sugar in the tea, stirred it, and handed it to Julia.

"I understand," Julia replied. She took a sip of the amber beverage.

"This is delicious, Juanita. It's just what I needed."

"Thank you. Is there anything else you need at the moment?"

"No, I'm fine. This tea will do."

"Then I'll leave you for now. You know where to find me if you need me," Juanita answered.

"I do indeed, and thank you again for the tea," Julia replied.

An hour later, Jim became more restless, tossing and moaning.

"Jim, I'm right here with you," Julia assured him, whispering. "I'm not letting you leave me, do you understand that, James Joseph Blawcyzk? You're not getting off that easily."

Julia wet a fresh cloth and placed it on his forehead. She talked softly to him while she stroked his sweat-soaked hair.

"Jim, do you remember our last trip to San Antonio?" she asked. "You got so jealous when that good-looking Mexican trumpet player in the mariachi band tried to flirt with me you wanted to toss him in the river. I had to stop you before you started a brawl. That wouldn't have looked very good, a Texas Ranger starting a fight over a woman, even if she was your wife."

Julia sighed when Jim only moaned a bit more loudly.

"Are you trying to tell me something? All right, if you don't want to think about San Antonio, how about the school social when you tripped over Mrs. Hunnicutt's dress and landed on your face under the pie table? I know all those old-fashioned petticoats she wears under her skirts are so stiff you could use them for a shelf, so it's understandable how you lost your balance when you stepped on her hem, but you still looked awfully silly sliding across the floor all sprawled out on your stomach. For a man who's so quick on his feet you looked awfully clumsy that night."

Julia laughed softly at the memory. She continued to stroke Jim's hair.

"Jim, I have something I've wanted to tell you

for some time now. It's about the cameo brooch you surprised me with for our last anniversary. I was so surprised when you gave me that brooch, and said I deserved some pretty things just like other women have. I honestly didn't know what to say, your gift was so unexpected. I told you the brooch was lovely but I didn't need fancy doodads to make me happy, and you shouldn't have spent the money. You must have scrimped for months to save enough to buy the brooch, and I sounded so ungrateful. You never said a word, but I could see the hurt in your eyes, and you barely touched your supper that night. You even offered to take the brooch back and see if it could be returned, but I wouldn't let you. I was so ashamed of myself, not realizing how much being able to buy me a beautiful piece of jewelry meant to you. You know I wore the brooch only once, to church that Sunday, then put it away. I told you it was for safekeeping until a really special occasion came along. The truth is, every time I look at that brooch it reminds me how much I hurt you that night. I promise you the next time we go to a dance or social I'll wear it. I'll wear it every chance I get from now on."

Julia took a cloth from the table to dab at a tear which trickled down her cheek.

"That's enough sad talk, Jim," she said. "Why don't I talk about your favorite subject instead . . . horses? We're going to have to look for a new stallion soon. Sonny still does his job, but he is getting a bit on in years. The next time you're in Dripping Springs why don't you talk with Joe Walier and ask him to locate a nice colored, well-put-together horse for us? Joe's honest and will know exactly what we're looking for."

Julia talked about horses, about friends, about Charlie being a Ranger and on the hunt for Tom Foley, anything she could think of until she finally fell asleep two hours later, just before Juanita returned. Seeing Julia dozing in her chair, Juanita covered her with a light blanket, checked on Jim, then turned down the light, leaving them undisturbed.

For three full days and nights Doctor Talmadge, his wife and nurses, Julia, and the women of San Leanna cared for Jim as he fought the infection ravaging his body. Several times Jim's temperature spiked so high Doctor Talmadge was certain the big Ranger would go into convulsions, but each time constant attention brought the fever back down. Finally, early the fourth morning Jim was resting comfortably. Doctor Talmadge smiled at Julia when he checked his patient.

"Julia, Jim's temperature seems almost back to normal, his pulse is slower, and he's breathing much easier," he said. "I would say his fever has broken, which means he's fought off the infection."

"Are you saying Jim is going to be all right, Doctor?" Julia asked.

"He's not completely out of the woods yet, but barring unforeseen complications, yes, Jim is going to survive. In fact, I would venture to guess in a few days he'll regain consciousness. Once that happens and he can take some proper nourishment, he should begin to recover fairly rapidly."

"Did you hear that, Jim? You're going to be all right!" Julia exclaimed. "Thank you, Doctor Talmadge. Thanks to all of you."

"You deserve as much credit as anyone, Julia," Talmadge answered, as he put his stethoscope to Jim's chest. "It was your determination as much as anything which pulled Jim through."

"I think we can thank the Good Lord also," Elmira Talmadge added.

"That's certainly true," Julia agreed. "Thank you, Lord, for helping Jim through this."

"Jim's heartbeat is good and strong," Talmadge noted.

"Of course it is," Julia answered. "Jim, you've got to get better quickly now. Charlie's joined the Rangers and is out there trying to find Tom Foley. He's with Smoky McCue, but I'd feel much better knowing you were also with him."

"Charlie's . . . a Ranger? Chasin' . . . Foley?" Jim murmured, his eyes flickering. "Dang . . . fool kid."

Chapter Nine

Five days and two hundred fifty miles after departing Comanche, Smoky and his comrades rode into the small settlement of Frio Town. The place was little more than a wide spot in the trail, yet it was the only town with any substantial population along a good stretch of the Frio River.

"These horses are in pretty bad shape from bein' pushed so hard, so we'll put them up first, then try and round up the town marshal," Smoky said. "He should be able to give us directions to the Bar 7."

"How about a room for ourselves?" Ty questioned.

"I doubt this town even has a hotel," Smoky answered. "If it does, I'd imagine it's not very clean. We'll be better off bunkin' in the livery stable's hay loft. Most stable owners'll let you do that for an extra four bits."

"I'm so tired I could sleep in the saddle while my bronc's gallopin'," Charlie chuckled.

"Don't laugh, you probably will before this trip is over," Smoky answered. He pointed down a side alley. "There's the stable. Looks like the owner's waitin' on us."

Sitting on an upended keg outside the unpainted, sagging barn was a middle-aged hostler.

"You gents lookin' for stalls for those cayuses?" he called.

"Sure are," Smoky answered as he reined up and dismounted. "Just for one night. I'm Smoky McCue. These are my pards Duffy McGlynn, Chip Blawcyzk, and Ty Tremblay."

"Frank Quinn. Rate's six bits a night, in advance." Quinn's battered hat covered long dark hair which hung lank and greasy to his shoulders, with a beard to match. He was dressed in a stained denim shirt and worn jeans, with run-over boots on his feet.

"Six bits? That's a bit steep," Smoky observed.

"Take it or leave it," Quinn shrugged.

"Reckon we've got no choice," Smoky decided. He dug in his pocket and came up with the amount demanded. "Any chance of bunkin' in the loft?"

"I ain't runnin' a hotel," Quinn replied. "That's the Frio House, two blocks west. You want grub and drinks, they've also got the only café and saloon in town. You can put your broncs in the last four stalls on the left."

"You're gonna make certain they get a good rubdown and feedin', aren't you, Quinn?" Smoky said. "My pardners and I sure would take it real personal if we found our horses hadn't been rubbed down properly and given plenty of grain and hay. They've carried us quite a few miles and need care."

Quinn started to frame a retort, but the glint in Smoky's eyes made him think better of it.

"I'll take good care of 'em," he answered. "Bring 'em on in."

A few moments later they were turning their horses into cramped stalls inside a damp, gloomy barn.

"Sure glad we won't be here more'n one night," Duffy muttered as he pulled the saddle off his bay. "I really hate leavin' Cactus in a sorry place like this."

"My dad'd be pretty displeased if he knew I was puttin' Ted up in a filthy barn like this," Charlie added.

"I know it's not the best, but these horses need to be in stalls for the night, where they can rest without worrying about wolves or mountain lions," Smoky answered. "Sometimes there's just no getting around it. Your dad and I have had to use stables as bad as this one, sometimes worse, plenty of times. You just have to make certain the owner knows what you expect from him, and that you won't put up with any neglect or skimpin' on the feed. We'll come back and check on the horses before we turn in for the night, just to make certain."

"It still sticks in my craw," Ty responded. "But I guess long as Bandit's fed and watered, he can stand one night here."

"He'll manage just fine," Smoky assured him,

as he shouldered his saddlebags. "Let's head over to the hotel."

"That hostler was a real surly son of a gun," Charlie complained while they walked up the alleyway. "Sure don't trust him with our horses."

"He'll take care of 'em," Smoky assured him. "He knows what'll happen if he doesn't. I've dealt with his kind before, and know how to handle them."

The hotel was less than a five-minute walk away. As Smoky had expected, the two-story building was unpainted, its porch sagging. The door swung open into a dingy lobby.

The clerk on duty was bent over the counter, dozing, head pillowed on his arms. He roused himself at the Rangers' approach.

"Can I help you gents?" he asked, looking them over and wrinkling his nose slightly with disdain. Smoky couldn't much blame him. After days on the trail, he and his partners didn't look all that much better than Quinn the liveryman. Their clothes were coated with dust, and they hadn't had a bath, haircut, or shave since leaving Austin. Their hair hung over their collars, while Smoky's beard thickly shadowed his jaw, and Duffy had coarse blonde whiskers stubbling his face. Even the youngsters, Charlie and Ty, sported scraggly beards.

"Yeah, we'd like two rooms," Smoky responded.

"Sorry, you're out of luck," the clerk answered.

"There's only one room left, take it or leave it."

"I reckon we'll take it," Smoky answered. "Been on the trail so long it won't matter much crowdin' into a single room, 'cause we sure don't hanker to spend another night sleepin' on the ground."

"Suit yourselves," the clerk shrugged. "That'll be a dollar. Sign the register."

"Sure thing," Smoky agreed. He tossed a silver dollar on the desk and signed for the room while the clerk took a key from the rack behind him.

"Number 13, up the stairs and down the hall on the right."

"Much obliged," Smoky said, taking the key. "We're gonna clean up a mite, then grab some chuck and a few drinks. By the way, where would we find the town marshal? Didn't spot his office on our way in."

The clerk's eyes turned murky.

"Marshal Stewart? You got any particular reason to be lookin' for him?"

"Just want to get some information and directions from him, that's all," Smoky explained.

"I guess that'll be all right then. This town's too small for a proper marshal's office, so Jake Stewart works out of his house. When he makes an arrest he locks the prisoner in his root cellar, until he can get him over to the county seat in Pearsall. Jake'll be startin' his rounds shortly, so if you hang around the saloon long enough he'll be stoppin' by."

"Thanks again," Smoky answered. "We'll be leavin' first thing in the morning."

"G'night, gents," the clerk muttered.

Room 13 was about what Smoky expected, a small chamber with faded cabbage-rose patterned wallpaper and a dusty braided rug on the floor. There was a bed with a sagging mattress, two ladder-backed chairs, and a washstand with a chipped pitcher and basin, backed by a cracked mirror.

"You certain we wouldn't be better off bunkin' behind that livery stable, Smoke?" Duffy asked.

"No, I'm not, but that liveryman would probably pepper our hides with buckshot if we tried," Smoky answered. "We'll just have to make the best of it. Only thing we have to decide is whether we're all gonna crowd into that bed or a couple of us'll get our blankets and throw 'em on the floor."

"Hey, Ty'n me are good friends, but we're not that close," Charlie objected.

"Then sleep on the floor if you want," Duffy answered. "As for me, I'm takin' the bed. I've crowded into a bed with three or four other fellas more'n once at the end of a trail drive. When you're worn out and dog-tired it don't matter how many are sharing a bed with you, long as you've got a soft mattress and pillows instead of the hard ground and your saddle."

"Same here," Smoky agreed. "Charlie, you and Ty can sleep on the floor if you prefer, but I'd recommend takin' the bed. It'll be crowded, but still better'n rollin' out your blankets on that old wood. You'll wake up so full of splinters you'll look like pincushions if you do."

"Chip, I think we should take Smoky's suggestion," Ty advised. "Heck, I'm so tired I couldn't walk back to the stable for my bedroll anyhow."

"All right, I'll give it a try," Charlie conceded.

"Now that that's settled, let's clean up and get our supper," Smoky said. He pulled off his hat and shirt, then poured water from the pitcher into the basin.

After a rudimentary washing, and beating the dust from their clothes, hats, and boots as best they could, the Rangers headed for supper.

Much to their surprise, the meal in the hotel's small dining room was unexpectedly good. The beef stew was hearty and well-seasoned, containing plenty of meat, potatoes, carrots, and onions. It was accompanied by still warm, freshly baked bread and newly churned butter. Dessert was a specialty usually found further east, pecan pie. All four men had double helpings of everything, plus several cups of coffee. After days on the trail eating mostly bacon and beans, plus a few grouse Duffy had bagged, this supper was satisfying indeed. With their stomachs full, they stepped outside for some fresh air, Smoky and Duffy also enjoying a smoke, then went next door to the Frio House Saloon.

Since it was a Wednesday the place wasn't crowded, so they were able to easily find a spot at the bar.

"Evenin', gents. Welcome to Frio Town, such as the place is," the bartender greeted them. "I'm Tad. What'll you have?"

"Evenin' yourself," Smoky replied. "Smoky's my handle, and my pards are Duffy, Chip, and Ty. I'll have a whiskey."

"Same here," Duffy said.

"I'll have a beer," Ty answered.

"Beer also," Charlie ordered.

Smoky looked askance at Charlie, one eyebrow cocked.

"Beer, Chip? Are you certain about that? What would your dad have to say if he knew you were drinkin' beer, or worse yet, that I let you?"

"Dad wouldn't mind. He's always told me just because he won't use alcohol he doesn't object to anyone else takin' a drink. He said when I was old enough I could make up my own mind about liquor. 'Course, he's also told me if he ever found me drunk he'd tan my hide, then pull it off, turn it inside out, and tan the other side no matter how old I was," Charlie chuckled. "I've been havin' a beer or two once in a while for a year or so."

"That part about your dad tannin' your hide I can believe," Smoky grinned. "All right; if you say so. Barkeep, that's two whiskeys and two beers."

He spun a coin on the mahogany.

"Comin' right up."

Two glasses of whiskey and two foaming mugs of beer were soon placed in front of them.

"You gents are new to Frio Town," the bartender noted. "Stayin' in town for a few days, or just passin' through?"

"We'll be pullin' out in the morning," Smoky answered. "Only stopped here for a night's rest, and to see your marshal. The clerk at the hotel told us he'd stop in here sooner or later."

"Marley's right about that. Jake Stewart'll stick his nose in here in about an hour or so. If you don't mind my askin', is there any particular reason you're lookin' for the marshal? If it's none of my business, just say so," Tad hastened to add.

"You're not out of line." Smoky smiled to assuage the saloon man's concerns. "We're lookin' for directions to the Bar 7 Ranch. Need to meet a feller up there about a job."

"Heck, you don't need to see the marshal for that," Tad replied. "You're a bit far south, though. The Bar 7's fifty miles or so north of here, about a two day ride. It's just outside Concan, up in the Frio River Canyon."

"That figures," Duffy muttered, as he took a sip of his whiskey. "We've been chasin' our own tails this whole trip. Why am I not shocked we're still two days away from the Bar 7?"

"I wouldn't fret about it none," Tad noted. "I'm not surprised the Bar 7's hirin'. It's a good-sized spread, one of the largest in these parts and mighty prosperous too, or so I hear tell. If y'all have any skills with a rope and handlin' cattle, you'll be put on right quick."

"That's good news," Smoky said. "I'd hate to think we rode all this way for nothin'. Appreciate the advice. With that settled, we can just take it easy and enjoy ourselves tonight. Reckon we'll still say howdy to your marshal, though. Most lawmen like to know when strangers are in town."

He tossed back his whiskey and banged the glass on the bar.

"I'll take another," he said.

"Sure." Tad refilled his glass.

They lingered over their drinks while awaiting the marshal, Smoky and Duffy rolling and smoking several cigarettes. Duffy's attention was caught by a buxom red-headed saloon woman beckoning to him. The big, blonde, good-looking Ranger had always been irresistible to most women.

"Looks like that gal wants my company," he muttered. "I'll see you boys later."

"Not too much later," Smoky cautioned him. "Remember, we're ridin' out first thing in the morning."

"I won't stay out too late," Duffy assured him, picking up his glass. "Don't wait up for me either, though."

"Reckon me or you'll never get a gal like that, Chip," Ty complained while he watched Duffy cross the room. "We ain't good-lookin' enough."

While he and Charlie did have rugged good looks, they were not what most would consider handsome.

"You don't want any women like that, leastwise not tonight," Smoky advised him. "Just relax with your beers until the marshal gets here."

Smoky ordered another whiskey for himself and two more beers for Charlie and Ty. They worked the drinks slowly, mostly in silence. Smoky noted that Charlie was becoming more morose and withdrawn as the evening passed.

"Somethin' bothering you, Chip?" he finally asked.

"Yeah, I reckon so," Charlie replied. "Just wonderin how my dad's doin', because we haven't had word about him since we left Austin. I thought mebbe there'd be a wire for us up in Comanche, but nothing."

"Your dad's gonna be fine," Smoky tried to

reassure him. "It's just gonna take a mite of time. Heck, he took two slugs, one right through his middle. It'd take anyone a while to recover from bein' shot up like that."

"I know," Charlie said. "I just wish I could be certain, that's all."

"Chip, if you want to head home to be with your dad and mom, go right ahead," Smoky told him. "We'll all understand, and there'll be no hard feelin's. No one could blame you for ridin' out."

Charlie shook his head.

"There's not a chance of that," he snapped. "I started a job, and I'm not quittin' 'til it's finished."

"Then you have to try'n stop worryin' so much about your dad and concentrate on what needs to be done," Smoky advised. "I know it won't be easy."

"You're right, it won't be, but I'll be okay," Charlie assured him. "Just a bit homesick, that's all. It's been a rough couple of days."

"Looks like our day might be gettin' better," Ty noted, gazing with interest at two women approaching. One was a brunette, the other a brassy blonde, both full-figured and wearing low-cut dresses.

"Howdy, boys," the brunette announced. "I'm Louise, and this is my friend Ophelia."

"Evenin', ladies. What can I do for you?"

155

Smoky questioned, politely putting two fingers to the brim of his hat in greeting.

"Not you," Louise replied. "We're told you're married, not that it matters to us. However, your friend over there with Marguerite said your two companions might be looking for some feminine company."

From across the room, Duffy raised his glass and grinned.

"These young'ns?" Smoky scoffed. "They ain't nowhere near ready for the likes of you gals. Besides, we've gotta get a real early start in the morning. We'll be headin' for our bunks real soon."

"You their father?" Ophelia demanded.

"No, just their friend," Smoky admitted.

"Then why don't we let them decide for themselves?" Ophelia said. She wrapped her arms around Ty's waist.

"You can start with buyin' me a drink, cowboy," she suggested.

"I . . . I dunno," Ty stammered, blushing.

"It'll be just fine, Mister; I won't bite . . . much," Ophelia promised.

"How about you, hombre?" Louise asked Charlie, draping an arm over his shoulder. "Wouldn't you like to buy me a drink? Then we can have more fun, just the two of us."

"I'm not certain, ma'am," Charlie answered. He flushed a deep red.

"Ma'am?" Louise laughed. "I can't recollect the last time anyone's called me 'Ma'am'. Now how about that drink?"

"I'll buy you those drinks, but you'll leave these boys alone, ladies," Smoky insisted.

"How about you keep your nose out of this, and we'll let the boys decide," Louise retorted. "They look old enough to make up their own minds. How about it, cowboy? You gonna let this hombre wet-nurse you all your life?"

"He's not my wet nurse," Charlie grumbled.

"Well, he's sure actin' as if he were," Louise answered. She kissed Charlie full on the lips, hard.

"You still want to let him tell you what to do?"

"How about you?" Ophelia asked Ty. "Are you gonna let that old man boss you around all your life?"

"Chip, Ty . . ." Smoky began.

"Stay out of this, Smoky," Ty warned him.

"Yeah, stay out of it," Charlie repeated. "If Ty and I want to have some fun with these ladies, we'll have it."

"That's telling him, honey," Louise said.

"Two beers for our lady friends, bartender," Ty called.

"Comin' right up," Tad replied.

Smoky stood by, helpless against the unfamiliar, overpowering emotions the two young Rangers were feeling, the stirrings in their bodies which they'd never before felt so strongly. He seethed while the two women worked their wiles, knowing Charlie and Ty would be defenseless against the charms of the two experienced saloon entertainers. Desperate, he finally came up with the one argument he hoped would prove effective.

"Chip, what would your dad think if he saw you right now?" he asked. "This ain't exactly a beer or two you're foolin' with. You forgettin' about him lyin' in a bed with two bullets in him? What about your mom? You forgettin' her also, not to mention Mary Jane Jarratt? How would she feel if she knew what you were up to?"

"Don't listen to him, Chip," Louise urged, kissing him hard yet again. "No one'll know about us, unless you tell them."

"No!" Charlie shook his head and pushed the woman away. "I'd know. Dunno what got into me, less'n it's just from bein' so tired. I'm not gonna shame myself by doin' something I'll regret for the rest of my life. Take your beer and go find somebody else."

"You mean that?" Louise asked, in disbelief.

"I sure do," Charlie confirmed. "I've got a gal waitin' back home, one I swore I'd be true to. I nearly forgot that, until Smoky brought me to my senses. Thanks, Smoke."

"Don't mention it," Smoky replied.

158

Ophelia had loosed her grip on Ty's waist and stood staring at him.

"What about you, cowboy?" she demanded, tugging her dress lower, revealing even more of her full bosom. "You still want to have some fun?"

"I reckon not," Ty answered, swallowing hard. "Like my friend here, I nearly forgot myself. I've got a gal back home too, and she'd be some upset if I took up with another woman."

"You don't know what you'll be missin'," Ophelia insisted.

"Reckon mebbe I do at that, but it don't matter none," Ty replied. "We bought your beers, and we're not obliged to do anything more."

"You heard them," Smoky said. "So git!"

"If that's what they want," Louise answered.

"It's what they want," Smoky reiterated.

"Suit yourselves," Ophelia said. "C'mon, Louise, let's stop wastin' our time here."

Charlie and Ty watched as the two women flounced away, moments later attaching themselves to a pair of young cowpunchers.

"I'm sure glad you boys came to your senses," Smoky said. "The time'll come along when you'll make love to a woman, but it has to be the right time, and the right woman. This sure wasn't it, and they for certain weren't the right women."

"I know," Charlie replied. "Thanks for stoppin' me before it was too late, Uncle Smoky."

The chagrined youngster slipped back into the familiar term he'd called Smoky for years.

"Yeah," Ty agreed. "Same here. Thanks, Smoke."

"Don't mention it, but don't forget it either," Smoky answered. "Far as Duffy, wait'll I get my hands on him for sendin' those gals over here."

"Here he comes now," Ty said, watching Duffy approach, still accompanied by the red-head.

"What's the matter?" Duffy asked, "Didn't you two like those gals?"

"Lady, get lost," Smoky ordered the red-head.

"Smoke, she's . . ."

"You heard me, McGlynn. Tell the lady good night."

Duffy started to retort, then decided against it, seeing the grim set of Smoky's jaw.

"Marguerite, I reckon you'd better leave," he said.

"All right," Marguerite shrugged. She turned to search out another prospect.

"McGlynn, what in blue blazes were you thinking?" Smoky demanded.

"Shucks, I was just havin' some fun," Duffy answered. "Thought mebbe Charlie and Ty'd enjoy havin' . . ." his voice trailed off when he noticed Smoky clenching his fist.

Smoky lowered his voice so it would be difficult for others to hear over the noise of the barroom.

"Duffy, we're after the man who murdered

Captain Trumbull and gunned down Lieutenant Blawcyzk," he reminded him. "It'd be one thing if you'd pulled a practical joke like you're so fond of doin', but the last thing we need is havin' these two youngsters all distracted, with their minds flummoxed by painted women. They're still wet behind the ears in plenty of ways, so until we've got Foley run to ground you remember that, hear me? Or else I'll whip the stuffin' outta you and send you back to Austin. Is that clear?"

"Yeah, I reckon so," Duffy answered. "Guess I made a mistake, Smoky. I didn't mean to start any trouble, and I won't let it happen again."

"See that you don't," Smoky answered. "I need you with us, and you're too good a Ranger to let something like this end your career. Since there was no harm done, it's forgotten. That goes for the both of you also," he told Charlie and Ty. "Meantime, since we're still waitin' for the marshal, I'll buy another round of drinks."

"You buyin' the drinks always sounds good to me, Smoke," Duffy grinned.

It was about twenty minutes later when the batwings swung open and a grizzled man wearing a town marshal's shield stepped into the saloon. Tad had a beer poured and waiting for him in the time it took the lawman to cross the room and belly up to the bar, at the opposite end from Smoky and his partners. He took a large swallow

161

from the beer and nodded to acknowledge the Rangers' presence.

"Evenin', Jake. Town all quiet tonight?" the bartender asked.

"Evenin' yourself Tad. Yep, it is," Stewart answered. "See we've got some strangers here. They say who they are?"

"Yeah, they're drifters who stopped for the night, and are headin' for the Bar 7 first thing tomorrow. Said they'd check in with you once you showed up."

"You think they're anything more than they're lettin' on?"

"I don't believe so," Tad answered. "Appears to me they're just chuckline ridin' cowpokes."

"I'll talk to 'em in a bit," Stewart said. He reached inside his shirt to pull out a folded sheet of thick paper.

"What've you got there?" Tad asked, as the marshal unfolded the poster.

"It's a wanted notice for Tom Foley, that renegade Ranger who killed his captain and shot down another man at Ranger Headquarters," Stewart explained. "Seems the state of Texas is offerin' a thousand dollar reward for his capture. I'd appreciate your allowin' me to put this up in here, just on the off chance Foley might show up here in Frio Town."

"Sure thing, Jake," Tad readily agreed. "Hang it on the post at the end of the bar."

"Gracias."

Stewart pulled his gun from its holster and several nails from his pocket. Most of the saloon's patrons gathered around him as he used the butt off his pistol to hammer the poster in place. The crowd murmured at the size of the reward offered for Foley's capture.

"I could sure use that thousand," one man said. "It'd go a long way toward payin' off the balance on my ranch."

"You wouldn't stand a chance against a man like Foley, Mike," one of his friends pointed out. "He'd put a bullet through your guts before you even knew what happened."

"Yeah, and that poster doesn't say 'Dead or Alive' another man noted. "You think you'd have any hope of capturin' that renegade alive and gettin' him to a cell before he killed you? That thousand would come in handy for me, too, but it ain't worth takin' a couple of slugs for. I figure I'll leave trackin' down Foley to the law."

"If it were up to me, I'd give Foley the reward for gunnin' down those two Rangers, instead of him havin' a price on his head. I ain't got any use for those law dogs at all," a tall, lean rancher loudly complained. "All they are is bandits hidin' behind a badge."

Charlie slammed down his beer and started for the man, only to stop short when Smoky put a restraining hand on his arm.

"Easy, Chip," Smoky warned. "Just let him spout off. We don't want to start any trouble."

"You've had a mad on for the Rangers ever since they wouldn't run those squatters off your land, Lyle," Marshal Stewart said. "That don't give you any call for bein' glad to see one of 'em's killed."

"I'm not satisfied because Foley killed one Ranger," Lyle retorted. "Far as I'm concerned he didn't finish the job. He should've made sure both of 'em were dead."

Hearing those words, Charlie couldn't restrain himself any longer. He pulled away from Smoky's grip, crossed the barroom in eight long strides, pulled the Colt from its holster on his left hip and jabbed the barrel into Lyle's belly. The rancher grunted from the impact, gasping as air was driven from his lungs.

"That other Ranger you want dead is my father, Mister!" Charlie snarled. He pulled back his right fist and punched Lyle squarely in the mouth. Blood spurted from the rancher's smashed lips, and he staggered back, spitting out several pieces of teeth before toppling to the floor. He tried to rise, but his eyes glazed and he settled onto his back, out cold.

Stewart started to pull his gun, but stopped when Charlie turned to face him, his blue eyes cold and deadly. The young Ranger had his Colt leveled an inch above the marshal's belt buckle.

"Careful, Marshal, I don't mean to cause you or anyone else any trouble," Charlie advised. "Take your hand off your gun and I'll put up mine."

"All right, son," Stewart agreed. He deliberately lifted his hand from the butt of his gun, holding it several inches to the side. Charlie slowly replaced his own gun in its holster.

"I'm sorry, Marshal," Charlie apologized. "I just couldn't listen to that hombre sayin' he wanted my dad dead."

"I can sure understand that," Stewart agreed. "Lyle always did have too big a mouth for his own good, but I can't have strangers ridin' into my town and stirrin' things up. You and your pards had better leave as soon as you can saddle your horses."

"We'll be leavin' at sunup like we'd planned, Marshal, not a minute sooner," Smoky spoke up. "Our room and horses' board have already been paid. We've been on the trail for quite a spell and need a good night's rest. More importantly, so do our horses, which're plumb wore out. We'll leave now and go upstairs, so that way you needn't worry about us causin' any more problems."

"I reckon that'll be all right," Stewart conceded. "You mind givin' me your names, just for the record?"

"I'm Smoky McCue. My pards are Duffy McGlynn and Tyler Tremblay, and that young hothead is Chip Blawcyzk. Like he said, his dad's Ranger Lieutenant Jim Blawcyzk, who's still in bad shape from the two slugs Foley put through him."

"I reckon I can't blame him for what he did to Lyle Cavendish, but that also makes me suspicious you're not just driftin' cowpokes like you claim."

"I guess there's no use tryin' to keep it a secret now," Smoky admitted. "We're Texas Rangers, on Tom Foley's trail. Last word we had is he was headed in this direction."

Several of the bystanders muttered in astonishment.

"Tad claims you were headin' for the Bar 7. Any particular reason?" Stewart questioned.

"Foley used to work there, before he was a Ranger. Our information states he might have gone there before movin' on to Mexico."

"That makes sense," Stewart agreed. Behind him, Lyle Cavendish moaned. "I'll take care of Cavendish, but I'd rather you're gone before he comes to."

"Of course," Smoky said. "Thanks for understandin', and good night, Marshal."

Once they had returned to their room, Smoky confronted Charlie.

"Chip, I know for a fact your dad must have told you never to pull your gun unless you intended to use it. What you did downstairs was plumb foolish. What the devil were you thinkin'?"

"I guess I wasn't," Charlie admitted. "When I heard that hombre sayin' those things about my dad, I just couldn't stop myself. I couldn't let him get away with that."

"You're gonna have to learn how to let some things roll off your back or you'll get yourself killed pretty quick, goin' off half-cocked like you did," Smoky warned him. "You might also get your pardners killed. I didn't want it known we're Rangers, and you knew that. Suppose one of Foley's friends was in that crowd? He'd get word to Foley as soon as he could, which'd give Foley enough warnin' so he could get away again . . . or set us up for a nice ambush. Dunno about you, but I'm not hankerin' for a bullet in the back. I'm sure Duffy and Ty aren't either."

"Don't be so hard on the kid, Smoke," Duffy said. "If I were in his boots I'd probably have done the same."

"No, Smoky's right," Charlie answered. "I shouldn't have gone after Cavendish like I did. You want my resignation, Sergeant?"

"Don't be ridiculous," Smoky replied. "You've got the makin's of a fine Ranger, Chip. You're just like your dad in so many ways, but there's one big difference. You've got one heckuva temper, which your dad doesn't . . . well, except when it comes to someone abusin' a horse."

"Yeah, that does tend to set him off," Charlie agreed. "Not to mention that time when those renegades invaded our ranch, shot me and dad, attacked my mom, and left us all for dead. He got more than a bit angry then, in fact he pretty much lost all sense of reason for a spell."

"Seein' a horse being mistreated does indeed set him off, and as far as the raid on your home, that would drive any man a bit loco," Smoky said. "My point is that most times, no matter how angry your father becomes, he usually manages to keep his temper in check. You're gonna struggle with that, kid. I can see it in your eyes whenever you're about to lose control of yourself. There's something in them I've never seen in your dad's."

"Sometimes a man needs righteous anger to help him through a situation, Smoky," Ty observed.

"That's correct, Ty," Smoky conceded. "However, there's a huge difference between controlled righteous anger and just plain flyin' off the handle. Chip needs to learn that, and fast."

"I can't promise it won't happen again, Smoky," Charlie said. "All I can promise is I'll try and make sure it doesn't."

"That's all I ask," Smoky replied. "Now it's been a long day, and we've still got two more hard days' ridin' before we reach the Bar 7, so I suggest it's time we turn in."

"You won't get any argument from me there,"

Ty chuckled. He sat on the edge of the bed and began tugging off his boots.

Soon, all four had removed their boots, hats, and gunbelts and crowded into the room's one bed.

"Quit shovin', Duffy," Ty complained. Duffy grunted when Ty put an elbow into his ribs. Those were the last words Smoky heard before he drifted off to sleep.

The sun was still low on the eastern horizon when the Rangers departed Frio Town, their route taking them along the winding Frio River. As they followed the river northwestward, the land gradually rose in elevation. The mostly level, virtually featureless plain they had been traversing for the past few days gradually became more rolling, and interspersed with low but rugged hills. The vegetation likewise changed, the grasses, scrub brush, and cactus becoming more sparse, replaced with bigger shrubs, mesquite, even cottonwoods and live oaks in spots. The Frio was generally shallow, mostly no deeper than knee high, if that, with a lazy current broken in spots by gentle rapids. In places where the river did run deeper, it was often shaded by towering cypress trees, which provided welcome relief from the constant heat and blistering Texas sun. Except for an occasional small settlement, which usually consisted of a smattering of ramshackle houses surrounding a general store and saloon, they passed no signs of civilization. The trail itself showed no evidence of recent travelers.

About an hour before sundown, Smoky called a halt.

"I figure we've covered enough ground for today," he announced. "This looks like a good spot to camp for the night. We'll get another early start tomorrow, which should find us at the Bar 7 before nightfall."

The spot Smoky had chosen was at a bend in the Frio, where it ran more deeply than in most places. Huge cypresses rose over the streambed, while a good-sized area of grass promised decent grazing for the horses.

"Looks like a good place to cool off," Charlie observed.

"That's exactly why I decided to call it a day," Smoky replied. "Once we care for the horses I figure we can take a nice, relaxin' swim."

"That sure sounds good to me," Ty stated, as he swung off Bandit's back. "I can hardly wait to scrub off some of this trail grime."

The horses were quickly unsaddled, rubbed down, watered, and picketed to graze. Once that was done, Smoky dug in his saddlebags and came up with a bar of harsh yellow soap. The men stripped off their gunbelts, boots, and clothes, then dove into the cool, crystal turquoise waters of the Frio.

"This sure feels good," Charlie said, while he relaxed neck deep in the river and let the refreshing liquid soothe away the aches of long days in the saddle.

"I believe I've washed off ten pounds of dirt," Duffy added, running the soap over his chest.

"Don't hog all that soap, Duffy," Ty warned. "I want some of it too."

"I'm just about finished," Duffy replied. "Here."

He tossed the bar to Ty, who had to make a diving catch, landing face-down with a huge splash.

"Thanks a lot, pard," Ty spluttered when he surfaced.

"Don't mention it," Duffy laughed.

They had been in the river for nearly an hour, unwinding from the stress of the past days, when Duffy got up and emerged from the water.

"Gotta take a break," he announced. "Nature's callin'. I'll be right back."

"Don't rush," Smoky called after him. "We ain't goin' anywhere."

Duffy disappeared behind the cypresses. He had been gone for about five minutes when a heart-stopping war-whoop ripped the air, followed by a blood-curdling scream. Duffy staggered into the clearing, his hands wrapped around an arrow's shaft which protruded from his stomach.

"Indians! Comanches!" Duffy gasped, then

plunged to the dirt, rolling onto his back, stopping just short of the river. At the same moment, Smoky screeched in pain and terror. He fell back into the Frio, his body slowly drifting with the current.

"We're sittin' ducks. What'll we do, Chip?" Ty shouted.

"I dunno, but I'm not goin' down without a fight," Charlie answered. "Let's try for our guns."

He lunged from the river and dove for his gunbelt, grunting when he hit the ground hard. He grabbed his pistol, yanked it from its holster, and rolled behind a downed log. In the meantime Ty had also managed to reach the shore. He dropped to his hands and knees, crawled to where he'd left his outfit, retrieved his Colt, and pulled himself along on his belly until he reached the same log where Charlie had taken cover.

"You see any Indians, Ty?" Charlie asked.

"No, but they're out there, just waitin' to take our scalps," Ty answered. "You see any way out of this fix?"

"No." Charlie shook his head. "Not with Smoky and Duffy dead. All we can do is take as many of those renegades with us as we can before they get us."

"Sure is quiet," Ty noted. "Wish they'd get this over with."

"They're bidin' their time, tryin' to rattle us,"

Charlie answered. "They'll come outta those trees soon enough. Bet a hat on it."

From the riverbank, there came a muffled guffaw.

"What the devil was that?" Ty questioned. "Didn't sound like any Comanche to me."

Charlie turned to locate the source of the sound. Duffy was still lying on his back, but now his body was quivering with mirth while he tried to stifle his laughter. In the river, Smoky's body had hauled up on the bank, a short distance downstream.

"That wasn't any Indian, it was Duffy," Charlie answered. "Looks like he's still alive, but he can't last long, not with an arrow in his gut. I reckon I should finish him off before those Comanches get to him and torture him."

Charlie raised his Colt and aimed it in Duffy's direction.

"Chip, don't shoot!" Duffy called. "There ain't any Comanches. I was just funnin' you and Ty."

"There ain't any Indians?" Ty repeated.

"There sure aren't," Smoky confirmed, stepping out of the water. "Duffy pulls the same trick on most of the rookies who ride with him. It's kind of an initiation. He asked me if I'd go along with his gag, and naturally I couldn't resist. You gonna let him up now?"

"I reckon," Charlie grudgingly conceded.

Duffy rolled onto his stomach and pushed himself to his feet.

"Duffy, you . . ." Ty growled.

"Wait a minute. What about that arrow in your gut?" Ty then asked.

"That arrow's only a stick, with the feathers from my hatband tied onto the end," Duffy explained. "It looks real enough to fool most anyone, long as they're not too close."

Duffy burst into laughter once again.

"You two should've seen the looks on your faces when you thought I'd been killed and there was a whole passel of Comanches ready to swoop outta the trees."

"I'm glad you think it was so funny," Ty answered. "I sure don't."

"Don't take it so hard, Ty," Smoky advised. "Duffy's pulled that stunt on plenty of new Rangers. It doesn't hurt anything, except mebbe some pride."

"Yeah, Ty," Charlie agreed. "You've gotta admit Duffy sure had us buffaloed. Besides, we couldn't have looked much funnier than Duffy did when he thought I was gonna plug him."

"You knew?" Duffy said.

"Not until you started laughin'," Charlie admitted. "When you did it gave you away, so then I figured I could pull a little joke of my own. You've gotta admit for a second you really thought I was gonna finish you off, pardner."

"I guess you got me there," Duffy conceded.

"Still took ten years off my life," Ty said, now grinning.

"Yeah, but next time Duffy pulls this off you'll get the chance to help him," Smoky said.

"That's right," Duffy added. "It always works better when I have a couple other men to play along with the gag."

"Or we can pull something on you, Duffy," Ty warned, with a chuckle. "Better watch your back."

"That's always good advice," Smoky said. "Dunno about the rest of you, but I'm famished. Let's get dressed and round up some firewood. I'll handle the cookin' tonight, 'cause I've got a surprise for you. Back in Frio Town I bought the fixin's for my famous sinker flapjacks. I was gonna make 'em for breakfast, but I can't wait to chow down on those hotcakes."

"Duffy, Ty, it's a good thing Smoky isn't waitin' until breakfast to make those flapjacks," Charlie said, grinning. "They're so heavy you'll give your horse a swayback—that is, if you can even climb onto your horse weighted down with Smoky's flapjacks in your belly."

"They're not that heavy," Smoky objected. "They do stick to your ribs, I'll grant you that, but heavy enough to break a horse's back? You're exaggeratin' a mite there, Chip."

"Then why did the United States Navy ask

you to make up a batch of 'em for them to try as armor plate for their ships?" Charlie retorted.

"Hey, I've never seen you turn down my flapjacks," Smoky shot back. "In fact, you usually down at least a half dozen of them."

"I never said they weren't tasty, just that they were heavy," Charlie answered.

"Why don't the two of you stop jawin' so Smoky can start cookin', before we plumb starve to death?" Duffy said.

"You've got a point, Duffy," Ty agreed. "My bellybutton's sunk in clean to my backbone, it's been so long since I've had any grub."

"All right, I'll start cookin' soon as you ranahans round up some firewood and get it burnin'," Smoky said.

"We'll have that fire goin' in a jiffy," Charlie promised.

They quickly dressed, and while Smoky got the flapjack supplies from a sack he'd tied on his saddle the others gathered downed twigs and branches. While Smoky mixed the batter, Charlie and Ty got the fire burning. A short while later, they were chewing on flapjacks sweetened with molasses and downing cups of hot black coffee.

Duffy swallowed a last helping of flapjacks, lit a quirly, and leaned back against his saddle, rubbing his stomach in satisfaction.

"Smoky, Chip was sure right about your hotcakes," he remarked. "They're mighty tasty, but I wouldn't want to try'n outrun a band of renegade Indians after eatin' a mess of 'em. Feels like I've got a ton of lead sittin' in my belly."

"Which just matches the lead in your backside, lard butt," Ty chuckled.

"At least I've got a butt," Duffy retorted. "You're so skinny a good breeze'd pick you up and blow you clean to the Gulf of Mexico. Dunno how your gunbelt stays on your hips."

"Not with Smoky's flapjacks in him, that wind wouldn't," Charlie answered. "Bet a hat on it."

"I've gotta agree with you there, Chip," Duffy conceded.

They spent the next hour relaxing, talking and watching the moon rise. Finally, when the fire had just about died out, they spread out their blankets and settled in for the night. As usual, Ty was the first one asleep, while Smoky and Duffy enjoyed a final smoke and Charlie murmured his evening prayers. A short while later, all four were softly snoring, their breathing the regular rhythm of men sleeping peacefully.

About four the next afternoon the Rangers rode into the small town of Concan. The settlement had been established around 1840 in the rugged hills of northern Uvalde county, and was supposedly named for the old Mexican card game of Con Quien, which had been corrupted to Coon Can. It had an idyllic setting deep in the Frio

River Canyon. Numerous springs in the area, over eleven hundred according to some residents, provided plenty of water sources in this parched region.

"We'll only stop for a few minutes, to give the horses a breather and make sure we're headin' in the right direction. Give your broncs a drink while I see the marshal," Smoky ordered. "It shouldn't be too much further to the Bar 7."

While the others headed for a horse trough in front of the general store, Smoky reined up in front of the town marshal's office. The arrival of four strangers in any town as small as Concan was sure to attract attention, and by the time Smoky had dismounted the marshal was already standing on the boardwalk in front of his office, waiting for him. He was young, no more than in his late twenties, with sandy hair and gray eyes. Smoky didn't miss the challenging look in the local lawman's eyes, nor the wanted poster for Tom Foley nailed to the wall behind him.

"Howdy, Marshal," Smoky said.

"Afternoon, Mister. What brings your bunch to Concan?" the marshal answered, his voice flat and expressionless. He kept his hand on the butt of the Smith and Wesson hanging on his right hip, while his gaze never wandered from Smoky's face.

"We're headin' for the Bar 7 Ranch, and need some directions," Smoky explained.

"You got business out there?" the marshal questioned.

"You might say that," Smoky replied. "We're Texas Rangers on the trail of Tom Foley, that hombre on the poster behind you. I'm Sergeant McCue, and my pardners are Rangers McGlynn, Blawcyzk, and Tremblay. We have information that Foley used to work at the Bar 7, and might've headed there. You haven't seen him, have you?"

"Hank Barton, and I can't say as I have," the marshal answered. He relaxed, taking his hand off his gun at hearing Smoky's identity.

"You recollect ever seein' him out there?"

"No, but that doesn't mean anything. I've only been marshal here for a couple of years, so if he worked there it was before my time. Besides, the Bar 7's out of my jurisdiction, so I've got no call to ride out there."

"I understand," Smoky replied. "Can you at least point us in the right direction?"

"Sure. Just keep following the river trail north, about four miles or so. You'll see a turn-off to the left, marked with a big Bar 7 sign nailed to a post. The main house is just down that turn-off. You can't miss the place."

"Appreciate that, Marshal," Smoke said. "Much obliged."

"Anytime, Ranger," Barton answered.

Smoky remounted and rejoined his companions,

still waiting by the horse trough. He allowed Soot to dip his muzzle in the trough, the gelding greedily sucking up the tepid water.

"What'd the marshal have to say, Smoke?" Duffy asked.

"First, he hasn't seen Tom Foley. Second, we're not all that far from the Bar 7. It's only a few miles north of here," Smoky answered. "Let's get ridin'," he continued, as Soot lifted his dripping muzzle from the trough. "We can be there in less than an hour."

He put Soot into a trot, the others close behind, following the road out of Concan.

As the marshal had said, a bit more than four miles later they arrived at the Bar 7 ranch, which stood on a rise overlooking the Frio. The main house, as well as the bunkhouse, were sturdily constructed of cypress logs, the roofs of cypress shingles, a style prevalent in this part of Texas. A low-roofed porch surrounded the main house on three sides, providing welcome shade. The view from the porch took in a spectacular panorama of the surrounding low hills and plains, as well as the meandering river. The outbuildings were likewise well constructed, as were the corrals. In one of these a wrangler was working a young sorrel while several cowboys sat on the fence, observing as he attempted to saddle and mount the spirited animal.

"Nice lookin' place," Duffy noted.

"Sure is," Smoky agreed. "Let's head on down there."

He heeled Soot into a walk. A few moments later, they rode up to the corral where the sorrel was being worked. The cowboys nodded to the new arrivals, then turned their attention back to the man and horse in the corral.

The wrangler was a black man of indeterminate age, tall and stocky. He'd lost his hat while trying to saddle the sorrel, revealing a completely bald head. He'd finally managed to tighten the saddle in place, and now stepped into the stirrup and swung onto the horse's back. The sorrel immediately exploded into a frenzy of bucking and spinning.

"Stay with him, Jeff!" one of the cowboys yelled, while the others whooped and shouted their encouragement. "You've got him now."

The wrangler stuck like glue to the sorrel's back while it went through a series of bone-jarring bucks, sunfishing and twisting, then rearing high in the air and coming down stiff-legged, the impact jolting every nerve in the rider's body. Jeff grimaced with pain, but remained planted firmly in the saddle as the horse went into another series of violent bucks.

"Stick with him, Jeff!" "You've got him now!" "Ride that ornery critter!" "Ain't seen a cayuse yet you haven't been able to ride, Jeff!" The cries of encouragement continued, urging the wrangler

181

to finish his ride. Finally, the exhausted sorrel gave one last half-hearted jump, then settled into a steady trot around the corral's perimeter.

"Atta boy, Jeff," one of the cowboys called. "You showed that bronc who's boss."

The wrangler rode the sorrel around the corral a few more circuits, then dismounted. He stroked the sorrel's neck and rubbed its muzzle, speaking to it quietly, reassuring the horse.

"Nice ride, Mister," Smoky called.

"Thanks," the wrangler replied, smiling pleasantly. He looked over Soot with a practiced eye. "Nice steeldust you've got there. That goes for the rest of you, too. Those are all good-lookin' broncs you boys are forkin'."

"Thank you," Smoky answered. "By any chance are you the owner of this place?"

The wrangler chuckled appreciatively at the compliment which Smoky had just given him, asking if he owned the Bar 7.

"Me, the owner? Heck no. I'm Jeff King, the head wrangler on this spread. Brendan and Jeff Nichols are the owners."

"From the way you handled that sorrel I can sure understand why you're the head wrangler around here," Smoky answered. "Where might I find one of the Nicholses?"

"Jeff's up at the house, goin' over the books," King replied. "Brendan rode into town this mornin', then was headin' to check some of the stock on the south range. There's a crew cuttin' out dries over that way. He should be back any time now, but if you're lookin' for jobs you don't want to see either of them. Bill Hennessey's the foreman, and he does all the hirin' and firin'. He's also on the south range, and'll probably ride in with Brendan."

"That's not why we're here," Smoky answered. "We're Texas Rangers. I'm Sergeant Smoky McCue, and my pards are Duffy McGlynn, Chip Blawcyzk, and Ty Tremblay."

"Rangers?" King echoed. "The Nichols brothers ain't in any trouble, are they?"

"Not at all," Smoky assured him. "We just need to talk with them a spell, about an hombre who used to work here."

"In that case, head on up to the house," King said. "I'm done here for today, so you can turn your horses into this corral until you can take care of 'em. In the meantime, we'll water 'em and toss 'em some hay. While you're unsaddling, I'll introduce you to the rest of the boys."

He looked at Charlie and shook his head.

"Chip . . . Bluh . . . ?"

"Bluh-zhick," Charlie offered. "It's Polish, and my given name's Charles. Lot easier to just call me Chip."

"I won't argue that point," King chortled. "Well, get down off those horses and light and set a spell."

The horses were unsaddled and turned into the corral, where they rolled in the sand, then trotted over to munch on their hay.

"Duffy, there's no need for all of us to go up to the house," Smoky said. "You and Ty stay here and take it easy. Me'n Chip'll talk with Nichols."

"It's gettin' late," King noted. "Y'all might as well stay to supper, and you're welcome to spend the night. There's plenty of room in the bunkhouse."

It would be impolite on any ranch not to offer travelers a meal and place to stay for an overnight's rest. The Western code of hospitality dictated such.

"We'll take you up on that offer," Smoky agreed. "Much obliged. C'mon, Chip, let's go."

They trudged up the hill to the main house, climbed the steps, and knocked on the front door. A plump, elderly Mexican woman answered.

"Yes? May I help you gentlemen?" she asked.

"We would like to speak with Mister Nichols," Smoky explained. "We're Texas Rangers."

"Rangers? I will tell Senor Nichols you are here. Wait on the porch, por favor."

"Gracias, Senora."

The woman turned back inside the house, closing the door behind her. Smoky rolled and lit a quirly while he and Charlie awaited her return. It was only a few moments before the door opened again.

184

"Senor Nichols will see you. Follow me, por favor."

"Gracias, Senora."

Smoky crushed out his cigarette on the rail and tossed the butt into the dust. He and Ty followed the woman down a long paneled corridor. She stopped at the end of the hallway, and motioned to a door on the right.

"Senor Nichols is in there. Enter, por favor. If you will excuse me, I must get back to my work."

"Bring us some coffee, Jacinta," a voice called from the room.

"Si, Senor Nichols. Senores, I will return shortly, with refreshments."

"Of course. Muchas Gracias, Senora," Smoky answered. He and Charlie stepped into the room indicated, a room dominated by a heavy pine desk and decorated with Navajo rugs along with various Indian artifacts. Waiting for them was a burly man in his thirties, lantern-jawed and barrel-chested. His eyes were a bright blue/gray, his hair sandy. His face lit in a ready smile when he shook Smoky's hand with a powerful grip.

"Howdy, I'm Jeff Nichols. Welcome to the Bar 7," he greeted them.

"Thank you. I'm Sergeant Smoky McCue, and this is Ranger Chip Blawcyzk. Prosperous lookin' place you've got."

"Thanks, we manage to do all right. I'm pleased to meet you both, but what brings you here? No one's accused any Bar 7 hands of rustlin', have they?"

"I wish it were that simple," Smoky answered. "You've probably heard by now about the shootin's at Ranger Headquarters."

"Just recently. News takes a while to reach us this far out," Jeff explained. "Hard to believe someone could gun down a couple of Rangers right inside your headquarters."

"One of 'em was my dad," Charlie softly said.

"Your dad? I'm really sorry, son. Was he killed?"

"No, he's still hangin' on the last I knew," Charlie responded. "He was shot up pretty bad though, and still might not make it."

"I sure hope he does," Jeff said. "I'm not certain what those shootin's have to do with the Bar 7, however."

"Are you aware it was another Ranger, Tom Foley, who killed Captain Trumbull and shot Jim Blawcyzk, Charlie's father?" Smoky questioned.

"I'd heard that, yes," Jeff said.

"We've been trackin' Foley from Comanche. He was spotted up there and got into a gunfight with one of the town deputies. He shot the deputy and got away, but his partner, Junie Blaisdell, was captured. According to Blaisdell Foley's headed for Mexico, but he was planning on stopping here first. Blaisdell claims Foley used to work on the Bar 7, and kept in touch with his friends. Blaisdell says Foley figured he could count on help here."

"It's true, Tom Foley did work here before he joined the Rangers," Jeff admitted. "He came back to visit whenever he got the chance. In fact one time he was with your father, Chip. He hasn't been by here for months though, at least not that I'm aware of. Knowing he killed a Ranger and tried to kill another, he wouldn't be welcome here in any event. We run an honest operation here, except for mebbe brandin' a few mavericks just like every rancher does, and don't tolerate lawbreakin'."

"What about your brother, or any of the men? Would Foley have tried to meet them without you knowin' it?" Smoky pressed.

"It's possible of course, but I doubt it," Jeff answered. "He must have realized that by now we'd heard that he'd gunned down a couple of men, and wouldn't want him on the Bar 7. My guess is he headed straight for Mexico."

"You're probably right," Smoky conceded. "We'd still like to talk with your brother, though, and question your hands."

"Of course. Brendan should be back any time now, as well as Bill Hennessey, our foreman, and his crew. Why don't we wait on the porch for them to return? They should be here just in time for supper. The meal's a bit late tonight, since we're waitin' on my brother and the rest. I know it's a bit unusual holding a meal until later, but our cook insists it's easier on him to serve as many of the men as possible at the same time. Instead of that coffee, I'll have Jacinta bring us some whiskey."

"That sounds good," Smoky agreed. "Better make it somethin' less potent for Chip here, though. He doesn't drink anything stronger'n beer."

"I don't have any beer around the place right now, but the water from our well is really cold," Jeff answered. "How's that?"

"That sounds fine, Mister Nichols, or I'll still have some coffee," Charlie said.

"All right then, I'll stop by the kitchen and have Jacinta bring everything out to us. How about a cigar, too? My brother and I have them brought in specially from New Orleans."

"I'll try one, but Chip doesn't smoke," Smoky answered. "I've got two other men with me, by the way. If you don't mind, could they wait with us?"

"Not at all," Jeff answered. "I'll simply have Jacinta bring out more."

A few moments later they, along with Duffy and Ty, were seated in wooden armchairs on the front porch, watching the sun descend toward the western horizon, Smoky, Duffy and Jeff sipping whiskey and smoking cigars, while Charlie and Ty worked on cups of strong black coffee, which was accompanied by a tray of ginger snaps.

"This is a fine cigar," Smoky praised, leaning

back in his chair and sending a ring of smoke toward the porch ceiling. "Mighty good whiskey, also."

"You can thank my brother for that when he arrives," Jeff answered. "He's the one who orders the smokes and liquor."

"I'll be sure to do that," Smoky said. His eyes narrowed when he spotted a smudge of dust on the horizon. "Riders comin'. Reckon that's your brother now?"

"It's gotta be," Jeff said. "That's the direction he'd ride in from."

The sun was gilding the western horizon in spectacular shades of gold, orange, and red when Brendan Nichols and his companions finally rode into the yard. They unsaddled their horses and turned them into a corral, then a man Smoky took to be Brendan walked up to the house.

"Howdy, Brendan, how was your trip to town?" Jeff asked.

" 'Bout the same as always," Brendan answered. "See we've got some company."

"We sure do. These are Rangers Smoky McCue, Duffy McGlynn, Chip Blawcyzk, and Ty Tremblay. Rangers, meet my older brother, Brendan."

The resemblance between the two brothers was striking. Like Jeff, Brendan was stockily built, with the same lantern jaw and barrel chest, and there was only a couple of inches difference in their heights. Brendan's hair was slightly darker than Jeff's, more of a light brown than sandy-colored. His jaw was framed by a close-cropped beard. Where the similarities ended were Brendan's eyes, which were an unusual green/hazel shade.

"Rangers, huh? What brings the Texas Rangers out this way?" Brendan asked. He climbed onto the porch, took out a cigar, and poured himself a glass of whiskey.

"We're on the trail of Tom Foley, the renegade Ranger who murdered Captain Hank Trumbull and badly wounded another man, Jim Blawcyzk, Chip's father," Smoky explained. "We have information that Foley's headed for Mexico, but that he might have stopped here first, lookin' for some help."

"He sure wouldn't find any help here after gunning down two men," Brendan growled. "We wouldn't have any truck with an hombre who'd do that."

"How about any of your hands?" Smoky asked. "Think any of them might try'n help Foley?"

"Anything's possible, but I doubt it," Brendan answered. "Our men are hard-workin' cow-punchers, not gunmen. The most excitement they have is ridin' into town on payday for some drinkin' and gamblin', mebbe a visit with a woman. No, I honestly don't believe Tom Foley would be welcome here any longer."

"Looks like this was a wild goose chase," Ty muttered.

"I'm afraid it was," Jeff answered. "Sure wish you had found Foley here. We'd have helped you bring him in."

"He's probably crossed the Rio Grande by now," Brendan surmised.

"By the way, Jeff, speaking of Mexico, I got the wire we were waitin' on from that cattle buyer in Del Rio. He wants to meet with me to discuss a deal as soon as possible, so I'll be ridin' for Del Rio first thing in the morning."

"I didn't expect to hear from him so soon," Jeff answered.

"Neither did I, but I'm sure glad we did," Brendan said. "We're way overloaded with stock, so we need to turn some of these cows into cash as quickly as possible."

"We do quite a bit of cross-border cattle tradin' with the Mexicans, both at Ciudad Acuna and Piedras Negras," he explained to the Rangers. "Plenty of money to be made in that trade, which is why our spread is so prosperous. There's ready cash, and we don't have to drive our cattle anywhere near as far as we would to the Northern markets."

"That makes sense," Smoky agreed.

From the cook shack alongside the bunkhouse, a triangle rang out. A grizzled old cowpuncher appeared in the doorway.

"Come and get it, before I throw it to the hogs," he yelled.

"Danby means it, too," Brendan chuckled. "We'd better get on down there before he does just that."

"My brother and I usually take our meals with the hands, unless we've got special company," Jeff explained. "Not that you Rangers aren't guests," he hastened to add. "It's just that we weren't expectin' you."

"Eatin' with your men is just fine with us," Smoky answered. "We do most of our eatin' on the trail anyway, so just bein' under a roof for our supper makes it special."

The triangle rang again.

"Danby's gettin' impatient. Let's go," Brendan urged.

"You don't have to ask us twice," Duffy replied.

Quite a few more men had ridden off the range for the evening meal, and were introduced to the Rangers. The Bar 7 hands were the typical mixture seen on most Southwestern ranches, a mix of white cowboys, Mexican vaqueros, and black men, most of those former slaves who had drifted west after the demise of the Confederacy. They were a group of various ages, ranging from rambunctious young waddies to grizzled old cowhands. A few of them appeared tougher than the rest, more handy with their guns, but that was not unexpected on a remote spread, where rustlers and the occasional marauding band of Indians, the latter becoming more rare with each passing year, were a constant threat.

One of the younger hands reached for a biscuit, only to have Danby whack the back of his hand with a wooden spoon.

"We've got guests tonight, O'Malley, and they'll be served first. You forgotten your manners, boy?"

"Reckon I did for a minute. Sorry, Danby," the cowboy murmured.

Danby was, as were most ranch cooks, a former cowboy, now too old to ride the range punching cattle, and like most ranch cooks, ran his kitchen with an iron hand. At mealtime the ranch cook was the absolute boss. Not even the ranch owner or his foreman dared cross the cook.

"Rangers, step right up and fill your plates," Danby invited.

"Don't mind if we do," Smoky said.

The meal was the usual ranch supper, consisting of plenty of beefsteaks, boiled potatoes, beans, biscuits, and gravy, accompanied by plenty of black coffee. Dessert was thick slices of dried-apple pie.

"Danby, that was the best meal we've had in a month of Sundays," Smoky praised.

"Sure was," Charlie added.

"See boys, these here Rangers know good vittles when they taste 'em," Danby declared. "Sure is an honor cookin' for men who appreciate my hard work, rather'n a bunch of cow nurses who complain all the time I'm not feedin' 'em right."

"That's 'cause you left the sand outta the grub for once, Danby," Bill Hennessey retorted.

"Just for that you get your own breakfast tomorrow, loudmouth," Danby snapped back.

"It's a deal. Mebbe I won't have a bellyache for a change," Hennessey laughed. He ducked out the door when Danby picked up a cast iron frypan and threw it at him. Danby let loose with a string of curses when the pan bounced off the wall.

"Danby, we'll help you clean up," Smoky offered. Just as the Western code of hospitality dictated travelers must be offered a meal and overnight bunk, it also obligated those travelers to reciprocate by lending a hand with the chores.

"Nah, O'Malley's gonna do that for tryin' to sneak that biscuit," Danby replied. "You men just go down to the bunkhouse and get settled in."

"Much obliged," Smoky replied. "We'll check our horses and grab our bedrolls."

"I'll come with you," Jeff King offered. "I want to check on that sorrel I was workin' anyway."

"Thanks," Smoky answered, "Lead the way."

Once the horses were checked and their blankets retrieved, Smoky and his companions accompanied King to the bunkhouse.

"Take any of the empty bunks," Bill Hennessey said.

"Gracias, Bill," Duffy answered. He chose a bunk in the far corner, rolling out his blankets. The others followed suit.

One of the cowboys pulled out a fiddle, another a harmonica, and were soon giving their off-key but lively rendition of "Turkey in the Straw." Others tended to the nightly chores which never seemed to be finished. Several were mending clothes or darning socks, while three or four labored with heavy needles and thread as they repaired torn leather or restitched worn tack. Two of the men pulled out rags and cans of saddle soap and began cleaning their saddles and bridles.

"How about some cards?" Billy Newly, one of the veteran hands, invited Smoky and the other Rangers. "We've got a couple of tables ready."

"Sure, deal us in," Smoky agreed.

They played a friendly game of poker for the next two hours, while one by one the other men drifted to their bunks. Finally, Smoky yawned and stretched.

"I don't mean to cut the evenin' short, but we've gotta be on the trail by sunup," he said. "Reckon it's time to call it a night."

"That's just as well," Will Williams answered. "We've got a long day ahead of us too."

The lamps were extinguished, except for one turned low. Fifteen minutes later, the only sound in the bunkhouse was that of men snoring softly or settling more deeply into their bunks.

Chapter Ten

Two days after leaving the Bar 7, the Rangers were on the northern bank of the Rio Grande. They had dismounted in a small clearing, surrounded by thickets of brush.

"We'll camp here for the night, then cross the river at sunup," Smoky ordered. "Since I don't want to chance anyone recognizin' us, particularly me or Duffy, we're not gonna use the crossin' between Eagle Pass and Piedras Negras. There's a ford about four miles north we'll take instead. That's about a mile from where we are right now. We sure can't afford to have anyone realize there's four Texas Rangers crossing into Mexico."

"Smoke, what if Foley decided not to head directly for Zaragoza, but chose to remain on this side of the border for a while?" Ty questioned. "Shouldn't we check around Eagle Pass first, just in case?"

"My hunch is Foley wouldn't hazard being spotted in any of the border towns," Smoky explained. "Don't forget, all the local authorities have been notified to be watchin' for him, and now there's that thousand dollar reward out too. It'd be too big a risk for Foley to take, especially since he's got friends already waitin' for him in Mexico, accordin' to Blaisdell."

"That makes sense, I reckon," Ty conceded.

"There's also the biggest reason I'm certain Foley avoided Eagle Pass, which is there's a Texas Ranger, Matt McCarthy, who's stationed there. That's also why we're not ridin' into town. Matt'd have to try and stop us if he knew we were planning on crossin' the Rio, or failing that, report what we were up to. Once he got word to Austin, they'd most likely notify the rurales, and we'd be up to our necks in trouble."

"Cap'n Huggins wouldn't turn us in," Charlie objected.

"He'd stall as long as he could, but sooner or later word'd get out he was coverin' for us, then it'd be his hide along with ours," Smoky said.

"Smoke, wouldn't it be smarter to ford the river tonight, under the cover of darkness?" Duffy asked.

"Not at all," Smoky replied. "First, it's gonna be a clear night, so even without a full moon there'll be enough light to skyline us while we're crossin'. We'd be clear targets for any bushwhackers hidin' in the shadows along the riverbanks, and we sure wouldn't be able to see them. I'm not much worried about an ambush anyway, since no one should know where we're at. More importantly, the ford we'll be takin' is real hazardous, doubly so at night. It's really just a narrow sandbar, so if your horse makes one misstep you could get swept away by the current and drowned real easy, especially with the Rio runnin' high like it is now. As it is, the horses are gonna have to swim part of the way. We'll have a much better shot at getting across safe by goin' in the daylight."

"Better take care of your horses and get some rest," he ordered. "There'll be no fire tonight, since we can't gamble on anyone seein' a fire or smellin' smoke."

"What about you and Duffy and your cigarettes?" Charlie asked.

"Those we'll shield with our hats," Smoky answered. "The smoke from a quirly shouldn't drift much outta this thicket, either, unlike wood smoke. Now let's settle the horses, grab some chuck, and turn in."

Once the horses were groomed and picketed to graze, the men ate a cold supper of jerky and hardtack, washed down with water from their canteens. Before dusk had completely fallen, the sky fading to indigo in the east, but still flaming with the reds and oranges of the setting sun in the west, they were already stretched out, heads pillowed on their saddles.

"Chip, Ty, make sure you check your boots in the morning, to see if any critters have crawled into 'em durin' the night," Duffy warned. "This is prime scorpion country."

"You're not gonna fool me again, Duffy," Ty responded.

"He's not kiddin' this time," Charlie answered.

"That's right," Smoky agreed. "Scorpions, spiders, and sometimes even sidewinders and rattlers like to crawl into dark, warm places . . . and your boots are just that," he said. "I'm surprised you didn't know that, Ty."

"Ty ain't traveled around as much as you and Duffy," Charlie said. "There ain't quite so many snakes up our way, and hardly any scorpions. Reason I know about them is my dad telling me."

Charlie paused and laughed.

"Besides, Ty's boots smell so awful bad no critter's about to make a home in 'em."

"Boy howdy, that's for dang certain," Duffy chortled. "Never gave it a thought before, but now that you mention it, I sure wouldn't want to sleep downwind from those boots."

"Givin' those boots a good dip in the river tomorrow'll help some," Smoky chuckled.

"Yours don't exactly smell like roses and lilac water, Smoky. In fact, that also goes for you and Chip, Duffy," Ty retorted.

"I guess we've got to give you that, Ty," Duffy conceded. "Another occupational hazard of bein' a trail-ridin' Ranger, filthy dirty clothes and smelly boots."

"Not to mention stinkin' of old leather and horse sweat, too," Smoky added. "Leastwise our smell keeps some of the flies and mosquitoes away."

"And attracts others," Duffy muttered, smacking a horsefly which had landed on his cheek.

"If it's any comfort, tomorrow we can add in the odors of chiles and Mexican spices stickin' to us too, first stop we make for a meal," Smoky added.

"You hombres gonna keep jawin' all night, or will you shut up so I can get some shuteye?" Ty complained.

"All right, you've got a point," Smoky answered. "We need to be ready to ride soon as it's light enough to read the river currents, so it's time to say buenas noches."

" 'Night, Smoke, Duffy, Ty," Charlie said. He rolled on his side, then began his evening prayers, while his companions drifted off to sleep.

The morning shadows were still long, mist still rising off the river when they reached the ford Smoky intended to use. The Rio Grande had risen another six inches overnight.

"That's one mean lookin' river, Smoke," Duffy observed. "It's runnin' real fast."

"Yep, it sure is," Smoky conceded. "Must've been some real heavy cloudbursts upstream for it to have risen that much so quickly."

"We still gonna be able to get across?" Charlie asked.

"I know you're anxious to track down Tom

Foley, Chip, but no more so than the rest of us," Smoky answered. "I'd say wait if I thought we couldn't make the other side. The horses'll have to swim a bit more'n I thought, but your dad and I have crossed here when the Rio was runnin' even higher, so we'll make it all right. We'll have to hold our rifles over our heads to keep 'em dry. There's not much we can do about our six-guns, though. We'll dry them off once we reach the other bank."

"What're we waitin' for?" Ty asked as Bandit fidgeted under him.

"Not a thing," Smoky replied. "Just remember this ford is treacherous even under the best of circumstances. We'll have to cross single file, so no matter what don't let your horse try'n pass the one in front of him, or we'll be liable to get tangled up and all go down. I'll take the lead, Duffy you go right behind me, Chip and Ty you follow him. Let's go."

He pulled his Winchester from its scabbard and laid it across the pommel of his saddle, then lightly touched his spurs to Soot's flanks. The steeldust snorted in protest, then plunged into the river. Cactus danced a bit before following, while Ted, Charlie's paint, stepped into the water without hesitation. Bandit stamped his feet, reared a bit, then under Ty's firm hand went along with the others.

The water rose rapidly, soon over the horses'

knees, then up to their bellies. Before reaching midstream their riders had to raise their rifles overhead to keep them out of the muddy, swirling water.

"Keep those horses in a straight line right behind me," Smoky ordered, shouting to be heard over the rushing water. "We'll be swimmin' 'em real soon."

He continued urging Soot forward. Just when they reached the most dangerous part of the crossing, where the horses would need to swim, a volley of rifle fire erupted from the Mexican riverbank. Smoky was knocked from his saddle by a bullet which took him high in the chest. When he fell, his right foot became entangled in the stirrup, pulling Soot off-balance and nearly dragging the steeldust under. The gelding floundered, struggling to keep his balance against the raging current.

Duffy leveled his rifle and got off a shot. His bullet found its mark, and one of the hidden gunmen screamed, staggered from the brush with both hands clamped to his belly, then tumbled into the river. His body was rapidly swept downstream.

"Chip, Ty, cover me!" Duffy shouted. He shoved his Winchester back into its scabbard, then dug his spurs sharply into Cactus's ribs, sending the startled bay lunging against the current. While Charlie and Ty kept up a covering fire, Duffy managed to come abreast of Soot. Leaning far over in the saddle, he grabbed Soot's reins, pulling him around.

"I just hope Smoke's foot stays hung up in that stirrup," he muttered, as Soot's hooves got a better purchase on the sandy bottom.

"All right, I've got him. Let's get back to Texas!" Duffy shouted to Charlie and Ty. They fired several more shots, then turned their horses, leaned low over their necks, and headed back for shore, the mounts struggling while their riders drove them as hard as they could against the fierce current.

The ambushers kept up a steady fire while the Rangers attempted to make their way to safety. Just before Duffy reached the Texas riverbank, several more shots rang out. Bandit reared when a bullet tore along his shoulder, and dumped Ty into the river. Another slug struck Duffy squarely in the middle of his back. He slumped over Cactus's neck, hung on for several strides, then toppled from the saddle, hitting the mud at the river's edge and rolling several times before coming to a stop, face-down. Soot, dragging Smoky, and Cactus ran for several more yards before halting, trembling with exhaustion and cold.

Bandit had reached shore, but Ty was still struggling in the foaming water, weighted down by his clothes, heavy boots, and gunbelt. Charlie tossed his rifle aside, grabbed his lariat from the saddle, and rushed back to the riverbank. He quickly built a loop in the rope and tied one end to his saddlehorn.

"Here Ty, grab it," Charlie cried, tossing the rope toward his friend. Years of experience working horses and cattle paid off, and Charlie's throw was true, landing within inches of Ty's outstretched hand. Ty lunged for the loop and grasped it.

"I've got you, pard," Charlie shouted. "Back, Ted, back." Muscles straining, the well-trained cow horse kept the lariat taut, backing until he dragged Ty out of the river's grip and into shallower water. Ty stumbled from the river, gasping for breath.

"Thanks . . . Thanks, Chip," he stammered.

"No time for that now," Charlie answered. "We need to see about Smoky and Duffy. I'll check Smoky; you get Duffy out of that river."

Duffy's lower torso and legs were still in the water, waves lapping over them while the current threatened to drag his body back under.

"All right," Ty answered.

"Stand hitched, boy," Charlie urged Soot as he approached Smoky's horse. The steeldust stood quietly while Charlie grew near, but shifted sideways when Charlie reached him. The movement turned Smoky from his back onto his side, causing water to dribble from his mouth and nose.

He's not breathin', Charlie thought. Not knowing what else to do, he pounded Smoky sharply on the back, between his shoulder blades. Smoky began choking, expelling a good volume of water.

"Take it easy, Smoky," Charlie said. "I'll have you loose in a minute."

It only took a moment for Charlie to twist Smoky's ankle so his foot slid from the stirrup, then roll him onto his back. He opened Smoky's shirt to examine the bullet hole in his chest.

"You . . . all right, Chip?" Smoky spluttered.

"Yeah, I'm fine; so's Ty."

"What about Duffy?"

"Dunno about Duffy. It appears he got shot in the back. Ty's checkin' on him. Looks like you're hit pretty bad, Smoky."

"Don't worry about me, I'll be okay. You go find out about Duffy."

"I've gotta try and stop this bleedin'," Charlie objected.

"Let me be for now. You make sure of Duffy," Smoky ordered.

"All right. I'll be back soon as I can," Charlie answered.

Ty had pulled Duffy from the river and turned him onto his back. Blood was oozing copiously from the exit wound in the young Ranger's chest. Ty looked at Charlie and shook his head, eyes moist with unshed tears.

"Guess . . . this was my last . . . ride," Duffy stammered.

"Don't even think that," Charlie replied. "We're gonna get you to a doc, Duffy. You'll be laid up for a bit, that's all."

"Don't try'n kid . . . me, Chip," Duffy gasped. "I'm all . . . tore up . . . inside. I can't feel . . . anything . . . in my legs. Reckon . . . that slug must've . . . clipped my . . . spine. I'm finished."

"Duffy," Charlie began to answer.

"Nothin' to say, pardner," Duffy said. "Do me . . . one last . . . favor. Make sure Cactus is cared for. He's been a darn good horse—and friend."

"Of course," Charlie assured him. "I'll take Cactus back to our ranch, so he can spend the rest of his days lazin' around, eatin' and gettin' fat."

"Good. Thanks, pard," Duffy answered. "Say, get my . . . tobacco and make . . . me a smoke . . . You'll have . . . to put it . . . between my lips . . . for me . . . my arms . . . ain't workin' either."

"I'll do that for you," Ty offered. He reached into Duffy's shirt pocket to remove a water-logged sack of tobacco.

"Sorry, Duffy," Ty said. "Your makin's got soaked."

"That's . . . all right, kid," Duffy said. "Gotta ask . . . one more favor."

"Sure, Duffy, what is it?" Ty asked.

"Next new recruits you . . . work with . . . pull

that . . . phony Indian attack . . . stunt . . . for me, will ya?"

"That's a promise," Ty assured him.

"Good . . . I'm countin' on . . . you."

A grin crossed Duffy's lips. He shuddered, then sighed while his blue eyes slowly closed. The gregarious, happy-go-lucky Ranger died with a smile still on his face.

"He's gone, Ty," Charlie said.

Ty sobbed, then turned and dropped to his knees, retching violently.

"I'm goin' back to Smoky," Charlie told him. "Join us when you're ready."

Ty waved a hand in reply.

"Well, how about Duffy?" Smoky demanded once he saw Charlie returning.

"He's dead," Charlie replied. "Didn't have a chance. That slug caught him plumb in the center of his back."

"Where's Ty?"

"Losin' his guts. He's never seen anyone killed before," Charlie explained. "It'll be hard on him for a while, bet a hat on it. Right now let's worry about you. You're still bleedin' pretty heavily. I've gotta try and stop it."

Charlie took the bandanna from around his neck, folded it, and placed it over the wound in Smoky's chest. He pulled out his shirt tail and tore strips from that, using them to tie the bandage in place.

"That's the best I can do for now," Charlie noted. "We've got to get you to a doctor, and right quick."

"Nearest one's . . . in Eagle Pass," Smoky answered. "Mexican . . . doc named . . . Jacinto Torres, on Portales Street, near Refugio. He's better'n . . . any of the Anglo medicos . . . when it comes to . . . diggin' out slugs or . . . patchin' up knife wounds. He's discreet, too. Won't let on . . . we're in town . . . if we ask him . . . not to."

"All right," Charlie answered. "We'll get Duffy on his horse and get movin'. I'll be back in a jiffy."

Charlie found Ty kneeling alongside Duffy's body, still silently crying.

"Ty, Smoky's in real bad shape," Charlie said. "We've got to get him to a doc as fast as possible. Even then I don't know whether he'll pull through."

"Okay, Chip," Ty answered. He pulled himself to his feet. "What about Duffy?"

"We'll take him into Eagle Pass and make arrangements there," Charlie said. "Get his horse."

"All right."

Cactus was retrieved and brought to where Duffy lay. He sniffed his rider's body and nickered mournfully. Duffy was loaded onto his back, draped belly-down over the saddle. Once that was done, Charlie returned to where Smoky lay waiting. He was somewhat surprised to find Smoky still conscious.

"You want to try and ride, Smoky?" he asked.

"I'm not gonna be able to hang on. You'd better tie me in my saddle," Smoky answered.

"I've got a better idea," Charlie responded. "I'll get you onto Ted and we'll ride double. That way you can lean on me. I'd rather see you sittin' upright as much as possible rather'n lyin' over Soot's neck. That'll help control the bleedin', at least a bit."

"That makes sense," Smoky agreed.

"Good. I'll get my horse."

Charlie went back to where Ted was patiently waiting. He led the paint back to Smoky, and helped the badly wounded Ranger onto Ted's back. Charlie tied a lead line onto Soot's bridle, looped it around his saddle horn, and climbed into the saddle. Smoky wrapped his arms around Charlie's waist, leaning his head against his shoulders.

"You ready?" Charlie asked.

"I reckon," Smoky answered.

"I'll take it as easy as I can," Charlie said.

"Don't worry about the jouncing, I can handle it," Smoky replied. "Just get me to Doc Torres before I bleed to death."

"I promise you that," Charlie answered. He put Ted into a walk until they reached where Ty, already mounted and with Cactus's reins tied to his saddlehorn, awaited.

"Let's get movin', Ty," he ordered.

Charlie heeled Ted into a smooth, ground-covering lope.

In broad daylight, it was impossible to ride unnoticed into town with a dead man slung over his horse and a wounded man clinging to another rider. Inquisitive passersby followed along as Charlie and Ty headed for Doctor Torres's office.

"They were ridin' pards, but got liquored up last night, started arguin' about nothing much in particular, and Sam shot poor Dave in the back," Charlie responded in answer to their shouted questions. "Then Dave managed to plug Sam before he died."

His explanation satisfied most of the crowd, so by the time they reined up in front of the doctor's office, the majority had drifted away. Shootings weren't all that uncommon in border towns anyway; so once their curiosity had been satisfied, most people lost interest. Besides, it could be quite unhealthy asking too many questions. Better to just go about your own business was the reasoning, rather than get involved in a dispute among drifting strangers. Since the shooting had evidently taken place outside of Eagle Pass, no one even bothered to notify the local law. Sooner or later, word would get back to the marshal or one of his deputies.

"We'll go around back, rather'n leavin' Duffy's body out here on the street in plain sight," Charlie told Ty. He rode around the small adobe house, to a walled courtyard.

"Open the gate for me, will you, Ty?" Charlie requested.

"Sure."

Ty dismounted and opened the heavy, wooden arched gate, so Charlie could ride into the yard. Ty followed, closing the gate behind him, which completely blocked any view of the small, enclosed space.

When Charlie dismounted, Smoky, who had passed out somewhere along the trail, slumped over Ted's neck. Ty and Charlie lifted him from the saddle and carried him onto the flower-bedecked patio. Ty knocked on the door. A moment later, a young Mexican woman answered.

"May I help you, senores?" she inquired.

"We have a badly wounded man out here," Ty answered. "He needs to see the doctor right away."

"Of course," the young woman answered, not even hesitating. She swung the door wide. "This way, por favor."

They followed the woman down a whitewashed hallway. She gestured to a door on the left.

"In there. I will get the doctor."

211

Ty and Charlie carried Smoky into the spotlessly clean room and laid him on the table. A
moment later, the woman returned, accompanied
by Doctor Jacinto Torres. The physician was in
his middle fifties, a bit on the short side, with
thick black hair and penetrating dark eyes.

"Corrina tells me you have a gravely wounded
man here," he stated.

"Yes, we have, Doctor," Charlie answered. "It's
Ranger Sergeant Smoky McCue, who's been shot
in the chest. He asked us to bring him here. I'm
Ranger Chip Blawcyzk, and this is Ranger Ty
Tremblay."

"My compadre Smoky McCue? Let me see
what I can do for him," Torres answered. He
stepped up to the table, shook his head, and
removed the bandage from Smoky's chest.

"This is a very serious wound, very serious,"
he stated. "I'll have to perform surgery immediately, to try and remove the bullet. Who did
this?"

"We don't know," Ty answered. "We were dry-
gulched upriver a ways."

"Corrina, I will need lots of boiling water,"
Torres ordered.

"Yes, Papa," the young woman answered. "I
will prepare it at once."

"Let me get to work," Torres said. He took
down several bottles from a shelf, then a clean
cloth to wipe blood from Smoky's wound. When

212

he ran the cloth over the Ranger's chest, Smoky stirred, and his eyes flickered open.

"Doc Torres," he murmured.

"Yes, Ranger McCue. I am always happy to see you, but I wish this visit were under more fortunate circumstances," Torres replied. "You are badly wounded, amigo mio."

"I've been shot worse'n this," Smoky answered, managing a wan grin. "My partners, are they here?"

"Si, they are."

"I need to talk with them before you start diggin' for that slug," Smoky said.

"I cannot delay your treatment," Torres answered. "You are already weak from considerable loss of blood."

"I've gotta talk to 'em first," Smoky insisted.

"All right," Torres conceded. "However, only for a few moments."

"That's all I need," Smoky said. "Ty, Chip."

"We're right here, Smoky," Charlie said.

"Listen to me, both of you. I want you to look up Matt McCarthy and let him know what's happened. He'll need to notify Austin. You're to remain here in Eagle Pass and await further orders from Captain Huggins."

"I was figurin' on getting a bit of rest, then headin' after Foley again," Charlie objected.

"Don't even think about that," Smoky retorted. "Aren't you satisfied you nearly got killed once today? Under no circumstances are either of you to cross into Mexico. Do you hear me?"

"Yeah, I hear you, Sergeant," Charlie muttered.

"Let me put that plainer, Chip. Are you listenin'? Do you understand me?"

"Yeah, I sure do," Charlie bitterly replied. "Sticks in my craw, though. Bet a hat on it."

"I know it does," Smoky sympathized, "but we took a long chance as it was. Don't worry, Foley will eventually be brought to ground."

"I'd really like to know why those drygulchers were waitin' for us," Ty said. "Sure seems like an awful long coincidence."

"Mebbe it was just bad luck," Charlie speculated. "They were probably just a bunch of robbers waitin' to prey on anyone who took that crossin'."

"It wasn't a coincidence," Smoky answered. "I spotted Tom Foley just before I got hit. They were waitin' for us, all right."

"But how would they know where we'd try crossin', and when?" Ty wondered.

"Someone tipped 'em off," Charlie replied. "But who?"

"There's plenty of possibilities," Smoky pointed out. "Someone from the Bar 7, or mebbe even the marshal or his deputy up in Comanche."

"Or someone in Frio Town who found out we were Rangers when I lost my head," Charlie added. "That's probably it. It's my fault we got ambushed, and Duffy killed."

"You have no way of knowin' that," Ty said.

"Ty's right," Smoky agreed. "Don't go blamin' yourself, Chip. It could've been any of a dozen men who warned Foley. Heck, mebbe he was even followin' us all along, just waitin' for his chance to gun us down, while all the while we thought we were trailing him."

"Ranger McCue, I must insist this conversation end right now," Doctor Torres broke in. "I have to begin surgery."

"All right," Smoky conceded.

"Wait a minute. What about Duffy?" Charlie asked.

"Doc here'll take care of him," Smoky answered. "Doc, one of my men, Duffy McGlynn, was killed by those bushwhackers. Will you make the necessary arrangements for his funeral and burial?"

"Si, of course," Torres replied. "I will bill the state, as usual. Where is the body?"

"Duffy's still on his horse, in your courtyard, Doc," Charlie said.

"Bueno. There is a small room just off the hallway where you came in, which I use for the dead. It is the first door on the right when you enter. Bring your comrade's body in there. There is also a stable where you may leave his horse, as well as Ranger McCue's."

"Muchas gracias, Doc," Smoky murmured, starting to once again lose consciousness as his ordeal took its toll. "Chip, Ty . . . remember, you stay right here in Eagle Pass until you hear from Austin. Those are orders."

"All right, Smoky," Charlie agreed. "We'll see you soon as you come around."

"Good. I'm ready, Doc," Smoky whispered.

"You must leave now," Torres ordered Charlie and Ty. "You may wait in the front parlor if you wish."

"Gracias, doc, but we'll take care of Duffy, then report to Ranger McCarthy," Charlie said.

"Bueno, and vaya con Dios."

"Adios, Doc."

Charlie and Ty removed Duffy's body from his horse and took it into the room Doctor Torres had indicated, laying it on a dark wooden table. They removed their hats and paused a moment in prayer for their companion's final journey to be with the Lord.

"Reckon that's all we can do here," Charlie said. "Let's go, Ty."

They headed outside to their horses.

"Ty, dunno about you, but I sure ain't stayin' around here with Foley still on the loose and laughin' at us," Charlie said. "You stay here if you want, but I'm headed for Zaragoza."

"What're you even sayin' that for, Chip?" Ty answered. "We've been friends and pardners for years. Your dad was almost as much a father to me as my own dad, so I'll be ridin' with you.

There's only one problem. We could well be ridin' our way right outta the Rangers if we disobey Smoky's orders and head into Mexico."

"That doesn't matter to me at all," Charlie snapped, his blue eyes glittering with that unholy fury. "The only thing which does is runnin' down Tom Foley and shootin' him like the mangy coyote he is. Are you still comin' with me?"

"The only way you could stop me is by gut-shootin' me," Ty declared.

"Good, then let's get outta town before Ranger McCarthy finds out what happened."

They led their horses outside, swung into the saddles, and put them into a gallop.

"Chip, you ain't intendin' to try'n use that same ford again, are you?" Ty asked.

"Not a chance," Charlie answered. "No one here knows us, except Smoky and Doc Torres and his daughter. We'll use the regular crossing right here between Eagle Pass and Piedras Negras. Far as anyone is concerned, we're just a couple of cowpokes headin' for some fun down in Mexico."

"Hope you're right," Ty muttered.

"Bet a hat on it," Charlie grinned.

Half-an-hour later, they had made the crossing into Mexico, and were riding through the bustling city of Piedras Negras, which translated in English as Black Stones. The city had been named for the vast coal deposits in the region.

"Looks like they're fixin' to build a railroad," Ty noted.

"Seems so. I recall my dad sayin' something about coal minin' startin' up around these parts," Charlie answered. "Both sides of the river, for that matter. Speculators are lookin' into opening a coal mine just outside Eagle Pass, I seem to recollect. If that happens, they'll need a railroad."

"This area'll sure boom in that case," Ty noted. "Where we headed first?"

"I'm figurin' on ridin' straight to Zaragoza," Charlie said. "That's where Foley's supposed to be, so that's where I'm goin'."

"Chip," Ty asked. "What're you planning on doin' if we catch up to Tom Foley?"

Charlie's eyes glittered with anger when he replied.

"You mean when, not if. I'm gonna gut-shoot him, that's what. I'm gonna put one bullet into his belly, just one, real low, so it tears up his guts but he lasts a long time, and dies real slow and painful."

"What about capturing him and bringin' him back for trial?"

"There's not a chance of that. First of all, we don't have any authority down here. Second, I want Foley to linger as long as possible, and suffer a whole lot, before he dies. The no-good sidewinder's gonna get the same chance he gave my dad and Captain Trumbull."

"Foley might plug you first," Ty warned. He shivered slightly at the fury in Charlie's voice.

"Don't matter," Charlie answered. "He might fill me fulla lead, but I'll kill him before I die. Bet a hat on that."

"All right, that's settled," Ty answered. "Meantime, I'm plumb starved. We haven't had anything to eat since before sunup."

"I know, I'm pretty hungry too," Charlie admitted. "Soon as we reach Zaragoza we'll stop at the first likely-lookin' place for some grub."

"That sounds reasonable," Ty answered. "If we ever find our way outta this town."

"We'll just ask how," Charlie replied. "That gentleman over there looks like he can give us directions."

A half-block along, they reined up in front of a distinguished, elderly man.

"Pardon, Senor, can you give us directions to Zaragoza, por favor?" Charlie asked, in Spanish.

"Zaragoza? Si," the man replied. In rapid Spanish, he provided the information.

"Gracias, Senor," Charlie said when he concluded.

"Por nada. Adios."

"Adios."

Charlie and Ty kept their horses at a lope most of the way to Zaragoza, so they were soon riding into the small village.

"There's a likely-lookin' place, Chip."

Ty pointed to a bright blue painted adobe, with La Casa de Cazar Ratas Cantina emblazoned over its door in red, gold, and green.

"I reckon so," Charlie shrugged. "Since I'm so hungry I could even eat a rat."

"What're you sayin'?" Ty asked.

"La Casa de Cazar Ratas . . . The House of the Hunter Rats," Charlie translated, chuckling. "That's a loose translation, but it's close enough."

"Suddenly I'm not so hungry," Ty replied.

"Well I still am, so let's chance it," Charlie retorted.

They reined up in front of the cantina, allowed their horses a drink from the trough there, and tied them to the rail, then ducked under the rail and stepped into the cantina. In contrast to the blazing Mexican sun, the cantina's interior was dim and cool. Behind the bar was a buxom blonde woman, who beckoned a greeting when they entered. Only a few other patrons were in the cantina, most seated at tables.

"Welcome to my place, boys," she called, in perfect English. "C'mon in. I'm Kris Blake. "That's Kris as in Kristin, with a K."

Charlie and Ty crossed the room and stepped up to the bar.

"What the devil are those?" Ty exclaimed. In a large cage on a shelf behind the bar were three rats, two of them practically naked, their skin covered only by a fine peach fuzz.

"Those? Those are my boys," the barwoman explained. "Templeton, Yul, and Telly. Templeton's the one with the hair."

"The other two look like plucked chicken legs with feet and eyes," Charlie said.

"They sure do," Kris laughed appreciatively.

"Unusual names you gave them," Ty added.

"I just made them up," Kris explained. "I like the sound of them. Enough about my rats, though. What're you boys havin'? And speaking of names, you didn't give me yours."

"I'm Chip, and my pard here's Ty," Charlie answered. "I'll have a cerveza, and whatever grub you've got."

"I've got chili and tortillas," Kris answered.

"That'll be fine."

"What about you, cowboy?" Kris asked Ty.

"Same here."

"I'll have your food right out."

Kris poured two mugs of beer, then disappeared into the kitchen, returning a few minutes later.

"Jorge is cookin' up your meal now," she said. "How about a refill in the meantime, or perhaps some tequila?"

"No tequila, thanks," Charlie replied. "But we will take that refill."

"Comin' right up."

Kris refilled their mugs, waited while they downed the contents, then refilled them again.

"Your food should be ready," she said. "I'll have it out in a minute."

Once again she disappeared into the kitchen, this time returning with two bowls filled with steaming chili, and accompanied by stacks of corn tortillas. These she placed on the bar in front of them.

"Here you go, boys. Hope you enjoy it."

"It sure smells tasty," Charlie answered. He dug a spoonful of chili from his bowl and popped it into his mouth.

"Tastes good, too. Nice and spicy."

"Just like me," Kris laughed.

"I reckon," Charlie agreed, blushing slightly.

"What brings you boys to Zaragoza?" Kris asked. "It's kind of an out of the way place."

"I was just about to ask you the same thing," Charlie answered. "How'd an American gal like you come to own a cantina in Mexico?"

"I had a good job up in Connecticut, but got tired of stayin' in one place," Kris explained. "So one day I packed up and left. I traveled for a spell, then came down here. I never looked back, and I've never regretted it. Now, how about you answer my question?"

"Sure," Charlie agreed. "We're lookin' for an hombre named Tom Foley. Ever heard of him?"

"Tom Foley? Can't say as I have," Kris answered, her eyes suddenly shadowed. "What's he look like?"

"Tall and thin, dark brown hair and eyes, has a big bushy mustache," Charlie answered. "Wears a cross-draw holster, and rides a black gelding he calls Indigo. Real good-lookin' hombre, who loves the ladies. Supposed to have a place down this way."

"Oh, you mean Tomas," Kris exclaimed. "Sure, now I know who you mean. What do you want with Tomas?"

"My dad sent us to find him," Charlie answered. "He's known Tom for years. We've been havin' a problem with rustlers on our spread, so Dad wants to hire Tom to help clean 'em out. He claims Tom's real good with his gun."

"Why didn't your dad come looking for him?"

"Because those rustlers shot him and left him for dead," Charlie answered. "He'll be laid up for quite a spell."

"I see," Kris answered.

"Does Foley come in here very often?" Ty asked.

"Only once in a while," Kris replied. "You'd be better off ridin' to his place. I'm not exactly sure where it is, but I know it's on the Real Ciudad Acuna, about fifteen or twenty kilometers north of here."

Charlie downed the rest of his beer, then banged the mug on the bar.

"Much obliged, Kris. We'll find the place. C'mon Ty, let's go."

"Aren't you going to finish your meal?" Kris asked.

"No time. I want to try'n locate Foley before dark," Charlie answered. "We'll stop back if we get the chance."

"Make sure you do," Kris answered. "Good luck."

"Thanks."

With their horses still tired from the long ride that day, Charlie and Ty held them mostly to a trot, occasionally allowing them to lope while they traveled northward along the Real Ciudad Acuna. About twenty minutes after leaving Zaragoza, they became aware of a large group of riders to their rear. They rode on for another mile, the riders shadowing them.

"Wonder what those hombres want?" Charlie said.

"Probably just headed in the same direction," Ty answered.

"I dunno. They've been keepin' the same pace we have, and remaining the same distance behind us for a couple of miles now," Charlie disagreed. "Let's stop and see what happens."

He pulled Ted to a halt, Ty doing likewise. The riders kept coming, slowing as they approached.

"They're pullin' out rifles," Charlie exclaimed. "Let's get outta here!"

He unshipped his own Winchester, jacked a

shell into the chamber, and dug his heels into Ted's flanks, sending the startled gelding leaping into a dead run.

Charlie and Ty pounded down the trail, their tired horses no match for the riders' fresh mounts. Slowly but surely their pursuers narrowed the distance between them and their quarry, inexorably closing the gap. Long-distance shots from their rifles began searching out the two Rangers. Charlie and Ty held their fire, knowing at this distance and on galloping horses any chance of making a hit was practically nil.

"This way, Ty!" Charlie shouted, when he spotted a side trail. He pulled hard on Ted's reins, sending the paint into a sliding turn to the right, then slapped him across the rump. Ted responded to Charlie's urging, somehow finding a fresh burst of speed. With Bandit on his heels, Ted galloped up the narrow trail, which soon began climbing steeply.

For several minutes they raced up that trail, until Ty slowed Bandit to a trot, then a walk, and finally stopped.

"Wait a minute, Chip. I think we've lost them," he called. "I don't see any sign of them."

"We're awful lucky if we did," Charlie answered. "Let's keep movin', just in case. We'll stick to a walk, though."

After several more minutes with no sign of their pursuers, Charlie and Ty finally relaxed a bit.

"I guess we did give 'em the slip," Charlie decided. "Funny they gave up that easily."

"I'm not complainin'," Ty said. "Don't stop quite yet, though. Let's push on a bit more."

"We can't stop here anyway. There's not enough room," Charlie said. The trail they were following had continued its upward climb, and was still narrowing, so that it was barely wide enough for the horses to plant all four hooves. To their right was a sheer drop of about fifty feet, while to the left was a scrub-covered slope, too steep for a man, let alone a horse, to climb.

"We'll keep goin'."

Charlie put Ted into a walk yet again.

"Wonder why those hombres were after us?" Ty said.

"That gal at the cantina must've set 'em on our trail," Charlie answered. "I guess she didn't buy my story about wantin' to hire Foley. I should've known better. She saw right through us, and is probably back there laughin' about that right now."

"It's too late to do anything about it. We'll just have to ride on outta here, then figure our next move," Ty replied.

The trail kept climbing and narrowing, the brush-covered slope closing in from the left, the drop to the right continuing to heighten. Ted stopped when he came to a washed-out section, a gully which reached a depth of forty feet or more.

"What do you think, Ty? Should we keep goin' or try'n turn back?" Charlie asked.

Before Ty could respond, Ted calmly stepped over the washout, not fazed at all by the drop.

"I guess we'll keep goin'," Ty answered when Bandit nonchalantly followed Ted across the gully.

"Reckon so," Charlie shrugged.

They had gone about another quarter mile when the trail abruptly stopped at a rock wall which rose straight up in front of them, thirty feet high. While a person could possibly, with luck, scramble up that wall, it was impossible for a horse to traverse. Charlie dismounted, squeezing between the slope and Ted's side while he pondered their predicament.

"Ty, we're in big trouble," he finally said. "There's no way past this cliff. You'll have to turn Bandit around so we can get outta here."

"I can't," Ty answered. "There's nowhere near enough room to turn him. In fact, your horse's right hind foot is hangin' half off the trail. You've gotta keep him calm, no matter what, while we figure a way outta this mess."

"If you can't turn your horse, you'll have to back him up to that wider spot," Charlie said. "I sure can't turn Ted until you do."

"I'll give it a try," Ty shrugged. He tugged on his reins. "C'mon, Bandit, back."

Ty's mustang-quarter horse cross backed

several steps until, with a snort of protest, he shot up the steep slope, crashing through the brush.

"Easy, Ted," Charlie soothed his horse, fearful the paint would take the sound as a predator and bolt. "Just back up, slow and easy."

He gently pushed on Ted's chest, urging him to back up.

"You all right, Ty?" he called, when the sound of brush being splintered stopped.

"I'm fine, but I'm sittin' in the middle of a bush," Ty shouted back.

"What about Bandit?"

"I can see him. He stopped in a clearing up ahead. Once I get outta this brush I'll get him. He seems to be okay. I'll catch up to you in a minute. How about you?"

"We're makin' our way back," Charlie answered. A few moments later, he reached a slightly wider place in the trail, where he was able to turn Ted around and remount. A minute later, Ty rejoined him.

"You okay, Ty?" Charlie asked.

"Seem to be. Bandit's got a few scrapes, but nothin' serious. How about you?"

"I'm fine on the outside, but I'm shakin' inside," Charlie answered.

"That goes double for me," Ty nervously laughed. "Reckon we've got no choice but to head back the way we came."

"I reckon not, which explains why those

hombres stopped chasin' us," Charlie conceded. "They knew this trail led nowhere. I'll bet my hat they're waitin' for us at the bottom."

"I'm not takin' that bet, 'cause I'm positive you're right," Ty grumbled.

"Well, there's no use in keepin' those boys waitin'," Charlie said. "We sure ain't gonna rush down this trail, though. It was too close a call as it was."

"Boy howdy, that's for certain," Ty agreed.

They put their horses into a slow, careful walk. Sure enough, when they reached the bottom of the slope their pursuers emerged from the brush and surrounded them, rifles pointed at the Rangers' chests.

"Senores, unbuckle your gunbelts and let them fall to the ground, por favor," the leader requested. "Then remove your rifles from their scabbards and drop them also. After you have done that, raise your hands shoulder high. Andale, por favor."

With no choice, other than being shot out of their saddles on the spot, Charlie and Ty complied.

"Gracias, senores. I am Bernardo Jalisco, alcalde of Zaragoza. These men, as I am sure you have noticed, are members of the Federal rurales. You are both under arrest for violating the sovereign territory of Mexico."

Chapter Eleven

Once Jim's fever broke and he regained consciousness, his recovery moved rapidly, so much so that Doctor Talmadge was able to send him home much sooner than he'd imagined to complete his recuperation. As the days went by, Jim grew more and more frustrated with his enforced home confinement.

"Jim, you seem more somber than usual," Julia noted one morning, while they lingered over a last cup of breakfast coffee. "I know you want to be out on the trail, but I sense something more is troubling you. What is it?"

"I'm just gettin' more and more concerned about Charlie, that's all," Jim answered. "Smoky, Duffy, and Ty, too. There hasn't been a word from them since Comanche. Dunno why not. I just hope nothing's gone wrong."

Alongside him, Charlie's collie Pal lifted his head and thumped his tail on the floor at the mention of his owner's name.

"I know, you miss Charlie too," Jim told the dog, patting his head.

"Jim, I hate to say this, but now you know how I feel when you're gone, and I don't hear from you or Headquarters for days or weeks on end. It's simply maddening."

"I know there are times you must be sick with worry when I'm away and can't get in touch with you," Jim answered. "I wish I could settle down, but every time I try it's only a couple of weeks until I have to be on the move again."

"I know that, and I've always accepted it," Julia said. "It's just a bit ironic seeing you get a taste of your own medicine."

"I guess I deserved that," Jim replied.

"I didn't mean it as harshly as it sounded," Julia replied, "but perhaps now you'll understand what I go through a little better."

"I believe I already do," Jim smiled ruefully. He drained the last of his coffee. "Well, breakfast's done. Let me give you a hand with the dishes."

"Thank you, but don't you have some chores you'd rather get to?"

"Always used to, but not right now. The horses are fed, eggs gathered, you milked the cow, and I got in some more firewood. Everything that needs fixin' around here has been fixed, so I've got nothing to do until I put some hay out later. Besides, I need to rest just a mite. I'm hurtin' a bit where that slug's in my chest."

"All right, you can dry the dishes," Julia agreed.

The dishes were done and put away. When Julia got out her broom to sweep the kitchen floor, Jim pulled it from her grasp.

"I'll do that for you," he said. "You just rest a spell."

"Jim, give me back that broom," Julia said in exasperation. "You've been underfoot for a week now, and it's driving me crazy. You're not supposed to be working as it is. If Doctor Talmadge ever knew you were up on the barn roof repairing it, he'd have a fit. As it was you nearly fell off when you got that cramp in your belly while you were up there. You know neither of your wounds, particularly that one, are completely healed. Please do what the doctor asked and rest. Go sit on the porch, or take a nap."

Jim handed her the broom.

"I'm all rested out, darlin', but if that's what you want."

"It is," Julia insisted. "Stay out of this house until I call you for dinner."

"Reckon you're givin' me no choice," Jim shrugged. Silently, he turned and headed outside.

"Jim," Julia whispered after him. "Oh, Jim."

Shortly before noon, Julia opened the front door to call her husband to the mid-day meal.

"Jim, where are you at? I'm putting dinner on the table," she called.

"I'm out here, workin' with one of the colts," Jim shouted back. "He still doesn't care for havin' his feet picked up, so I've been showin' him it's not so bad. I'll be in soon as I wash up."

"All right. Don't take too long or the food will get cold."

"Time to call it a mornin'. You did fine, boy," Jim praised the overo yearling he was working with. "Go back with your friends."

He led the young horse from the corral and turned him into the pasture. The colt nuzzled Jim's shoulder, then trotted off to join his stablemates.

Jim headed for the wash bench out back of the house. While they had installed an indoor pump and sink several years back, he still found it easier to clean up outside, unless the weather was too chilly or he wanted to take a full bath.

Jim pumped water into the trough, then stripped off his shirt. He picked up a bar of soap and a washcloth from the bench, then ducked his head into the refreshing liquid. He ran the soap through his hair, washed his face, then scrubbed his upper torso. He was again ducking his head in the trough when he felt two arms wrap around his waist.

"Julia?" he spluttered, still half-blinded by the soap in his eyes.

"Who else did you think it would be?" Julia's soft voice answered. "And you'd better not name another woman!"

"I wouldn't think of it," Jim chuckled. "I'm too fond of livin'."

When he straightened up, Julia snuggled against his broad back. She began to gently massage his belly.

"Jim, I love you," she murmured. "I didn't mean to be so hard on you this morning. I realize how frustrating it must be for you, stuck here when you'd rather be out looking for Tom Foley. Add in your worry about Charlie and it has to be doubly aggravating."

"There's no need to apologize," Jim answered. "I know I'm not the easiest man to live with, especially when I'm tied down. Time's just gonna keep draggin' until I can get back in the saddle again."

"Honey, I know exactly how to kill some of that time," Julia whispered. She kissed Jim on the nape of his neck.

"Really? How?" Jim teased.

"I thought I would start like this."

Julia commenced running a fingertip around the rim of Jim's bellybutton. His stomach muscles tightened in anticipation, then he flinched slightly.

"Did I hurt you?" Julia asked.

"It was only a twinge. Don't worry about it."

"All right."

Julia put her right hand on Jim's left breast, fingering his nipple.

"Does that give you an idea?"

"I'm not sure," Jim said.

"Perhaps this will make things clearer."

Julia's left hand dropped lower and she unbuttoned his jeans, causing a stirring in his groin.

"Now do you know what I mean, cowboy?"

"I believe I do, but what about dinner? You were worried it would get cold," Jim answered.

"Not any longer, and do you really care about that?" Julia asked.

"Not one bit. Bet a hat on it," Jim replied. He turned, wrapped his arms around Julia, and crushed her body to his.

Two days later Julia was working with the same overo yearling who had given Jim trouble about his feet. She was working the horse on a long line while Jim stood outside the pen, watching intently. Two of the barn cats were rubbing against his boots, meowing for milk. The youngster Julia was training obeyed her commands instantly, breaking smoothly from a jog to an easy lope when asked.

"Boy howdy, Pecos sure is a handsome colt," Jim noted. "He's one good-lookin' fella."

"What did you say?" Julia questioned.

"I said he's one good-lookin' horse," Jim answered. "Then again, so is the trainer."

"Whoa, boy." Julia brought the yearling to a stop, before turning to face Jim, her brown eyes wide with indignation.

"That's not what you said," Julia replied. "You said Pecos is a handsome horse, not he. And what do you mean his trainer is a good-lookin' horse?"

"Not a horse," Jim protested, "Just real good-lookin'. I'd never call you a horse. A filly, mebbe, but never a horse."

"You'd better quit before you get in even deeper trouble," Julia warned. "Obviously you've forgotten about not naming the foals, since now you've given this one a name, too. That means you're thinking of keeping him. Don't you dare. We have to sell at least six youngsters before the winter."

"Aw, honey, I can't give 'em all up," Jim grumbled. "Pecos looks like he'll have the makin's of a good Ranger mount. I'd like to see Charlie ridin' him in a couple of years."

"Jim, there'll be others. We can't afford to keep this horse for two or three years only to find out he's afraid of gunfire, or has some other trait which makes him unsuitable for law work."

"But I really like Pecos's potential," Jim objected. "You like every horse's potential," Julia pointed out. "Jim, I really need to work with him some more, and the longer you hang around here watching the more you'll fall in love with this horse, which means the more you'll want to keep him. It's not that I don't want you here, but don't you have something to keep you busy for a while?"

"Nope," Jim cheerfully answered, grinning. "There's nothing I'd rather do than watch a handsome horse bein' worked by a beautiful woman."

"Couldn't you find something, please?" Julia persisted.

Jim shoved back his Stetson and ran a hand through his sweat-soaked hair.

"It is a mite hot," he noted. "I reckon I could head for the swimmin' hole for a dip. I guess I'll take Pal along with me."

"Now that's a wonderful idea," Julia agreed. "By the time you return I'll have supper waiting."

"Fried chicken?"

"Fried chicken. Now would you please let me get back to working this colt?"

"As you wish, m'lady," Jim grinned, with an exaggerated bow. "See you at supper."

Jim ambled over to the corral which held Sizzle and Sam. He whistled sharply, and both paints trotted up to the fence.

"Let's go for a little ride, fellas," Jim said, as he dug in his hip pocket and came up with a peppermint for each horse. "Matter of fact, I've got an idea."

Jim took a halter and lead rope from a post and ducked under the railings. He slipped the halter over Sam's head and led the gelding alongside the fence.

"Sam, I know you can't carry me very far, but I'm gonna give you the chance to take me to the creek," he said. Sam had been badly injured by outlaws who had invaded the Blawcyzk ranch several years previously, and left with a permanently crippled leg. He still accompanied Jim on his assignments, but only as a pack horse.

Jim climbed the fence, swung a leg over Sam's withers, and settled onto his bare back. Sam turned his head to look questioningly at his rider, nuzzled Jim's foot, and whickered.

"I knew you'd like this," Jim said. "Just let me know if it's too much for you. Let's go."

Jim leaned from Sam's back to open the gate. Sizzle stood in the corral, nickering curiously when Jim rode out of the enclosure.

"Siz, you comin' with us, or are you just gonna stand there all day?" Jim called to him. "C'mon if you're goin' to."

Sizzle tossed his head and whinnied, then trotted up to Sam's side.

"All right, then." Jim heeled Sam into a walk. He waved to Julia when they passed the corral where she was still working the colt. She smiled and waved in return. Jim whistled for Pal, who bounded off the porch. Once the collie was alongside Sam, Jim put the horse into a slow jogtrot.

A short while after Jim headed for the creek, Julia had finished working the colt and was sponging him down. She looked up at the sound of approaching hoof beats. A moment later Captain Jim Huggins rode into the yard. He reined up alongside the corral, remaining astride Dusty, his sorrel gelding.

"Good afternoon, Julia," he called. "That sure is a pretty animal you've got there."

"Captain Huggins, hello. I didn't expect to see you today. Have you gotten any news about Charlie?" she replied.

"I'm still Jim, remember? I'm only acting Captain," he reminded her. "Yes, I do have news about Charlie and Ty. They're both doing all right, as is Smoky McCue. Is Jim around? I rode over to talk with him."

"He went out to the swimming hole to cool off," Julia answered. "If you follow the creek about a quarter mile upstream you'll find him. He'll certainly be glad to see you, especially since he's bored out of his mind, and is driving me a bit crazy. He even wants to keep this colt, which is the last thing we need. In fact, he's already named him Pecos. Do you have any idea when Charlie will be home? Has Tom Foley been captured yet?"

"I'm afraid I have to answer no to both of your questions, Julia," Huggins said. He paused, studying the overo yearling. "However, I may be able to solve one of your problems. I really like the looks of that colt. If the price is right, I might take him off your hands."

"Do you mean that? I was going to ask two hundred dollars for him. I know that's a bit steep, but he will be a fine riding horse once he's developed. For you I'd let him go for one hundred and seventy five dollars."

"Make that one hundred fifty and it's a deal," Huggins countered.

"I'll settle for that as long as you take him home today, before Jim has a chance to object too much," Julia agreed. "Although perhaps he won't be as upset once he knows it was you who bought this colt."

"I don't have that much money with me," Huggins said.

"I'm not concerned about that. You can get the money to me or Jim whenever you have the chance. While you're talking with Jim, I'll draw up a bill of sale."

"That'll be fine, Julia. I'll see you in a bit."

Huggins turned Dusty and put him into a lope. As Julia had promised, by following the creek which traversed the JB Bar he soon came upon Jim's retreat, a small meadow alongside a wider and deeper stretch of water.

Jim was lying propped against a low boulder, barefoot and bare-chested. Alongside him Charlie's collie lay flopped on his side. Beyond them Sam and Sizzle were busily cropping the grass. Jim was so intent on watching the dragonflies flitting over the creek he didn't hear

Huggins approach until the captain was almost on top of him. Jim rolled onto his side, reached for the Colt on his left hip, then grinned sheepishly when he realized it wasn't there.

"What do you mean, sneakin' up on a man like that, Jim?" he complained. "You're lucky I wasn't wearin' a gun or I might've drilled you plumb center. Bet a hat on it."

"You're even luckier I wasn't some renegade lookin' to plug you," Huggins retorted. "Bein' as it appears you forgot you weren't wearin' a gun, and your mind was so far off in the clouds you didn't even know I was comin'. I could've shot you real easy, and you never would've known what happened."

"I reckon you're right," Jim conceded.

"I am, and you know it," Huggins declared. "You mind if I join you?"

"Pull up some grass and set a spell," Jim invited.

"Thanks."

Huggins dismounted, slipped the bridle off Dusty's head, loosened his cinches, and with a gentle slap on the rump sent his sorrel off to join Jim's horses.

"Jim, you're getting awful lazy," Huggins chided as he stretched out in the grass. "What're you up to, out here in the middle of the day doin' absolutely nothing?"

"I didn't have anything to do around the house

except get underfoot, so I decided to come out here for a swim," Jim answered. "Far as what I'm doin' now, I read some philosopher's words awhile back. He said everyone, man or woman, should just take a day every so often and relax, belly to the sun, and do nothin' but forget the rest of the world. So, I'm doin' just that."

"Makes sense," Huggins conceded. "So much sense I hate to have to end it for you."

"I figured you didn't ride out here just to make small talk," Jim answered. "What is it? Have you heard from Smoky? How's Charlie?"

"Yes, I have heard from Smoky. I've also gotten word of Charlie and Ty," Huggins answered.

"Where are they? Are they all right?" Jim demanded.

"Hold on and I'll tell you everything I know," Huggins answered, adding, "As long as you promise not to go off half-cocked on me until I'm done."

"Just tell me about my boy," Jim answered.

"Okay. Charlie and Ty Tremblay are alive and well, as far as we know. That's the good news. The bad news is they're in a Mexican prison, just outside Piedras Negras. They're bein' held in Zaragoza, to be precise."

"Mexico? What in blue blazes were they thinkin', ridin' into Mexico? Where were Smoky's brains at, letting those boys cross into Mexico? Why didn't he or Duffy stop 'em?"

"Jim, what'd I warn you?" Huggins scolded.

"You're right. Sorry, Jim, finish your story."

"All right. First, Duffy McGlynn's dead, and Smoky's laid up in Eagle Pass, badly wounded. He'll be out of action for quite a spell."

"What happened?"

"I'm comin' to that, if you'll just shut up," Huggins retorted. "Evidently Smoky got word up in Comanche that Tom Foley was headed for Mexico, where supposedly he has friends in Zaragoza. That much you knew. Smoky's information claimed he'd stop at the Bar 7 Ranch, outside of Concan, first, so they went there lookin' for him. According to the Bar 7's owners, Foley never did, so Smoky and the others kept on toward Mexico. Apparently when they attempted to cross the Rio, they got ambushed. Duffy was killed, and Smoky took a bullet in the chest. Charlie and Ty managed to patch him up and get him to a doctor in Eagle Pass. Smoky ordered them not to try'n get into Mexico on their own, but obviously they didn't listen to him."

"You figure it was Foley and some of his friends who bushwhacked 'em?" Jim asked.

"According to Smoky, yes. He claims he spotted Foley just before he got shot."

"Which means someone tipped off Foley as to where and about when they'd be crossin' the Rio," Jim noted.

"Seems so."

"What's bein' done about gettin' Charlie and Ty out of that Mexican jail?"

"There's not much of anything we can do, you know that, Jim. Charlie and Ty violated international law once they crossed into Mexican territory. We can ask the authorities down there to return them, but other than that our hands are tied."

"Your hands might be, but mine sure aren't," Jim snapped. "Besides, what's got into you? We've gone into Mexico more'n once, you and me, and Smoky too, for that matter."

"Yes, but those were the old days," Huggins pointed out. "Things have changed. Regulations are tighter, and now goin' across the Border without permission might even get Washington involved. You know I have to order you not to head into Mexico," Huggins answered.

"Just like you know I'm not gonna listen," Jim replied.

"That's right, so officially you're not to go to Mexico under any circumstances," Huggins replied. "Unofficially, you're still on medical leave, so you can do pretty much what you want. Also unofficially, good luck."

"Thanks, Cap'n," Jim replied. "The Bar 7 Ranch. That's on the Frio River."

"Yeah, it is. You know the place?"

"I've been there once, along with Tom. He

was a cowpuncher there before he joined the Rangers," Jim explained.

"That doesn't mean anything," Huggins noted.

"Mebbe, mebbe not. There's been some rumors about the place, that it might be involved with runnin' wet cattle into Mexico, along with smugglin' other contraband. There was supposed to be an investigation a few years back, but nothing ever came of it, at least nothing I ever heard. Seems kind of odd Tom would stop there," Jim mused.

"Unless he knew something . . . or was involved with something," Huggins exclaimed. "That would explain a whole lot."

"It sure would," Jim agreed. "Especially if I'm recollectin' correctly, and Tom Foley was the man who was assigned to that investigation. We've wasted enough time. Let's get movin'."

Jim tugged on his socks and boots, came to his feet, and shrugged into his shirt, wincing when he slid his arms into the sleeves.

"Jim, are you sure you're in any shape for a long, hard ride?" Huggins questioned.

"With my boy's life at stake, yeah, I sure am," Jim answered. He whistled shrilly, and Sam trotted up to him, Sizzle and Pal close behind.

Huggins retrieved Dusty and rebridled the gelding, while Jim switched the halter from Sam to Sizzle, then used that low rock to climb onto Sizzle's back. He still got a pain in his belly where the bullet had hit whenever he tried to mount.

"Sorry, Sam, but you've been ridden enough," Jim apologized to the horse, "Besides, we're gonna move fast. You ready, Jim?"

"Sure am," Huggins replied.

"Good." Jim heeled Sizzle into a smooth lope, then a run. Five minutes later they pounded into the JB Bar's front yard. Julia was on the front porch, relaxing in a rocker. She leapt up at their approach.

"James Joseph Blawcyzk, what are you doing riding like that?" she shouted. "You're not even supposed to be on a horse yet, let alone be riding like a fool Indian!"

"I don't have time to argue, Julia," Jim answered, as he swung off Sizzle's back. "Charlie and Ty are in jail down in Mexico. I'm goin' to get 'em out."

"Charlie's in prison?" Julia echoed. "But you said he was all right, Captain Huggins."

"He is all right, so far," Huggins replied. "So is Ty Tremblay. However, Duffy McGlynn is dead, and Smoky McCue is badly wounded. I didn't want to tell you all that until Jim was with you."

"Can't you do anything about Charlie and Ty?" Julia asked.

"You know we can't, not officially," Huggins answered.

"But Jim still shouldn't be working," Julia protested.

"I'm not," Jim answered. "As a Ranger, I can't do a thing, but as a private citizen . . ."

"You can get jailed yourself, or even killed," Julia finished.

"That's right, but would you rather I let Charlie rot in jail, or mebbe face a firin' squad?" Jim answered.

"Of course not," Julia replied. "I only wish there were another way."

"There's not," Jim flatly stated. "Could you please get some clothes for me while I saddle the horses?"

"Of course. I'll pack some food for you also."

"Thanks, Julia. I can always count on you."

"Captain Huggins, you said Smoky was wounded?" Julia questioned.

"That's right, the telegram I received said he was shot in the chest. The doctor thinks he'll survive, but he can't promise that yet."

"Does Cindy know?"

"Yes, I stopped by to let her know on my way over here."

"Then once you and Jim are on your way, I'll go over to see her. She must be devastated."

"That's a good idea," Jim agreed. "It'll also be better if you're not alone right now. Do you want me to saddle Lucinda for you?"

"No, I'll do that. You won't want to lose any

time getting on the trail. I'll have your things ready in a few minutes."

Julia went inside, while Jim, accompanied by Captain Huggins, headed for the barn to retrieve his gear.

"You've got a real Ranger's wife there, Jim," Huggins noted.

"I'm well aware of that. Don't know what I'd do without her," Jim answered.

"Let me give you a hand," Huggins offered.

"Sure, Jim. Appreciate it. If you could, Sam's packsaddle is over there. Would you mind gettin' it on him?"

"I wouldn't, but he sure will," Huggins chuckled, referring to the one-man horse's wicked temper.

"I reckon you're right," Jim conceded. "Grab Sizzle's stuff instead. I'll handle Sam."

"With pleasure," Huggins agreed.

The horses were quickly readied, and by the time they were saddled and bridled, with extra supplies loaded into Sam's packsaddle, Julia had put together a packet of food and the clothing Jim had requested. These he put into his saddlebags, then pulled Julia to him for a long, lingering kiss.

"Jim, please be careful, and bring both you and Charlie back in one piece," she pleaded.

"I promise you that," Jim assured her. "Soon as I get him out of Mexico I'll send a wire."

"Make sure you do," Julia said.

"Bet a hat on it. Now I'd better leave."

Jim pulled himself into the saddle, wincing when a sharp twinge of pain shot through his gut.

"Jim, are you sure you're up for this?" Huggins asked.

"I'm positive."

"I hope you're right. I'll ride with you as far as the turnoff for Austin. Julia," he added, "I'll return for that package tomorrow."

"The package? Oh, the yarn for Cora," Julia answered, realizing the captain was referring to the colt he'd just purchased, without letting on to her husband. "That will be fine. I'll have it wrapped for you."

"Jim, if you're ready I'll stick with you a little further than that. I'm gonna make a slight detour before headin' south," Huggins told Jim. "Let's ride."

He turned Sizzle and put him into a lope.

Julia watched until Jim and Captain Huggins faded from sight, then wandered to a field at the boundary line of the JB Bar. This was her favorite spot on the ranch, a meadow which in early spring was covered with bluebonnets, their bright blossoms forming a carpet of vivid blue. Now, though, in the heat of summer, the field was dry and dusty, as bleak as the feeling in Julia's heart. She dropped to her knees in prayer.

Jim rode with Captain Huggins as far as the outskirts of Austin. While the captain continued on to Headquarters, Jim headed for a quiet cemetery at the edge of town. There he stopped and dismounted at Captain Hank Trumbull's grave. The captain had been laid to rest alongside his beloved wife, Maisie, and their daughter, Josie. Their sons, Michael and Jeremiah, had been buried near where they fell on the battlefield of Antietam.

Jim removed his hat and prayed in silence for several minutes.

"Cap'n, I'm gonna make Tom Foley pay for what he did. Bet a hat on it," he finally said. "You can rest easy knowin' that."

Jim made the Sign of the Cross and turned from the grave. He remounted, pointed Sizzle's nose southward, and put the horse into his steady, mile-eating lope, Sam right alongside.

Chapter Twelve

As much as Jim preferred travelling by horseback to riding the rails, he hopped an International and Great Northern Railroad freight train at the whistle stop of Kyle, a short distance south of Austin. Sizzle and Sam were placed in a boxcar, while Jim traveled in the caboose. Taking the train would shorten his journey from Austin to San Antonio from two days to a six-hour overnight run. Perhaps more importantly, it would be far easier on his still-healing wounds, allowing his body a bit more rest. It would also provide his horses with a much-needed respite before the hard run to Eagle Pass.

Once Jim left the train at San Antonio, he rode cross-country for almost three full days, arriving at Eagle Pass late in the afternoon. His first stop was at a small building hard by the river, which served as a makeshift office for Ranger Matt McCarthy. Captain Huggins had wired McCarthy to expect Jim's arrival.

McCarthy had been working on papers while watching for Jim to appear. He stepped out of the office before Jim had even dismounted.

"Jim, howdy. Good to see you again. C'mon inside and rest a bit," McCarthy greeted the lieutenant. He was a tall man in his early forties, with brown hair and eyes, and a bushy mustache.

"Howdy, Matt, it's good seein' you again also," Jim replied, as he swung out of the saddle, wincing slightly at a pain in his gut. "Wish it were under better circumstances."

"That's for certain," McCarthy agreed.

"You two wait here," Jim ordered his horses, tying them to the hitch rail. "You'll get supper and stalls in a bit, once I talk with Matt and visit Smoky."

He started to duck under the rail, but thought better of it when he felt another twinge in his belly, so he walked around the rail instead and followed McCarthy into the office.

"Have a seat, Jim," McCarthy offered, waving toward a battered wooden chair. "Coffee?"

"Don't mind if I do," Jim answered. He reversed the chair and straddled it, leaning his arms on its back.

McCarthy poured a cup of thick black coffee from a pot simmering on the corner stove, and handed it to Jim.

"Here you go."

"Much obliged, Matt."

McCarthy took out the makings and began rolling a quirly.

"Jim, I know you don't smoke, so I won't offer you a cigarette," he said. "How's that coffee?"

"Good and strong," Jim praised. "Best I've had

in a while. Matt, I don't mean to be rude, but I haven't got time for chewin' the fat. You have any more news about my boy and his friend? What about Smoky? How's he doin'?"

"Whoa, easy Lieutenant. One question at a time," McCarthy chuckled. "First, there's nothing new from below the border. Far as we know, your son and his friend are still locked up in the Zaragoza calaboose. Wilfredo Herrera's gonna meet you tomorrow morning, as you requested. He promised to do what he can to help, but he doesn't hold out much hope."

"Hold on a minute, Matt. What do you mean, tomorrow morning? I was figurin' on stopping to see Smoky, grab a bite of chuck, then push on into Mexico tonight," Jim objected.

"Sorry, Jim, but the best Wilfredo can do is tomorrow. He's tied up until then. Besides, you look pretty worn out. Those wounds you received must still be botherin' you some. I've got an extra bunk here in the office, so after we visit Smoky, who's recoverin' nicely by the way, you can put up your horses in the corral out back, then we'll have supper. You'll get a good night's rest, which beggin' your pardon but you look like you can use, Lieutenant, then start out fresh first thing in the morning."

"I reckon I don't have any choice," Jim muttered.

"That's right, you don't," McCarthy responded.

"So you might as well make the best of it. I'll get my horse and we'll head for Doc Torres's."

Jim rose from the chair.

"What're we waitin' for? Let's go."

Jim waited impatiently while McCarthy saddled and bridled his dun gelding.

"Took you long enough," he grumbled, when McCarthy led the horse out of the corral.

"I wasn't in any big hurry," McCarthy answered. "You can't go anywhere until morning, so I'm tryin' to slow you down a bit and force you to relax."

"I'll relax when my son is back on this side of the Rio, and not a minute sooner," Jim retorted. "C'mon."

He put Sizzle into his long-reaching lope. McCarthy had to scramble into his saddle and put his gelding, Dunny, into a gallop to catch up.

"Jim, it's only ten minutes from here to the doc's," he said.

"I know that," Jim answered. "But that's ten minutes too many."

He kept Sizzle at that ground-covering pace. Five minutes later, they were pulling up in front of Doctor Jacinto Torres's neatly kept home and office. They dismounted, tied their horses, and walked up to the front door. McCarthy knocked twice, softly. A moment later Corrina Torres appeared.

"Buenas tardes, Senorita Torres," McCarthy

said, touching two fingers to the brim of his hat in greeting. "Teniente Blawcyzk is here to see Ranger McCue."

"Buenas tardes, Ranger McCarthy, Teniente," Corrina returned. "Come inside, por favor. I will summon my papa."

"Gracias, senorita," McCarthy replied. He and Jim followed the young woman into the cool, dim interior of the thick-walled adobe structure.

"Wait here," Corrina ordered. "I will return shortly."

"Of course," McCarthy agreed.

A few moments later, Corrina returned, accompanied by her father.

"Ranger McCarthy, Teniente Blawcyzk, welcome. It is good to see you again, Teniente. Pardon my keeping you waiting; however, I wanted to make certain Ranger McCue was awake before I brought you to his room," Torres explained.

"No apologies necessary, Doc," Jim replied. "How is Smoky doin'?"

"He is doing very well indeed, I am pleased to say," Torres replied. "In fact, if his progress continues, I hope to be able to release him shortly. Of course, he will not be able to return to duty for quite some time. But enough of this talk. You wish to see your friend. Right this way."

Torres led them down a long corridor to a room on the right.

"In there, gentlemen."

"Gracias, Doc," Jim replied. He and McCarthy stepped into the room to find Smoky McCue sitting up in bed. The smoke-haired Ranger was propped up on his pillows, covered only to his waist. His flesh was extremely pale, almost as white as the bandage taped to his chest. However, he flashed a broad smile at seeing Jim.

"Jim! Matt told me you were on your way down here, but I didn't believe it was possible. Last time I saw you was back in Austin, where you were lyin' on the floor with two bullets in you. You're lookin' dang good pardner, considerin'."

"Yeah, but you didn't need to go and get yourself shot just because I did, Smoke," Jim laughed.

"Hey, you know we do just about everything we can together, Jim . . . includin' gettin' plugged," Smoky retorted.

"We might want to break that habit," Jim said. "Doc Torres tells me you'll be getting outta here pretty soon. That's good news."

"Can't be soon enough to suit me," Smoky answered. "Jim, I'm sure sorry about Chip and Ty. I gave them strict orders not to cross the border, but they didn't listen."

"Chip?" Jim repeated, puzzled. "You mean Charlie, don't you?"

"Sorry, Jim. Didn't anyone tell you Charlie got the nickname Chip hung on him when he signed on with the Rangers?"

"No, that wasn't mentioned, not even by Julia," Jim answered. "How'd he get that handle?"

"You'll appreciate this," Smoky replied. "Adjutant King said Charlie looks so much like you he's a chip off the ol' Blawcyzk, and it stuck."

"You're right, that's pretty good," Jim admitted.

"Jim, in case there was any doubt in your mind, I wanted to go after your son and his friend," McCarthy said. "I received definite orders not to make any attempt to rescue them."

"If I could've gotten out of this bed, I'd've figured something out," Smoky declared.

"I realize that, Matt, Smoky," Jim reassured them. "Now that's why I'm down here . . . to get 'em back. Unofficially, of course. As far as Austin is concerned, I'm still on medical leave," Jim answered. "Tell me exactly what happened, since I only have the information which was wired to Captain Huggins."

"I'll be as brief as I can," Smoky answered. "We had word Foley would try'n stop by the Bar 7 Ranch up on the Frio, then head for Coahuila. We swung by the Bar 7, but everyone there denied seein' Foley, so we lit our for here. When we tried fordin' the river, upstream from here—you know the spot I mean—we were bushwhacked. I got shot off my horse and nearly drowned. Duffy McGlynn managed to pull me out of the river, but he got plugged in the back. He died savin' my life, Jim."

Smoky paused, his voice cracking. Tears welled in his eyes.

"Take it easy, Smoke," Jim urged. "Wait until you're ready."

"There's not much more to tell. Chip and Ty got me here, and Doc Torres patched me up. They also brought Duffy back. Then they went after Torres and wound up in a Mexican jail."

"Duffy had a real nice funeral, and he was buried in a cemetery overlookin' the Rio," Matt interjected.

"That's good," Jim said.

"Least we could do for him," Matt replied.

"Jim, someone tipped Foley off where we were headed, and when. We were sittin' ducks in the middle of that river," Smoky continued. "I spotted him on the Mexican riverbank just before I took that bullet. It could have been any of several men who warned him."

"I think I can narrow that down," Jim replied. "Either of you have any idea whether Foley is still in Mexico?"

"We don't know for certain, but there hasn't been any word of him showin' up in Texas," McCarthy answered.

"You have any idea where he holes up in

Mexico, besides just Zaragoza, Matt?" Jim questioned.

"Supposedly he has a place not all that far out of town, that's all I know," McCarthy explained.

"Jim, what're you gonna do with Chip once you get him outta Mexico?" Smoky questioned.

"First I'm gonna make sure he's safe on this side of the border," Jim answered. "Then I'm planning on kickin' his sorry butt all the way from here to Austin. Bet a hat on it."

"Jim, think about what you're sayin'," Smoky advised. "Suppose the situation was reversed, and it had been Chip who had gotten shot, and the hombre who plugged him was holed up in Mexico? What would you do in that case?"

"I'd have done the exact same thing Charlie did," Jim admitted.

"So now what are you gonna do with him, bein' as he only did what you would've done?"

"I reckon I'll only kick his butt from here to San Antonio, instead of all the way to Austin," Jim laughed.

Just then, Doctor Torres poked his head into the room.

"Gentlemen, I do not wish to interrupt; however, it is time for Ranger McCue's bandages to be changed, then for his evening meal. Will you be much longer?"

"We're just about finished, Doc, unless Smoky has more to say," Jim said.

"I've told you all I know, Jim," Smoky said. "Wish it could be more."

"You've given me plenty to go on," Jim answered. "Besides, it's high time I took care of my horses and got some supper myself. I'll stop by in the mornin' before I leave, Smoke."

"I'll hold you to that," Smoky answered. " 'Night Jim, Matt."

" 'Night, Smoke. See you in the mornin'."

After leaving Doctor Torres's, Jim and McCarthy returned to the Ranger's small office, where Sam and Sizzle were unsaddled and rubbed down, turned into the corral along with McCarthy's gelding, Dunny, and fed. After that, the two Rangers ate a leisurely supper at a small café two blocks from the office, then returned to McCarthy's office. They talked for a while, catching up on old times, until they turned in shortly before nine o'clock. Jim would be awake with the sun, ready to ride into Mexico.

By the time the sun was barely an hour into its daily climb across the sky the next morning, Jim had already visited with Smoky, bid farewell to Matt McCarthy, and crossed into Piedras Negras. Waiting for him there was Rurale Captain Wilfredo Herrera.

"Jim, my friend, it is wonderful to see you again. It has been far too long."

Herrera was a tall, dignified man, who was

well-mounted on a long-legged palomino gelding, whose coat shone brilliantly in the early morning sun. The captain was impeccably dressed in his uniform, which was pressed and spotlessly clean. The high-peaked sombrero he wore also showed not a speck of dust. Herrera's dark eyes reflected his joy at seeing his Ranger friend once again.

"Buenas dias, Wilfredo," Jim replied. "You are right, it has been far too long."

"I am sorry for the circumstances which bring us together again," Herrera responded. "I wish I could have arranged the release of your son, so this journey you have undertaken would not have been necessary . . . a journey which I fear will prove fruitless, I must add."

"You don't think you'll be able to help me get Charlie and Ty out of prison?" Jim asked.

"Let us talk while we ride," Herrera said. "It is more than an hour's steady riding from here to Zaragoza."

"All right," Jim agreed.

While they kept their horses at a slow but easy lope, Herrera explained the difficulty of obtaining the two young Rangers' freedom.

"Jim, the alcalde of Zaragoza is a man named Bernardo Jalisco. He is a very powerful individual, who runs the town as if it were his own fiefdom. He is also a suspiciously wealthy man."

"Any idea where he gets that wealth?"

"There are rumors, word that he is involved in the movement of stolen cattle back and forth between Mexico and the States, as well as smuggling of other contraband. Unfortunately, there is no proof to back up the accusations and stories."

"Wilfredo, there are similar rumors on the Texas side of the Rio Bravo, most connected with a ranch outside Concan, the Bar 7. Tom Foley worked for the Bar 7 before he became a Ranger. As I recall, a few years back he was assigned to check out those rumors, but nothing ever came of his investigation. Do you think there's any possibility Foley and Jalisco are workin' together?"

"Of course," Herrera shrugged. "But again, where is the proof?"

"That's what we need to find . . . after I get Charlie and Ty safely back to Texas," Jim answered. "When did this Jalisco hombre become alcalde of Zaragoza? I don't recall his name, and he sure wasn't in charge the last time I was down this way."

"He arrived from Ciudad Acuna about two years ago, and immediately began befriending anyone he could. He now has most of the populace loyal to him, believing he will empower them, and obtain more influence for all of Coahuila with the government in Mexico City," Herrera explained. "As far as obtaining the release of your son and his partner, that will be much more difficult than you realize, my friend. You see, besides being very wealthy, Jalisco has great political ambitions. The capture of two Texas Rangers who entered Mexico illegally, two Rangers who were attempting to take back a guest of our country by force, is powerful ammunition for a man such as Jalisco. He will use their arrest and imprisonment for whatever advantage he possibly can in the forthcoming elections. So you see, he has no motivation at all to release your son and his friend. Indeed, Jalisco plans on making an example of them. He is arranging for a very public trial, presided over by a judge who allegedly is paid off by Jalisco, then having them sentenced to a long prison term . . . or execution by firing squad."

"You have any idea how Jalisco knew the reason Charlie and Ty were coming down here . . . or for that matter, how did he even know they were comin' at all?" Jim questioned.

"I believe you already have most of that answer," Herrera replied. "If, as I have been informed Smoky McCue claims, Tom Foley was one of the persons waiting when he and the other Rangers made their first attempt to cross the border, he undoubtedly told Jalisco to keep a watch out for other Rangers who might make the same attempt. No doubt somehow your son and his friend were recognized. Now I fear they will

263

be executed, and there is little if anything I can do to stop their deaths."

"Jalisco will die with my bullets in his belly before I'll ever let that happen," Jim vowed. "Bet your fancy sombrero on that, Wilfredo."

He kicked Sizzle into a gallop.

Forty-five minutes later, the Ranger and the rurale rode into Zaragoza, which was a sleepy town of adobes, clustered around a dusty plaza, which was fronted by the usual church. Passersby stared unabashedly at the two lawmen as they walked their horses through the fetlock-deep dust of the main street.

"The place sure hasn't changed much since the last time I was here, Wilfredo," Jim remarked. "Where'll we find Jalisco?"

"He owns that store over there," Herrera answered, pointing to a structure diagonally across the plaza. "This time of the day he is usually there. We'll allow our horses a short drink, then pay him a visit."

Sam, Sizzle, and Amarillo, Herrera's palomino, were given a moment to quench their thirst from the trough in the center of the plaza, then ridden to the alley alongside Jalisco's store, where there was a bit of shade.

"I won't be any longer'n necessary," Jim told his horses, giving each a peppermint. When Herrera took a step too close to the ill-tempered paint, Sam lunged at him, teeth snapping. Herrera jerked back just in time to avoid a wicked bite.

"I forgot about your horse, Jim," he said. "I see he still is as mean-spirited as ever."

"He's got reason to be," Jim answered. "Enough about Sam. Let's go find Jalisco."

"Certainly."

Herrera led Jim into the store's cool, dimly lit interior. Goods were piled neatly on counters or precisely arranged on shelves. To one side, a young woman was polishing a display of crystal glasses. Bernardo Jalisco was seated at a desk in the back, and looked up from the ledger he was examining when they entered. He was a short, pudgy man, slightly balding, with a thin mustache. Despite his rather plain appearance, the man exuded power, and his dark eyes glittered with cunning.

"Capitan Herrera, to what do I owe the honor of this visit, so early in the day?" he questioned, in a voice dripping with sarcasm. His dislike for the rurale was clearly evident.

"I have brought someone to see you, Bernardo," Herrera replied, his hatred for the alcalde also plain. "This is Texas Ranger Teniente Jim Blawcyzk. However, do not be mistaken about his capacity as a Ranger. He has come into Mexico strictly as a private citizen. His visit here is quite proper, and entirely legal. In fact, you may consider Teniente Blawcyzk my personal guest."

"Another Ranger!" Jalisco exclaimed, still using Spanish, his native tongue. "Blawcyzk? Could you possibly be related to the young Ranger who so brazenly invaded my country, and is now in a jail cell, awaiting trial for fomenting revolution?"

"The name's Bluh-zhick, not Blay-sick." Jim coldly corrected what he was certain to be a deliberate mispronunciation of his name by the alcalde.

"Charlie is my son," Jim continued, also in Spanish, which he spoke as fluently as English. "I have come to ask for his release."

Jalisco laughed wickedly.

"I must say you have nerve, Ranger, riding in here so boldly and expecting me to turn your son and his companion free, just because you wish it. However, your trip has been futile. Your son will be placed on trial within the next week. I am certain he and his friend will be convicted of their crimes."

"Senor Jalisco," Jim answered, fighting down the anger rising in his chest, "I came here not as a Texas Ranger, but as a father. Charlie came here seeking the man who shot me and left me for dead. Surely you can understand why he would do such a thing. Would you not have done the same for your father?"

"What I would have done does not matter," Jalisco sneered. "What does matter is your son violated the sovereign territory of Mexico, and for that he will pay. Now, I have much work to do. I ask that you leave my establishment at once."

"Senor, were you never impulsive in your youth?" Jim asked. "Didn't you ever do something foolish, something you later regretted? Charlie and Ty were merely doing what they thought was right. Can't you see that?"

"All I can see is they were Texas Rangers, invading my country illegally as the Rangers have done so many times in the past. They will be punished for doing so."

"All right, Senor, how much?"

"How much? What do you mean, Ranger?"

"You know exactly what I mean, Jalisco. How much money do you want for the release of my boy?"

Again, Jalisco laughed.

"You believe I can be bought, Ranger? I assure you, I cannot."

"Every man has his price, Jalisco."

"Indeed. And my price is your son's blood."

"Don't, Jim," Herrera warned, when the Ranger reached for the Colt on his hip.

"Bernardo," he said to the alcalde, "I advised Ranger Blawcyzk his trip was a waste of time. However, since he has traveled all this way, will you at least permit him to visit his son?"

"Visit his son?" Jalisco repeated. "Of course, Capitan. I am a compassionate and reasonable man. Come, Ranger, I shall take you to your son immediately. Maria, please watch the store until I return."

"Si, Senor," the young woman replied.

"The jail is just across the plaza," Jalisco told Jim. "In a moment you shall be with your son. Visit with him as long as you wish, for it will be the last time you will have the opportunity to do so."

With Jalisco in the lead, the three men crossed the plaza to the jailhouse, a squat adobe building with a single front window and heavy wooden door. Jalisco knocked, and the deputy inside slid open the door's shutter.

"Esteban, please open the door," Jalisco requested. "I have a guest here, Senor Texas Ranger Jim Blawcyzk, who wishes to visit with his son."

"Si, Senor Jalisco," the deputy replied. He closed the shutter, lifted the thick bar holding the door, and opened it.

"After you, Ranger Blawcyzk," Jalisco offered.

"Gracias," Jim grudgingly replied. He stepped into the small jailhouse, which held only a small office and two cells.

"Open the door to the cells, Esteban," Jalisco ordered.

"Si, Senor."

The deputy unlocked and swung open the heavy door separating the cells from the office.

Charlie and Ty were locked in the smaller of the two. Ty was lying on his bunk, while Charlie was sitting on the edge of his.

"Charlie, Ty," Jim called, then stopped short. "What the devil happened to you two? Jalisco, what's the meaning of this?"

Ty's shirt was open, revealing livid welts covering his chest and stomach. Charlie had stripped to his waist in the oven-like heat of the cramped cell, and his torso also was marred by welts across his chest and belly. In addition, Charlie's skin was covered with cigarette burns, and his navel was blistered and inflamed from what appeared to be where a lit butt had been pressed into it and held there, no doubt causing extreme pain. Both boys had also lost a considerable amount of weight.

"Dad! You're alive!" Charlie exclaimed. "How's Mom?"

"She's fine, but worried about you. We'll talk about her later, soon as I get this cell opened."

Jim turned to the alcalde, his blue eyes blazing with anger. He lifted his Colt halfway out of its holster.

"Jalisco, I asked you a question. What have you done to these boys? And give me the keys to this cell, pronto!" Jim demanded.

"They would not cooperate with us," Jalisco shrugged. "As far as opening the cell door, that is impossible."

Jim started to pull his gun the rest of the way, only to stop when he stared into the leveled revolver of Wilfredo Herrera, which was pointed directly at his stomach.

"Jim, we have been friends for many years, but I cannot permit you to make a mistake here. Please, put your gun back in its holster," Herrera ordered. "I do not wish to shoot you."

"Soon as that deputy gives me the keys to this cell," Jim persisted.

"I will make sure of that," Herrera promised.

"You're not in any position to give orders, Capitan," Jalisco objected.

"Listen to me, Bernardo, you might well be able to arrest these two boys under questionable circumstances, but if word should get out about how they've been treated, it will create quite a problem for you," Herrera shot back. "Austin will notify Washington, Washington will protest to Mexico City, there will be an investigation, and you will be hard pressed to explain how these boys were apparently tortured while in your jail. It would be far better to let Ranger Blawcyzk visit with them in the cell. What difference does it make whether he speaks with them from one side of the door or the other?"

"You make a valid point," Jalisco conceded. "Why invite trouble before the trial? Esteban, open the door."

"Si, Senor Jalisco."

"Jim, your gun," Herrera repeated. "You may keep it, but if I see any sign you are attempting to use it, I will have to kill you."

With a sigh, Jim let his Colt slide back in place. Once he had, the cell was unlocked.

"Dad, you don't know how glad I am to see you," Charlie exclaimed as soon as Jim entered.

"The same goes for me, Lieutenant Blawcyzk," Ty added. He stood up and shook Jim's hand.

"Don't worry about that," Jim answered. "I want to check these wounds. Some of them appear to be badly infected. Have you even seen a doctor?"

"No," Charlie answered. "They told us the only one in this town has been away for several days, treating an outbreak of illness on a ranch south of here."

"We haven't been eatin' too well, either," Ty added.

"So I suspected," Jim said. "Charlie, turn around and let me see your back."

Charlie turned his back to Jim, to reveal slashes across his back even deeper than the ones across his chest and belly, along with more cigarette burns.

"You had my boy whipped half to death, Jalisco," Jim accused.

"If he had answered our questions, that would not have happened," the alcalde answered. "We do not treat our prisoners as kindly as you Norte Americanos."

"If I ever get my hands on you, you'll see how kind I can be," Jim snarled. "Bet a hat on it."

"Careful, Jim," Herrera warned him again.

"All right . . . for now," Jim answered. "Wilfredo, in the saddlebag on the left side of my horse is a medical kit, along with a tin of salve and another of witch hazel. Could I trouble you to get those for me, por favor?"

"Of course, Jim," Herrera readily agreed. "I'll have those items right back."

"Gracias," Jim said.

"Ty, take off your shirt," he then ordered. "I want to check your back also."

"I'd rather not," Ty protested. "My back's not as bad as Chip's."

"Let me be the judge of that," Jim answered. "Now take off that shirt."

"All right," the youngster reluctantly agreed. He peeled off the garment, flinching when dried blood and bits of skin came with it.

"Ty, your back's cut to ribbons," Jim exploded.

"Ranger Blawcyzk," Jalisco called.

"What, alcalde?" Jim growled, struggling to keep his rising anger in check. Losing his temper now would only get them all killed.

"I did not realize just how badly your son and his friend had been treated. I assure you I did not mean for them to be injured so badly. The only solution I can see is to release them at once. They are free to go with you, right now."

"And as soon as they step out of this cell, they'll get bullets in their backs as escaping prisoners," Jim answered. "I'll also get one or two for helping them. The old ley de fuga, Jalisco. I'm not that stupid."

"The ley de fuga? What's that?" Ty asked.

"The law of flight. It's kind of like a lynching up in the States. The ley de fuga says that any man attempting an escape can be shot in the back, no questions asked," Jim explained. "Of course, that makes it real easy for the authorities to turn loose anyone they want to be shut of, then plug him in the back. If we walked out of this cell, you can bet your hat we wouldn't make three steps before we were cut down. Nice try, Jalisco, but no dice."

"It does not matter," Jalisco answered. "You are only postponing the inevitable, Ranger."

"We'll see," Jim snapped.

Several moments passed with no more words exchanged.

"I wonder what's keeping Wilfredo," Jim finally said.

"Mebbe Sam got him," Charlie speculated.

Just then the door swung open and Herrera entered, holding a small leather case, two tins, a bucket of water, and several pieces of cloth.

"Here you are, Jim. I apologize for taking

so long, but I also went to Jalisco's store and obtained some cloth for washing the boys' wounds and for bandages," Herrera explained. "I'm sure you don't mind, Bernardo, do you?"

"I will just send the bill to your commanding officer," the alcalde replied.

"Thanks, Wilfredo," Jim said, taking the supplies from him. "Ty, stretch out on your belly. I want to care for those wounds on your back first."

"All right, Lieutenant."

Ty complied, lying face down on his bunk. Jim began to wash out the slashes on his back.

"Charlie," he asked his son while working on Ty, "what exactly went on here? Is there a reason you and Ty were horsewhipped so badly?"

"Nothing in particular," Charlie answered. "Most of the guards have treated us real decently, except one. Some of 'em have even snuck a little extra food to us. The exception is Juan, the overnight guard. He was tryin' to get us to talk, and when we wouldn't, he took the whip to us. Since it appears that somehow it was already known we were after Tom Foley, there wasn't much more information we could have provided in any event. That didn't matter to Juan, though. He just kept whippin' us, first Ty, then me. After awhile it didn't seem to matter much whether we talked or not. Juan seemed to get a whole lot of pleasure from usin' that whip."

Ty took up the story.

"When Charlie wouldn't talk, Juan then started burnin' him with his cigarettes," he said. "Guess he was tryin' to scare me into talkin', figuring if he hurt Chip bad enough I'd be frightened into spillin' my guts."

"Ty didn't talk, Dad. Neither one of us did," Charlie concluded.

"I'm proud of you both for that," Jim said.

He continued working on Ty's injuries, washing them out with water, then witch hazel, drying them, and coating them with salve.

"All right, Ty. You can sit up," he ordered, once the slashes on the young Ranger's back had been treated. "You want me to take care of the cuts on your chest and belly, or can you handle that?"

"I reckon I can do that," Ty replied. "You'd better get to work on Chip."

"I still can't get used to that," Jim chuckled, shaking his head. "I'm gonna keep callin' my boy Charlie, like I have all his life. So, Charlie, you need to lie on your back first. I don't like the looks of some of those burns, particularly the one to your bellybutton. That one's definitely infected."

"Okay, Dad." Charlie lay down on his bunk, his hands behind his neck. Jim went to work, squeezing the flesh around Charlie's navel to expel accumulated pus and fluid, then washing it out with witch hazel, drying it, coating it with salve, and finally taping a bandage over it.

"Sorry if that hurt too much, Charlie," Jim apologized. "I went as easy as I could."

"It wasn't all that bad," Charlie answered.

"You're a mighty poor liar, Charlie," Jim retorted.

Jim continued treating Charlie's injuries, going through most of his medical supplies.

"That's the best I can do," he said, washing his hands. "With any luck we got those wounds treated in time to avoid blood poisoning."

"Dad, can we talk about you and Mom now?" Charlie questioned.

"Sure," Jim answered.

"You said Mom's all right?"

"She is," Jim confirmed. "She's just worried about me getting you home in one piece."

"How about my folks?" Ty asked.

"I've gotta be honest and say I'm not sure, Ty," Jim admitted. "When I got the news about you and Charlie, I left for here as soon as I could get the horses ready. I'm sure Captain Huggins has notified them by now about the situation."

"How about Smoky? How's he doin'?" Charlie asked.

"I stopped to see him before crossin' the border," Jim answered. "He should be up and around before too long, and back in the saddle before you know it."

"I have to say, I was real surprised to see you walk into this jail, Lieutenant Blawcyzk," Ty observed. "I figured you were still laid up."

"I was goin' stir crazy just hangin' around," Jim answered. "I'm just about all healed up, so a few more days rest wouldn't have made much difference."

"This is all very touching, Ranger, but you have overstayed your visit," Jalisco called.

"I'll stay here as long as I want," Jim answered.

"It's all right, Dad," Charlie said. "Don't stir up more trouble."

"Your son is giving you good advice. I suggest you take it," Jalisco said.

"I guess I'd better," Jim muttered. "Charlie, Ty, I'll see you tomorrow. I'll figure some way to get you out of this mess."

"I know, bet a hat on it," Charlie concluded, chuckling.

"That's right," Jim grinned.

"Get out of there, Teniente," Jalisco insisted.

"Don't push me, alcalde," Jim warned. Nevertheless, he left the cell, closing the door behind him. Esteban quickly turned the key in the lock.

"Let's go, Wilfredo," Jim said. "I can't stand the stink in this place any longer."

"I understand, Jim," the rurale said.

Much to Jim's chagrin, Jalisco insisted on accompanying them out of the jail.

"Teniente, you may believe you will be allowed

to visit the prisoners again, but I assure you that will not happen," he said. "You are to leave Zaragoza within the hour. Be certain that you do. Get back on your own side of the Rio Bravo, and stay there."

"I'm not goin' anywhere, except to take care of my horses, then get a room and meal," Jim answered.

"You intend to disobey my orders?" Jalisco asked.

"Bernardo, listen carefully," Herrera warned. "Jim Blawcyzk is my guest, and he will remain in Zaragoza as long as he wishes. Also, you are to allow him access to the prisoners for at least one hour every day. Is that clear?"

"You are overstepping your authority, Capitan," Jalisco answered.

"I am not, and you are well aware of that," Herrera retorted. "So, what will it be? Do you allow the teniente to remain here until the trial, and to visit his son and companion, or do I declare martial law?"

"You would not dare!" Jalisco exploded.

"Are you willing to take that chance?" Herrera rejoined.

"I . . . suppose not," Jalisco conceded. "You win, Capitan . . . for now."

He stalked off toward his store.

"Thanks, amigo, for your help," Jim told Herrera.

"It is only temporary," the rurale explained. "If Jalisco goes over my head, I am certain I will be ordered not to interfere in this matter."

"Well, at least you bought me some time, and I appreciate that, Wilfredo," Jim answered.

"I may also have bought you a bullet or knife in your back," Herrera replied. "As I must return to Piedras Negras, I cannot provide you any assistance. Please watch yourself, amigo mio. Be very cautious."

"I always am," Jim assured him. "Always."

Chapter Thirteen

After leaving the jail, Jim took his horses to the sole livery stable in Zaragoza.

"You wish stalls for your fine caballos, Senor?" the hostler, a middle-aged man who walked with a limp, asked, in passable English. "I am Jose Varbenas, at your service."

"Si," Jim confirmed. "Stalls, feed, and water. I'll rub them down myself. Sam here doesn't take too kindly to strangers."

"I can see that," Varbenas answered, when Sam pinned his ears and lunged at him. "I will be more than happy to let you groom him yourself. Bring your caballos inside. They will be placed in the first two stalls on the right."

"I'm not sure how long I'll be in town, so here's enough money for a week," Jim said, digging in his pocket. He came up with a five peso coin, which he handed to the liveryman.

"This is too much," Varbenas protested.

"I'm also looking for some information," Jim said, as he followed Varbenas into the stable.

"I will help if I can," Varbenas offered.

"There are two prisoners in the jail, Texas Rangers."

"Si senor, that is true," Varbenas agreed.

"One of them is my son, the other his friend,"

Jim explained. "I want to find their horses. When I return to Texas, those horses will be with me."

Varbenas suddenly lost his fluency in English. "Caballos? No entiendo, Senor."

"The Rangers' horses, a pintado and a palomino. Donde estan los caballos?" Jim demanded.

Varbenas shrunk back from the unbridled fury in Jim's eyes. His resolve wilted under the steady gaze of those cold blue eyes, which glittered like chips of ice.

"A pintado and palomino? They are in my back corral," Varbenas reluctantly admitted. "However, they no longer belong to the prisoners. Senor Jalisco has ordered them confiscated."

"Senor Jalisco has no right to those horses," Jim answered. "You will have them ready when I want them, or else. You understand that, hombre?"

"Si . . . si, Senor," Varbenas stammered.

"Bueno," Jim answered. "As soon as I get the gear off my horses, I'm going to check on those two. They'd better be in good shape."

"They are," Varbenas replied.

Jim stripped the gear from Sam, then Sizzle. He then gave each a peppermint.

"I'll be right back," he assured them, then headed out the back door of the barn.

As Varbenas had indicated, Ted and Bandit were in the far back corral, dozing in the sun. Ted jerked up his head at Jim's whistle. Jim whistled again, and Ted answered with a whinny, then trotted up to the fence, Bandit following.

Jim ducked into the corral and looked over the horses, running a hand over their backs, then down their shoulders and legs.

"You both seem all right," he said, giving each a peppermint. "I'll have you out of here in a couple of days, along with your buddies. Bet a hat on it."

Jim left them with a pat on their noses, then went back inside, where he found Varbenas already feeding his own mounts.

"They are in the condition I said, no, Senor?" Varbenas asked.

"They are, si," Jim agreed. "You appear to take excellent care of your charges."

"I try my best," Varbenas answered.

"Gracias, and remember what I said about who owns the pintado and palomino," Jim warned.

"I will, Senor," Varbenas promised.

"Bueno."

Jim entered Sam's stall and began grooming the gelding. He would spend the next hour making sure both his horses were thoroughly rubbed down.

Jim's next stop was the Casa de Cazar Ratas. The owner, Kris Blake, shouted a greeting to him the moment he stepped through the doors.

"Jim Blawcyzk," she called. "I'd heard you

were in town. I figured it wouldn't take you all that long to get here once you got word about your boy."

"Howdy, Kris," Jim returned, grinning. He stepped up to the bar and propped one boot on the foot rail.

"Your usual, Jim?" Kris asked.

"Yes, ma'am," Jim answered.

"Comin' right up."

The cantina's owner rummaged under the bar until she came up with two bottles of sarsaparilla. These she placed on the bar, opened, and poured the contents of one into a mug.

"There you go. That'll be two bits American," she said.

"All right." Jim spun a quarter on the bar. He glanced at the rats scurrying about in their cage behind the bar.

"I see you've got a new friend, Kris."

"Oh, you mean Templeton," Kris replied. "He's company for Yul and Telly."

"Interesting names," Jim noted. "How'd you come up with them?"

"I just liked the sound of Templeton," Kris explained. "As far as Yul and Telly, I tossed a bunch of letters in a sombrero, and pulled 'em out until I had enough to put together names."

"As good a method as any," Jim chuckled. He glanced around the mostly empty cantina, then lowered his voice.

283

"Kris, I want to thank you for gettin' word to Austin about my boy and his friend bein' taken prisoner and held here in Zaragoza," he whispered.

"Why Jim Blawcyzk, you devil!" Kris laughed, then also lowered her voice. "I figured you were the only chance they had," she continued. "I knew what had happened to you, of course, so I was sure hopin' you were in good enough shape to ride."

She boldly ran her gaze over the rugged Ranger.

"I can see I needn't have worried. You're lookin' good, sugar," she loudly proclaimed.

"Thanks, you're lookin' pretty good yourself," Jim answered.

"How'd you know Charlie was my kid?" he then asked, once again whispering.

"Are you kiddin'?" Kris softly replied. "First, he's the spittin' image of you. Second, no one would ever buy the cock and bull story he was peddlin' about trying to find Tom Foley to work for you, helping clean out a passel of rustlers. There were several of Foley's friends in here when your boy started asking about him. When they left real sudden-like, I knew your kid and his friend were in for some tall trouble. Sure enough, it wasn't long before they were brought in by a bunch of rurales, with Bernardo Jalisco leading the pack. I let Wilfredo Herrera know what had happened as fast as I could."

"I sure appreciate that," Jim said.

"Like Wilfredo, I have no great love for Jalisco either," Kris stated. "Foley too, for that matter."

"You used to, for Foley," Jim reminded her.

"The biggest mistake of my life," Kris said.

"What about Jalisco? You think he's workin' with Foley?" Jim asked.

"I wouldn't be surprised," Kris replied. "They've been friends for a long time."

Jim downed the contents of his mug, which Kris then refilled.

"Kris," he inquired. "Do you still have those rooms for rent out back?"

"I sure do," she confirmed. "You want to take one for the night?"

"Make that a couple of nights," Jim answered.

"Whatever you wish," Kris answered. "That's two dollars American."

Jim dug in his pocket and came up with the requested amount. He held the two silver dollars just out of Kris's reach. Once again he lowered his voice, but kept it just loud enough to be over-heard.

"How much for the room if you spend the night with me?" he suggested.

"Ranger, how dare you?" Kris hissed. She slapped him soundly across the face.

"I guess I deserved that," Jim muttered, rubbing his cheek. Quietly he added to Kris, "If anyone wonders what we were whisperin' about, that should fool 'em."

"Mister, you can still have that room, but keep your dirty paws off me," Kris ordered.

"Yes, ma'am," Jim answered. "Is there a chance I could at least settle for some grub?"

"I've got steak and eggs, but if you want supper, you'd best figure on eatin' alone. There's a nice corner table you can use, right over there."

"I guess I better," Jim answered. He picked up his drink and stalked to the indicated place.

After supper, Jim sat outside the cantina until sunset, watching the comings and goings of the residents of Zaragoza. Confident Bernardo Jalisco would not dare make a move against Charlie and Ty with him in town, Jim headed for his room once full dark had descended.

Jim said his evening prayers, undressed, then stretched out on the bed.

"Gotta figure out some way to break Charlie and Ty outta that jail, and fast," he muttered. "I wonder . . ."

"It's been a long night," Kris Blake declared once the last customer had finally departed the Casa de Cazar Ratas, two nights after Jim Blawcyzk's arrival. "Lily, Ramon, Pedro, you may all just go home. We'll clean up tomorrow before opening. I'll lock up in a few minutes."

For a Tuesday night, the cantina had been

unusually busy, and it was now several minutes past two a.m.

"Si, Senorita Blake, and gracias," Lily replied for all of them. It was not that unusual for them to leave things be until the next day. "Buenas noches, Senorita."

"Buenas noches to all of you."

Once her employees had left, Kris turned off all the lights save the one closest to the door. She pulled her beaded reticule from its place on a shelf under the bar, opened it, and removed the two shot Derringer it contained. She checked the loads in the little pistol, nodded with satisfaction, and replaced it in the purse. She then took down her thin shawl from a wall peg and draped it around her bare shoulders. Finally, she took a bottle of tequila from behind the bar.

"I guess that's all," she murmured. After saying a final good night to her rats, she turned out the last light, closed and locked the door, and stepped into the darkened main street.

Juan de Vaca, the overnight deputy, was as usual sitting on a chair in front of the jail, smoking a thin cigar. His rifle was leaning against the wall alongside him. Kris nodded to him as she always did when she walked by the jail on her way home. De Vaca smiled and nodded in return.

Kris strode fifty feet past the deputy, then paused and turned as if having forgotten something. She went back to the jailhouse, stopped, and smiled at de Vaca.

"Senorita Blake, may I be of assistance?" he asked. De Vaca was a bit over average height, with very handsome features and a slim build. Women found him extremely attractive, and many had succumbed to his considerable charms. Much to the dismay of most, too late they would discover de Vaca also had a streak of extreme cruelty.

"I was hoping you could be, Juan," Kris replied, smiling. "You and I pass by each other nearly every night. We nod, then go about our business. I have been thinking lately, that is a real shame. We don't really know each other, yet it seems to me we are both very lonely people. I think we should change that situation. I would like to get to know you better, if I may be so bold."

De Vaca smiled broadly, revealing his even white teeth.

"I believe I would like that very much, Senorita Blake."

"Please, call me Kristin."

"Si . . . Kristin," de Vaca agreed. "As you say, we should become better acquainted. When would you like to have our first, shall we say, rendezvous?"

"What's wrong with right now?" Kris answered. "For two night owls such as ourselves, the night is still young. I have brought a bottle of my

288

finest tequila. We can talk, drink—perhaps a bit more."

De Vaca licked his lips in anticipation.

"You have tequila?"

"Si, Juan, right here."

Kris held up the bottle containing the fiery liquor.

"I am tempted, Kristin; however, I am on duty," de Vaca hesitated.

"Who is to know what we are doing?" Kris replied. "We can go inside the jail. There is no one about this time of night."

"There are the prisoners," de Vaca pointed out.

"They are no doubt sleeping, and you undoubtedly have the door to the cells closed and locked," Kris stated. "If we are discreet, they won't awaken. Even if they did, who would they tell, and who would believe the overactive imaginations of two young boys in any event? Juan, I have waited a long time to build up enough courage to approach you. After all that, you are not going to disappoint me, are you?"

"No, I will not. That would be very impolite of me," de Vaca said. "Come inside, swiftly."

"Now you're talking like my kind of man," Kris answered.

De Vaca picked up his rifle and let Kris precede him into the jail's small front office. He made one last check of the street, then quickly closed the door.

"Do you have some glasses here, Juan?" Kris asked. "I neglected to bring any."

"No, I am afraid I do not," de Vaca apologized. "We will have to make do with coffee cups."

"It seems a shame to put fine tequila such as this into coffee cups, but I suppose they will have to do," Kris answered. "Get them while I open the bottle."

"Right away," de Vaca agreed. He took two mugs from the shelf. Kris filled these half-way with the tequila.

"To us," she smiled, lifting her mug.

"To us," de Vaca answered. They touched the mugs, then downed their contents.

"That is indeed fine tequila," de Vaca praised. "It's quite excellent."

"More?" Kris offered.

"Certainly," de Vaca replied.

After several more drinks, de Vaca had become quite loquacious, his customary cautious nature a casualty of the powerful liquor.

"Kristin," he said, "it is true that at the moment I am a mere diputato, but before long I will be appointed jerife of this entire region."

"From deputy to sheriff for one so young?" Kris questioned.

"Si, it is true," de Vaca answered. "Senor Jalisco has promised me that for my loyalty to him. And Senor Jalisco is a very ambitious man, so who knows where I might go if I remain a valuable associate to him? You could also rise to better things along with me, if you wish."

"But I am older than you by several years, Juan," Kris pointed out. "Would you not prefer a younger woman?"

"Not at all," de Vaca declared. "Older women are wiser, and they are more experienced in the ways of pleasuring a man. I would much rather have a worldly woman such as yourself than a young, shy creature. I hope you will allow me to show how much excitement and delight I can provide you."

"Perhaps," Kris said. She removed the shawl from her shoulders, draped it around de Vaca's neck, and pulled it slowly and provocatively down his chest. She dropped it to the floor, then undid the top two buttons of her blouse.

"Juan, would you like to see something you've never seen before?" she purred.

De Vaca gulped, his blood racing and pulse pounding. He leered at the attractive, blonde cantina owner.

"Si, I would like that very much," he answered.

"Then I shall show you," Kris replied, her voice low and sultry. She leaned closer to the deputy and pulled her blouse a bit lower. De Vaca's eyes widened with excitement when she reached into her cleavage.

"Are you ready, mi corazon?" Kris huskily asked.

"I have been waiting for this moment," De Vaca answered, swallowing hard.

"Perfect," Kris said. She removed her hand from her bosom, showing de Vaca the pet rat she'd kept hidden, nestled in her cleavage.

"This is my friend Templeton," she said. "Isn't he cute?"

De Vaca recoiled in horror.

"That is a rat!"

"Of course it is," Kris answered. "He's a hooded rat, one of my pets. Wouldn't you like to hold him?"

"Senorita, no! Take him away, please. I am terribly afraid of rats."

"Templeton won't hurt you," Kris persisted, stroking the rat's dark brown and white hair. "He's very friendly, just like I am. Why don't you give him one little kiss?"

She held the rat directly under de Vaca's nose. The terrified deputy backed toward the door, trembling.

"Senorita, I have made a mistake," he said, his voice quaking with fear. "Please go now."

"Do you really mean you don't like Templeton?" Kris said.

"Senorita, I despise rats," de Vaca insisted. "Please, take him away."

"But he likes you," Kris retorted, stepping even closer.

"No! I beg of you, Senorita," de Vaca screeched.

He took several more steps backward . . . directly into the barrel of Jim Blawcyzk's Colt Peacemaker rammed into his spine.

"Don't move a muscle, deputy, or I'll blow your backbone in two," Jim snarled.

De Vaca gave a high-pitched scream, gasped, clutched his chest, and pitched to the floor. His body lay quivering in its death throes.

"Puerco! Cerdo!" Kris spat at the dead deputy.

Jim rolled de Vaca onto his back.

"I guess this hombre wasn't kiddin'. He really was scared of rats," he remarked. "Died of pure fright."

"Oh, like the gun you stuck in his back didn't have a thing to do with that," Kris sarcastically retorted.

"I suppose you could be right," Jim answered. "Thanks, Kris, and especially you, Templeton. Here, buddy, this is for you."

He placed a peppermint in Kris's hand, just under Templeton's nose. The rat sniffed at the candy, then began gnawing it with his razor-sharp teeth.

"We have to move fast, Jim," Kris reminded him.

"Right. Give me those keys, will you?"

Kris lifted a heavy ring of keys from a wall peg and handed them to the Ranger.

"Thanks, Kris. Now you'd better take Templeton and get outta here," Jim ordered.

"If it's all the same, I'd rather keep a lookout for you," she replied.

"That's not a bad idea, thanks," Jim agreed.

While Kris took up a position at the window, Jim unlocked the door leading to the cells.

"Charlie, Ty!" he hissed.

"Dad?" Charlie sleepily answered.

"Yeah, it's me," Jim confirmed. "Get your boots on and get movin'. I'm breakin' you outta this jail, right now. Hurry."

"All right, Dad," Charlie answered, now fully awake. He nudged Ty, who was still sleeping soundly.

"Ty! Wake up. We're leavin'."

"What?" Ty muttered. "What d'ya mean, Chip?"

"Ty, it's Lieutenant Blawcyzk," Jim half-whispered. "I'm unlockin' the cell, then we've gotta make a run for it. The horses are out back of the cantina. Hurry it up."

"Yessir, Lieutenant," Ty replied. He sat up and quickly pulled on his boots.

Jim turned the key in the lock and flung open the cell door.

"Get movin', you two," he ordered. "We'll take a minute to try'n find your guns, but then we have to git!"

Ty and Charlie grabbed their hats and shirts and followed Jim out of the cell. They stopped short at the sight of de Vaca's body.

"What happened to him?" Ty asked.

"Rat poisonin'," Jim muttered.

"Jim, hurry," Kris urged. "It's starting to get a bit light out there."

The first gray light of the false dawn dimly illuminated the eastern horizon.

"What's she doin' here?" Charlie demanded. "That's the witch who turned us in."

"She's hardly that, but there's no time to explain right now, except to say she helped me figure a way to get you two outta here," Jim said. "Try'n locate your guns."

"There's our Winchesters in the rack," Ty noted, "and I think they put our six-guns and gunbelts in the bottom left drawer of the desk."

"Get 'em," Jim said.

While Ty took their rifles from the rack, Charlie pulled open the drawer and removed their Colts and gunbelts. He checked to be sure the weapons were still loaded, then tossed Ty's to him. They quickly buckled the gunbelts around their waists.

"We're ready, Dad," Charlie said.

"Good. Kris . . . ?" Jim asked.

"I don't see anyone," she answered.

"Fine. You and Templeton go first," Jim ordered. "We'll be along in a couple of minutes. It wouldn't do for you to get caught with us."

Jim kissed her on the cheek.

"Thanks again, Kris. Once all this is over, I'll try'n stop by."

"Just get your hides back to Texas without gettin' 'em shot full of holes," Kris said. "Once you do, get word to Wilfredo that you're safe."

"Will do," Jim promised. "Now go!"

Kris slipped out of the jailhouse and into the darkness. The Rangers waited tensely for a few minutes, then followed. Sticking to the shadows, they made their way as rapidly as possible to the alley behind the Casa de Cazar Ratas.

"Quiet, Sam," Jim ordered, when the horse lifted his head and began to whicker a greeting. "Don't give us away."

He swung onto Sizzle's back, Charlie and Ty likewise mounting their horses, shoving their shirts under their bedrolls rather than sliding them onto their still tender skin.

"Keep at a walk until we reach the edge of town," Jim ordered. "Let's not stir anyone up."

He heeled Sizzle into a shuffling walk, the horse's hooves making virtually no noise in the thick dust. Charlie and Ty kept their horses just behind. Once they reached the edge of town, they pushed the mounts into a full gallop.

Jim kept the horses at that gallop for a full mile, then slowed the pace to a steady lope for another, finally slowing to a trot, then a walk for another half-mile. He then called a halt to allow the horses a short breather.

"I know you've got a lot of questions," he said

to Charlie and Ty, "and I'll answer 'em all, once we're back in Texas."

"Can you at least tell us how you got our horses back?" Ty asked.

"Sure. The hostler in Zaragoza's takin' a nice long siesta," Jim chuckled. "When he does wake up, it's gonna take him a while to wiggle out of the ropes holdin' him."

"Where're we headin' now?" Charlie questioned. "Seems to me we're not ridin' northeast toward Eagle Pass. We're headin' more due north."

"We're not goin' back to Texas, not quite yet," Jim confirmed. "Far as I've been able to determine, Tom Foley's still here. His place is about an hour's ride from here, accordin' to what I've been told. In addition, yesterday afternoon Bernardo Jalisco left town, headed in this direction. If he and Foley are workin' together, as I suspect, they probably met up last night. With any luck we'll catch 'em both with their pants down."

"I'd purely enjoy that," Ty said, laughing. "We could shoot 'em right where it'd hurt the most."

"Then we'd kill 'em," Charlie answered, then chuckled. " 'Course, after they were drilled right through their you-know-whats, they'd probably wish they were dead anyway."

"You might be laughin' now, but just remember we're gonna have a fight on our hands," Jim cautioned. "Bet a hat on it. Foley and Jalisco'll have the place well-guarded. If anything happens to me, you two are to turn tail and head straight back to Texas as fast as your horses will carry you. You got that?"

"I reckon," Charlie muttered. "Sure sticks in my craw, though."

"Better'n havin' a slug stuck in that craw," Jim retorted. "One thing. Either of you think you're not up to this after what you've been through?"

"After what Jalisco did to us, darn right we're up to it," Charlie answered. "Bet your hat on it, Dad."

"Same goes for me, Lieutenant," Ty agreed.

"Bueno. Get your shirts on, check your weapons, then let's ride. I want to hit Foley's place before full daylight."

Charlie and Ty made sure their guns were loaded and operational, then pulled on their shirts, wincing when the garments settled on their still-raw wounds. Once that was done, they again put their horses into a lope, while the eastern sky glowed ever brighter.

Forty minutes later, Jim reined in Sizzle.

"This is it," he said. "Foley's place is just ahead, over that rise. Dismount."

He swung out of the saddle, while Ty and Charlie did the same.

"What now, Dad?" Charlie asked.

"I'm gonna explain that to you," Jim answered. "Soon's I get what I need."

He went to Sam, gave him a peppermint, then

dug into the pack Sam carried, extracting two sticks of dynamite and a length of fuse.

"You're gonna blast those hombres out of there?" Ty asked.

"Wish I could, but it won't be that simple," Jim answered. "Kris Blake's been out here several times, since she and Foley had a relationship for a while. She drew me a rough sketch of the place. It's walled on all four sides, but there's only one gate. I'm gonna blow that gate down, then we'll charge the house in the confusion. With luck, some if not most of the men will still be asleep, and won't figure out what's happenin' until too late. Keep in mind we want Foley and Jalisco more'n anyone else. We'll try and grab 'em, then head for the border."

"That's an awful long shot, Dad," Charlie observed.

"Would you rather we just ride back home and leave Foley down here, ridin' high, wide, and handsome?" Jim replied.

"There's not a chance of that," Charlie answered. "I need to know before we start, though, exactly who or what is Kris Blake? Ty and I figured for certain she was the one who told Foley about us. She also said she didn't know where this place was."

"The quick answer is I've known Kris for years. She's a great gal, and a friend. Far as her claimin' she didn't know where Foley's hacienda was at, she was just tryin' to protect herself, in case Foley tried to figure out how you knew where to find him," Jim explained. "She's the last person who'd give you up to Foley or Jalisco. In fact, Kris is the one who got word to Austin about you bein' captured and jailed. If it hadn't been for her, we'd still have no idea what had happened to you two. You'd have been executed, then buried in an unmarked grave somewhere in the badlands, or more likely just left for the coyotes and buzzards. Did you ever think about that before you crossed the Rio?"

"No, I guess we didn't," Charlie admitted.

"I didn't think so. Now, here's what we're gonna do. I'll sneak up on that hacienda, get as close as I can, then dynamite the gate. Once you hear the explosion, ride up fast, shootin' as soon as you get within range. Just try to not plug me," Jim grinned. "That'd make your mom plumb upset, Charlie. It wouldn't make me too happy either."

"What about your horses?" Ty asked.

"They'll follow yours," Jim explained. "I'll rush that gate on foot anyway, so I won't need 'em right off. Any other questions?"

"I've got none," Charlie said.

"Me neither," Ty added.

"Good. One more thing, hold onto your horses real tight until the dust settles. They may try'n bolt when that dynamite goes off. And remember, if you see me go down, don't try and be heroes. Your orders are to get back to Texas alive," Jim stated. "Good luck."

With a pat to Sizzle and Sam, Jim disappeared into the scrub. Charlie and Ty waited tensely, their anxiety mounting with each passing moment.

"Sure hope nothin's happened to your dad, Chip," Ty said, as the minutes dragged by. Just then, a thunderous explosion shattered the morning calm.

"I guess nothing has," Charlie grinned. "Let's get 'em!"

He dug his heels into Ted's ribs, sending the startled gelding leaping forward.

Jim was flat on his belly, rifle in hand, firing rapidly through the shattered gate when Charlie and Ty topped the rise and charged down the slope, shooting. One of the guards had climbed the wall and was drawing a bead on Jim's broad back. Ty fired, and the man dropped his rifle, clutched his stomach, and toppled to the dirt. Another of Foley's men appeared through the dust of the explosion. Jim shot him through the chest, spinning him to the ground.

Jim leapt to his feet, giving the Rebel yell, waving Charlie and Ty through the opening and into the courtyard. They raced their horses into the yard, leapt off their backs, and rolled for cover.

As Jim had predicted, they had taken Foley's men completely by surprise. Two more attempted to gun down the Rangers, only to die with the lawmen's bullets in their chests, then the rest threw up their hands and tossed out their guns. A makeshift white flag appeared from one of the windows.

"They're givin' up awful quick, Dad," Charlie muttered.

"Seems so," Jim agreed. "Might be some kind of a trick."

He came to his knees behind the rain barrel where he'd taken cover.

"Are you men really surrenderin'?" he called.

"Yeah," a voice answered.

"Then all of you step outside, hands over your heads," Jim shouted back. "Any one of you makes a false move'll get a bullet through his guts. Bet a hat on it!"

"Lieutenant!" Ty shouted. Jim whirled, and a bullet smacked into the rain barrel, just missing his ribs.

Ty and Charlie fired as one, their bullets finding their mark. Bernardo Jalisco screeched in pain when Ty's shot struck him in the chest, while Charlie's ripped through his stomach. The impact of the slugs slammed him back against the wall, then he slumped to the verandah floor.

"Anyone else want to die here today?" Jim snarled.

"No. No sir, Ranger," one of the men stammered.

"Then let's have no more foolishness."

The surviving renegades were herded into the center of the courtyard.

"I don't see Tom Foley anywhere," Jim muttered.

"Of course you don't," one of the men bitterly stated, then spat in the dirt. "He's got a tunnel under the north wall. Once the shootin' started, he took off like a scalded hound. Why do you think we quit fightin' so easily? Foley left us here to keep you busy while he made his getaway, the no-good s.o.b. It wasn't worth dyin' for him."

"Charlie, Ty, let's go," Jim exclaimed. "We've gotta try and stop Foley before he reaches the Rio Grande."

"What about these hombres?" Ty asked.

"By now it's been discovered I broke you outta jail, and the rurales are on their way here, since they know I'd come lookin' for Foley once you two were free. My friend Wilfredo can figure out what to do with these men."

"The rurales?" Charlie questioned. "But that's the same bunch who arrested us. They're workin' for Jalisco, or I guess they were workin' for him, bein' as he's now dead."

"Those weren't the men in Wilfredo Herrera's command," Jim explained. "Wilfredo would never have stood for that. No more questions."

Jim whistled sharply, and a moment later Sam and Sizzle trotted into the courtyard. Jim climbed onto Sizzle's back, whirled him around, and, low over the big paint's neck, galloped him back out of the gate, Charlie and Ty right behind.

With the Rangers' horses having rested for the past few days, they still had plenty left for the long race to the Rio Grande. Several miles later, when they topped one of the few low rises in this mostly table-flat territory, Jim spied three riders in the distance, pushing their horses to the limit.

"That's Foley," he exclaimed. "We might have a chance to catch up with him after all."

Jim started Sizzle down the slope, then screamed, grabbed his gut, and toppled from the saddle. Charlie leapt from his horse and knelt at his father's side.

"Dad!" he cried. "What's wrong?"

"Dang . . . bullet hole in my . . . belly's . . . still not healed . . . up . . . all the way," Jim grunted. "Guess we won't catch Foley after all."

"We're not gonna worry about that," Charlie answered. "I'll get you to a doc's at Piedras Negras."

"No," Jim ordered. "You two are still down here illegally, and now, after breakin' you out of jail, not to mention going after Foley and Jalisco, so am I. We're ridin' straight for the Rio. We'll have to swim it, but we're not chancing gettin' caught down here. Help me up, will you?"

"Sure, Dad."

Charlie pulled Jim to his feet.

"You all right, Lieutenant?" Ty asked.

"Seem to be now," Jim answered. He pulled himself onto Sizzle's back, wincing at another sharp pain stabbing through his gut.

"We're losin' ground," he said. "We need to make the crossin' before dark."

"You're not still worried about Foley, are you?" Charlie asked.

"Nope, because I'm certain I know just where we'll find him," Jim answered.

They pushed the horses as hard as they dared, conserving both the mounts' and their own strength. They reached the Rio at a spot where it carved its way through high bluffs and steep slopes.

"Hold a tight rein on your horses, boys," Jim warned. "Keep their heads above water, no matter what, and leave some space between each other."

He edged Sizzle and Sam over the rim of a sheer drop, the horses sliding on their haunches until they plunged into the river. With Charlie, then Ty, following close behind, the horses swam strongly as they struck out for the Texas shore. A few moments later, and a hundred yards downstream, Jim's horses lunged from the water. He turned and shouted encouragement to Charlie and Ty. Shortly, both youngsters had ridden onto Texas soil.

"Boys, we're back home," Jim said, with a sigh of relief. "We're gonna spend the rest of the day right here, get some rest and lick our wounds. We'll light out again first thing in the morning."

"Thank the Good Lord!" Ty exclaimed.

"You've got that exactly right," Jim said.

Chapter Fourteen

After two long days of hard, fast riding, pushing the horses to their limits and riding cross-country to avoid the main trails and towns, the weary Rangers neared their destination—the Bar 7 Ranch.

"Charlie, you'n Ty have been here before," Jim noted. "What's the best way to approach the place without bein' spotted?"

"See that hill over yonder, Dad?"

Charlie pointed to a low rise, which was dotted with redberry junipers and cedars.

"Yeah," Jim said.

"We'll cross the river, then we can ride to the left around the base of the hill, which'll bring us onto a trail that'll take us through an arroyo, then winds between some more low hills. We'll come out of those hills right into the main house's front yard. With any luck, no one'll spot us until we're right on top of 'em," Charlie explained.

"You seem mighty sure of yourself after only one short visit here," Jim objected.

"Chip's right about that trail, Lieutenant," Ty confirmed. "It's the one we took when we left this ranch. Like he said, it'll put us practically on the Bar 7's front porch."

"I reckon you two know what you're talkin' about," Jim grinned. "Let's get on in there."

"Wait just one minute, Dad, please," Charlie requested.

"We're wastin' time," Jim answered.

"This won't take long," Charlie assured him. He reached into his shirt pocket and pulled out a Mexican five peso coin, which he handed to his father. The coin already had two wedges cut out of it, where Charlie had started to carve it into a silver star on silver circle.

"What's this for, Charlie?" Jim questioned.

"I was beginnin' to carve that coin into a Ranger badge," Charlie explained. "But after what Ty and I did, disobeyin' orders, ridin' into Mexico, and gettin' ourselves caught, I don't deserve to be a Texas Ranger."

"That goes for me, too, Lieutenant," Ty broke in. "Chip and I talked this over long and hard while we were in that cell, and we both agreed we're not fit to ride with the Rangers. Once we're back in Austin, we'll hand in our resignations."

Jim turned the half-finished badge in his fingers, hesitating while he formulated a reply.

"Charlie, Ty," he finally said. "It is true you disobeyed orders, that's a fact. You also broke the law when you crossed the border and rode into Mexico, with every intention of capturin' or killin' Tom Foley. However, there are other things to consider here. First, that's not the first time

Rangers have gone into Mexico after a fugitive—border and treaties be hung—and it won't be the last, bet a hat on it. Second, you stuck with your pardners through an ambush and didn't turn your backs on 'em. That means a lot. Third, you showed an awful lot of courage, and durin' that gunbattle at Foley's hacienda you showed you can fight, too. You're both men to ride the river with, bet a hat on it. So, Charlie, you can just take this badge back and finish carvin' it first chance you get."

Jim passed the coin back to his son.

"You really mean that, Dad?" Charlie asked.

"If bein' a Ranger still means so much to you, yes," Jim answered.

"Bet a hat it does!" Charlie exclaimed. "One more thing, though, Dad."

"Just what might that be?" Jim asked.

"You might want to change your shirt," Charlie grinned.

"Why? What's wrong with this shirt? Now that you bring it up, your mom hates this shirt too, for some reason," Jim protested.

"It's not that," Charlie said. "I kinda like that shirt, but that bright red color makes you a much easier target, Dad."

"Kinda like a turkey gobbler's red head," Ty added.

"There's nothing wrong with this shirt," Jim retorted. "It's one of my favorites, and I'm a plenty big enough target anyway, bet a hat on that. There's only one thing missin' from this shirt, now that I think of it."

Jim dug in his shirt pocket, extracted his Texas Ranger badge, and pinned it to the shirt.

"There. Forgot to pin on my badge," he said. "Now if you two don't have any more smart-alecky remarks, let's get a move on."

"All right," Charlie smiled.

They heeled their exhausted horses into a slow walk. This close to finding their quarry, there was no need to rush into an ambush, or to make a foolish mistake.

"Charlie, Ty, listen to me," Jim explained as they rode toward the hill. "When we reach the Bar 7, I'll handle Tom Foley, and the owners. You two are to keep an eye on their cowboys, just in case any of 'em decide to take a hand. Since it's gettin' close to suppertime, it's likely quite a few of the hands will be at the bunkhouse, washin' up or gettin' ready to eat. You see any of 'em go for a gun, you plug 'em. Is that clear?"

"It sure is," Charlie answered.

"That's assuming Foley's there," Ty pointed out.

"I'm almost one hundred percent positive he is," Jim answered. "It's his safe haven at this point, and if he's been smugglin' goods, like we suspect, he'd want to come back here and get whatever he could before takin' off for parts unknown. The only question is exactly where he'll be on this spread. Now no more talkin' until we reach the ranch."

They rode silently from that point, splashing their horses across the shallow Frio, then riding into the shadowy arroyo. A sense of foreboding pressed upon them, much like the beetling cliffs of the rocky defile, until they emerged unchallenged, now riding between brush-covered hills and rock outcroppings.

Jim ordered a halt, so they could check their weapons one last time, then once again the horses were put into an easy walk.

The Rangers rode into the Bar 7 yard to find Jeff Nichols on the front porch of the main house, in an animated discussion with the ranch's head wrangler, Jeff King. The pair turned at the sound of the lawmen's horses' hoof beats, narrowly eyeing Jim and the others while they approached. Nichols's gaze, in particular, settled on the silver star on silver circle badge pinned to Jim's shirt, glittering in the late afternoon sun.

"Afternoon, gentlemen," Jim said, touching two fingers to the brim of his hat while keeping his left hand on the butt of his six-gun. "I'm Texas Ranger Lieutenant Jim Blawcyzk. These are Rangers Charlie Blawcyzk, my son, and Ty Tremblay."

"I recognize you two!" King exclaimed. "You were here awhile back with two other Rangers, askin' about Tom Foley."

"That's right, they were," Jim confirmed. "You mind givin' me your names, just for the record?"

"I'm Jeffrey King, head wrangler here."

"I'm Jeff Nichols, one of the owners of this ranch, along with my brother," Jeff replied. "We explained then that we hadn't seen Foley for quite some time, so what brings you Rangers here again?"

"Mind if we dismount?" Jim requested.

"Suit yourselves," Jeff shrugged.

Jim, Charlie, and Ty got down from their horses. Once again, Jim flinched as pain shot through his belly when he swung his leg over Sizzle's back.

"Ty, Charlie, keep an eye on the bunkhouse," Jim ordered.

"Yessir, Lieutenant," Ty complied. He and Charlie pulled their Winchesters from their saddle boots, jacked shells into the chambers, and turned to face the men now gathering in front of the bunkhouse, curious as to the new arrivals' intentions.

"Just stand right where you are, boys," Charlie ordered, leveling his rifle in the cowboys' direction. "We're not lookin' to start any trouble, but if someone tries to pull a gun on us, he'll be the first man to die here today. Bet a hat on it!"

"You didn't answer my question, Ranger," Jeff grumbled.

"I'm about to, and ask you a passel of questions

myself," Jim retorted. "First and most important one: Where's Tom Foley?"

"I have no idea what you're talkin' about," Jeff retorted.

"You're lyin'," Jim shot back. "In case you've forgotten, I'm the man Foley shot and left for dead after he killed Captain Trumbull. His trail led here, then to Mexico. Charlie and Ty, along with the other two Rangers you mentioned, were ambushed by Foley and some of his confederates. Smoky McCue and Duffy McGlynn were gunned down without warnin'. Smoky was badly wounded, while Duffy was shot in the back and killed. That's the kind of man Foley is."

"That doesn't have anything to do with us," King objected. "Like Jeff says, Foley hasn't been around these parts for months."

"You're wrong, mister," Jim replied. "Someone had to tip off Foley when and where Smoky and his men would be crossin' the Rio, for him to be able to set up that drygulchin'. When these two boys here made the mistake of ridin' across the border on their own to try'n track down Foley, they were captured and tossed into jail. Again, someone must've given Foley a description of the men trailin' him, so he'd know who to keep an eye out for. That person had to be someone from this ranch."

"That's preposterous!" Jeff exclaimed. "Both my brother and I explained we knew that Foley had gone bad, and if he'd dared to show up here, we'd've turned him in."

"Is it?" Jim asked. "Once I'd been informed what had happened and was well enough to ride, I headed for Mexico myself, mainly to get my son and his friend out of that jail, but also searchin' for Foley. From what I learned, Foley had a place down there, just outside Zaragoza. There's been speculation for quite some time about cattle rustlin' and smugglin' takin' place between this ranch and Coahuila. I discovered Foley's been workin' with an hombre name of Bernardo Jalisco, the alcalde of Zaragoza."

"Ranger, this would be hilarious, if your accusations weren't so far off base. They're ridiculous," Jeff insisted. "In fact, Tom Foley investigated those charges and completely exonerated the Bar 7 from havin' anything to do with wet cattle or moving contraband across the Rio."

"Jeff's right," King concurred.

"More likely Foley decided it'd be a good deal to get a cut of the operation for himself," Jim answered. "After I got Charlie and Ty out of jail, we went lookin' for Foley at the place we mentioned. He was there, but got away before we could capture him. You see, some of his men put up a fight, even Jalisco, who was killed, but Foley had a tunnel out of his hacienda, so while his men kept us busy he ran like a scared rabbit.

We lit after him, but he had too much of a head start. We did manage to catch sight of him, just once. There were two other men ridin' with him, and one of 'em bore a strong resemblance to you, Nichols!"

Jim's voice snapped like a whip when he uttered that last line.

"Ranger, you've been ridin' in the sun far too long," Jeff sneered. "It's got your brain addled. I haven't been away from this ranch for months. Any of my men can tell you that."

"What about your brother?" Jim asked.

"Brendan? Sure, he's been away, on a trip to Saint Louis tryin' to arrange a deal for most of our cattle with a big packin' house there. He just got back late yesterday," Jeff answered.

"Where's he at now?" Jim asked.

"He rode into Concan this morning, along with our foreman, Bill Hennessey, to order supplies. They'll be back any time now."

"Are you certain that's where he was, St. Louis?" Jim questioned.

"Of course that's where he went, where else? My brother does a lot of travelin', buying and selling cattle, while I remain here and run the ranch," Jeff answered. "What reason would I have to lie to you?"

"To answer your first question, Mexico. To answer the second, the reasons I just gave you, cattle rustlin' and smugglin'," Jim retorted.

"Ranger, I've got nothing to hide," Jeff said. "You're free to search this whole spread if that's what it'll take to convince you we had nothing to do with Tom Foley or anything else you're accusin' us of."

"I intend to do just that, bet a hat on it," Jim answered. "After I talk to your brother. Since you claim he'll be back shortly, we'll just wait here for him, long as you don't object."

"Would it do any good if I did?" Jeff retorted.

"Not really," Jim answered. "We'll just set a spell and take it easy until he arrives."

"What about the men? It's almost suppertime," King pointed out.

"Sure, they can have their meal, long as they stay in the cook shack or bunkhouse," Jim agreed. "If we spot anyone of 'em tryin' to come this way, we'll blow his brains out. Is that clear?"

"As crystal," Jeff answered.

"All right, explain that to 'em," Jim ordered.

"Okay, Ranger."

Jeff lifted his voice and called to the gathered cowpunchers.

"Boys, these men are Texas Rangers. They're here to ask Brendan and me a few questions, then once they're satisfied with the answers, they'll be on their way. It's just a misunderstanding, which Brendan will clear up as soon as he gets back from town. In the meantime, you're to stay in the bunkhouse. Danby, finish cookin' supper so the boys can eat on time, but no one is to come near this house. Make certain of that."

There were a few murmured grumbles of disagreement from the cowboys, but realizing facing the unwavering rifles of the Rangers would be foolhardy, one by one they drifted back inside the bunkhouse.

"Unless you Rangers enjoy standin' around, you might as well make yourselves comfortable," Jeff said, once the cowboys were all settled. "We'll go up on the porch and sit down. There's plenty of chairs."

"We'll take you up on that," Jim agreed. "Charlie, Ty, c'mon up here and join us, but make sure you keep your rifles at the ready. You see anyone even try'n poke his head out of that bunkhouse, you plug him."

"All right, but what about the horses?" Charlie asked.

"Lead 'em up here and tie them to the rail," Jim ordered.

"You realize this is a complete waste of time," Jeff said, as they climbed the stairs to the porch.

"I'll be the judge of that, once I talk to your brother," Jim replied.

It was forty-five minutes later when two riders approached the Bar 7.

"That your brother, Nichols?" Jim asked.

"Yeah, that's Brendan, and Bill Hennessey, our

foreman. Mebbe now we can get this whole thing cleared up," Jeff answered.

"Just don't try anything tricky," Jim warned. "You'll get a bullet in your back if you do."

"No reason to do that, since we've done nothing wrong," Jeff answered.

"What's goin' on here? I see we've got company," Brendan remarked when he and Hennessey drew abreast of the house. He took a closer look at Charlie and Ty, who were still seated, but with their rifles at the ready.

"You two hombres look kinda familiar," he said.

"They should, they're the two Texas Rangers who were here not all that far back," King told him.

"That's right, I recognize them now," Brendan answered. "What's this all about? Who's the other hombre?"

Jim stood up, his left hand on the butt of his Colt. The rays of the westering sun glinted off the silver star on silver circle pinned to his chest. With his first good look at Brendan Nichols, he was struck by the strong resemblance between the two brothers.

"I'm Lieutenant Jim Blawcyzk," he told Brendan. "I've got some questions for you. You two light off those horses and stand hitched."

Jim nodded toward Charlie and Ty, who now had their rifles aimed straight at the two riders' stomachs.

"Don't try any sudden moves, 'cause if you do you'll get a couple of Winchester slugs in your guts for your trouble," he warned.

"We've got no reason to do somethin' like that," Brendan shrugged. They dismounted, keeping their hands well away from their guns, while Jim and the others came off the porch to join them.

"Charlie, Ty, watch those men down below," Jim ordered. At the sound of Brendan's and Hennessey's approach, the Bar 7 hands had once again gathered in front of the bunkhouse.

"You mind explainin' yourself, Lieutenant?" Brendan said. "I haven't got all day."

"The Ranger here has some fool notion that you and I are tied up with Tom Foley, and that the Bar 7's a base for runnin' wet cattle across the Rio, and smugglin'," Jeff told him. "I tried to explain to him that's ridiculous, but he won't listen to me. Mebbe you can talk some sense into him."

"That right, Ranger?" Brendan asked, his expression a sneering half-smile.

"That's right," Jim confirmed. "I'm not goin' over everything again, but four Rangers followed Tom Foley to Mexico, only to be ambushed while crossin' the Rio Grande. One of 'em was shot in the back and killed, another badly wounded, but not so bad he didn't recognize Foley as one of the bushwhackers. Someone had to tip Foley off

319

about those Rangers, and that someone had to be from this ranch."

"I won't even dignify that absurd allegation with a reply," Brendan snapped. "Except to say there are plenty of others who might've told Foley he was bein' trailed."

"That's not the least of it," Jim continued. "We tracked down Foley outside of Zaragoza, but he managed to escape. We did catch sight of him and two other riders, one of which I accused your brother of bein', but now that I see you I have to admit that rider could very well have been you, Brendan . . . and the third had just about your build, Hennessey. Their horses matched the ones you're ridin', too."

"But you can't say for certain those men were us, can you?" Brendan retorted.

"No, I can't," Jim admitted. "But they were headin' in this direction, last we saw of 'em."

"Dad," Charlie broke in, "I just thought of somethin' which might be important."

"What's that, Charlie?"

"When we were here last time and talked about Foley headin' for Mexico, Brendan here claimed he'd gotten a wire from a cattle buyer he was waitin' on, so he had to leave for Del Rio right away to meet him. Trouble is, his brother acted mighty surprised, as if he didn't expect any message from a buyer. Seems like a mighty powerful coincidence, Brendan lightin' out for

the border soon as he heard about us chasin'
Foley down that way."

"Good work, Charlie," Jim answered. "What
about it, Nichols? You or your brother care to
explain that?"

"Like that boy says, it was a mere coincidence,"
Brendan replied. "I'm constantly getting letters
and telegrams from cattle brokers, and sometimes
I neglect to tell Jeff about one, that's all. You
have nothing to go on, Ranger."

"I've got plenty of circumstantial evidence
to work with," Jim disagreed. "Besides, your
brother invited me to search your ranch, and I
intend to do just that, bet a hat on it. Listen to me
good, both of you. Right now the most I could
charge you with is cattle rustlin' and smugglin'.
Once the rurales down in Mexico go through
Foley's hacienda, I'm sure they'll find something
connecting you two to Foley. In addition, I'm
fairly certain I'll come up with some pretty
convincing evidence once I get a look around
here, and go through your books. However, if I
find Tom Foley on this ranch, then you'll both
be charged with obstructin' justice, harboring a
fugitive, and as accessories to murder. That last
one's a hangin' offense. You willin' to chance
that?"

"Ranger, like I told you, search all you want,
you won't find a thing on us," Jeff answered.

"Jeff's right," Brendan added. "Search to

your heart's content, Lieutenant. "You'll just be wasting your time . . . and ours."

"We'll see," Jim replied. "Meantime, there's still some daylight left, so we'll just take a look around. Don't plan on anyone leavin' here until we're finished with our investigation."

"You'll have our complete cooperation," Brendan assured him.

"I appreciate that," Jim answered. He turned to retrieve his horse, intending to make a quick search of the area immediately surrounding the house.

"Brendan, don't!" Jeff shouted, then two guns fired almost as one. Jim staggered from the shock of a bullet clipping the back of his right shoulder. He pulled his gun as the impact spun him around, cocking the hammer as he brought the Peacemaker level.

Jeff Nichols was facing his brother, his own gun smoking in his hand, but now pointed at the ground. Brendan had dropped his pistol to the ground, and was standing, staring dumbfounded at the red stain spreading around a bullet hole in his shirt, an inch above his belt buckle.

"Jeff, you . . . you shot me," he stammered. "Never . . . figured on . . . that."

Brendan pressed both hands to his middle, dropped to his knees, then pitched onto his face.

Charlie's rifle cracked, and Bill Hennessey went down, his pistol flying from his grasp.

Charlie's bullet tore through the foreman's left thigh, shattering his femur.

A number of the cowboys gathered in front of the bunkhouse started to move toward the Rangers, only to be stopped in their tracks when Ty put several bullets into the dirt at their feet.

"Next one who makes a move gets it through the guts," Ty warned. "Don't even twitch."

"Nichols?" Jim said, not quite understanding what had just happened.

"My brother was gonna shoot you in the back, Ranger," Jeff answered, his voice shaking. "I couldn't let him do that."

Jeff King rolled Brendan onto his back.

"He's still breathin', Jeff," the wrangler said.

"Why, Brendan?" Jeff half-sobbed, numb with shock. "Why'd you try'n kill this Ranger?"

"Because . . . he was . . . right, little brother," Brendan gasped. "Tom Foley and I've been . . . usin' this ranch . . . for rustlin' . . . and smugglin' . . . for years. The Ranger . . . had figured that . . . out . . . would've discovered . . . enough to . . . hang me . . . along with Foley . . . once he started diggin'. Thought mebbe . . . if I killed . . . him, Bill and I'd . . . get the drop on the other . . . two and finish them, also. Then . . . bury the bodies . . . make up story . . . to convince you . . . and men these hombres . . . weren't . . . really Rangers."

"Where's Foley now?" Jim asked.

"Not . . . not gonna . . . tell . . . you, Ranger."

Blood welled and gurgled in the dying man's throat. Brendan shuddered, his eyes wide with surprise. His body stiffened in a final spasm, then went slack.

"He's gone, Jeff," King softly said.

"Dad," Charlie called from where he now stood alongside Bill Hennessey. "This hombre wants to talk with you, pronto."

"I'll be right there, Charlie," Jim answered. "Nichols, King, you both mind givin' me your guns?"

"Not at all," Jeff replied, still appearing somewhat in shock when he handed his six-gun to the Ranger, who shoved it in his belt.

"I reckon not either," King added, pulling a .44 Remington from his holster and giving it to Jim. King's weapon was also shoved behind Jim's belt.

Jim headed over to where Hennessey lay, bleeding heavily from the bullet wound in his leg. Jeff and King trailed along.

"Ranger, I've gotta . . . talk to you before I . . . cash in my chips," Hennessey choked out.

"You're not gonna die, mister, at least not yet," Jim replied. "We'll splint that leg and get you to a doctor's."

"Mebbe," Hennessey said. "Know . . . you've got . . . lotta questions. First, I need to make you understand . . . Jeff here . . . had nothin' to do with . . . rustlin' and movin' wet cattle. He had no idea . . . what me'n his brother were up to."

"I'll take your word for that, Hennessey," Jim assured him. "How about any of the other men here?"

"No . . . not one of . . . 'em," the foreman explained. "Foley kept our crew at his . . . place outside Zaragoza. No one here . . . knew about that."

"I see," Jim answered, then called to Ty.

"Ty, you can let those men come up here now, but keep your rifle on 'em, just in case."

"Will do, Lieutenant," Ty agreed. He lowered his rifle and motioned to the cowboys they were free to move. They trudged up the slope to gather around the wounded Hennessey.

"Bill, you and Brendan sure had me fooled," King said.

"Yup," Hennessey chuckled. "I reckon we did."

"Brendan's the one who tipped Foley off about the Rangers on his trail, wasn't he?" Jim asked.

"Yeah, it was Brendan," Hennessey confirmed. "He rode hard, and since he knew exactly . . . where to find Foley, was able to . . . beat your pardners to him. Foley, since he . . . rode with the Rangers . . . for years . . . was pretty sure where . . . they'd cross, so he had men . . . watchin' at Piedras Negras . . . and all the fords . . . along that stretch . . . of the Rio."

"Hennessey, where's Foley now?" Jim asked. "He's somewhere on the Bar 7, isn't he?"

"Yeah, he is," Hennessey confirmed. "About a half-day's ride from here, there's an old line shack up a box canyon. We used that . . . shack for our headquarters. The canyon's a . . . perfect spot to . . . hide smuggled goods or . . . hold a herd of stolen cows . . . until it's safe to . . . move them. You just follow the river upstream roughly twenty-two miles. The canyon's on the left. You can't miss it . . . 'cause a rockslide . . . blocks its mouth. Foley'll be in there."

"You sure he hasn't already taken off for parts unknown?" Jim questioned.

"No," Hennessey said. "He was gonna lay low there for at least . . . a coupla' weeks, then me, him, and Brendan were planning on lightin' out for Mexico and stayin' there for good. He'll be there."

"I know that canyon," Jeff exclaimed. "That slide happened a few years back, and it completely blocked off the entrance. There's no way for a man to get in there on foot, let alone a horse and rider."

"You're wrong, boss," Hennessey replied. "Brendan and me found a . . . back way into that canyon . . . even though . . . it looks like a . . . dead end. It's a rough trail, but you can drive cattle or pack mules over it. We also found a passageway . . . just wide and high enough . . . for man leadin' . . . his horse. Ranger . . ." Hennessey's voice trailed off.

"What, Hennessey?" Jim pressed.

"Gotta talk . . . fast . . . 'fore . . . I pass out," Hennessey said. "You'll see . . . tiny space . . . right side . . . canyon mouth . . . looks like . . . impossible to . . . fit through . . . but you can squeeze . . . through . . . with your . . . cayuse. Rocks made kind of a tunnel . . . when they fell. Goes for . . . about a hundred and fifty feet . . . then opens up. That's the way . . . in. You'll have to get . . . your feet . . . wet, since the slide goes right down . . . to the Frio."

"Much obliged, Hennessey," Jim answered. The foreman gave a wan smile, then closed his eyes.

"Ranger, he needs a doctor, fast," Jeff said. "Mind if I send a man into town for Doc Withers?"

"No, go right ahead," Jim answered.

"I'll go," King offered.

"That's fine," Jeff accepted.

King headed for the corral to rope out a horse.

"Nichols, have a couple of your men carry Hennessey up to the house. Get a couple of boards to splint his leg until the doc arrives," Jim instructed. "Have 'em take your brother's body, too."

"Sure." Jeff chose six men to carry out the grim task.

"Put Bill on the bed in my room, and lay Brendan out on the sofa in the parlor," Jeff told them. "We'll bury him in the morning."

"Charlie, you and Ty are in charge here," Jim ordered. "I'm goin' after Foley. One of you stay with Hennessey at all times."

"Dad, you can't, not yet," Charlie objected. "You've been shot, and need to have that shoulder looked at."

"It ain't all that much," Jim protested, grimacing. "I've had worse."

"If it's not that bad, why the face?" Charlie retorted. "You patched me'n Ty up back in Zaragoza, so now it's my turn to return the favor. I want to look at your shoulder, and I will. Bet your hat on it."

"Ranger, Lord knows I don't want to cause you any more trouble," Jeff added. "However, it's gettin' pretty late in the day. The sun'll be down in less than an hour, and it's a new moon, so you wouldn't be able to get very far tonight in any event. In fact, it's already dusk in some of the canyons. Why not listen to your boy, and let him treat that wound? I'd hazard you should probably let Doc Withers check it after he tends to Bill. That way you and your horse can get a good night's rest, rather'n chancing your bronc stumblin' in the dark and throwin' you or mebbe breakin' a leg."

"That's good advice, Lieutenant," Ty agreed.

"All right," Jim conceded. "I reckon Tom Foley will keep until mornin'."

328

"Now you're makin' sense, Dad," Charlie said. "Bet . . ."

"I know," Jim grinned. "Bet a hat on it."

"Come into the house, Ranger," Jeff invited. "I've got medical supplies there, and I'll have Danby make coffee . . . or I can offer you somethin' stronger if you'd prefer."

"You sure you want that, after all that's happened?" Jim questioned.

"I'm certain, so don't argue the point," Jeff insisted. "C'mon in."

"All right," Jim shrugged. He, along with Charlie and Ty, followed the rancher inside, where he led them to the kitchen.

"Take a chair, Ranger, while I dig out those supplies," he offered. "Danby'll have the coffee ready in a few minutes. You want some whiskey, or a cigar?"

"Just the coffee, thanks," Jim answered.

"My dad won't touch liquor," Charlie explained. "You won't see him smokin' or hear him cussin', either."

"That's right, and I'd better not ever catch you cussin' or smokin' either, kid," Jim warned.

"Here's the stuff you'll need, son," Jeff told Charlie. He handed him a box holding bandages, bottles of medicine, and salve.

"Thanks," Charlie answered, then ordered Jim, "Dad, get outta your shirt."

"I guess I've got no choice," Jim grumbled. He

unbuttoned the shirt and pulled it off, wincing a bit when he handed it to Ty.

"Dad, I told you not to wear that red shirt," Charlie chuckled. "See, I was right. It did make you a good target. You're just lucky that bullet didn't catch you plumb in the middle of your back."

"I reckon I've got Nichols here to thank for that," Jim somberly replied. "Which reminds me, I haven't thanked you properly for savin' my life. I'm much obliged. Your brother had me dead to rights, and would've drilled me dead center for sure if you hadn't stepped in and, well . . ."

"You can say it, Ranger. I had to shoot my own brother," Jeff answered.

"Yeah. Anyway, I appreciate what you did . . . Jeff," Jim answered. "I can't imagine how hard that was."

"Dad, this doesn't look too bad," Charlie noted, as he washed blood and dirt from the bullet slash across Jim's shoulder. "I'll have you patched up in no time."

"Ranger . . ." Jeff started. Tears were welling in his eyes and his voice cracked as the reality of the day's events began to settle in.

"My name's Jim, unless you'd rather keep usin' Ranger," Jim offered.

"All right . . . Jim," Jeff agreed. "I want you to know I feel kinda responsible for everything that's happened. I know, Hennessey told you I

330

didn't know anything about what was goin' on right under my nose. The truth is, I did, or at least I long suspicioned Brendan was involved in some kind of shady dealin's. However, I didn't want to believe my own brother could be involved in anything dishonest, so I turned a blind eye to things around here. I reckon I should have tried to stop him years ago, but he was my brother. I just couldn't bring myself to face the facts. I'm also sorry I was so harsh with you, when you were tryin' to convince me about what was goin' on."

"I can understand that, Jeff, and I can't really blame you," Jim sympathized. "There's nothing wrong with being loyal to your kinfolk, to a point. Far as you bein' harsh with me, I was pretty hard on you, also, and it turned out my accusations were dead wrong, at least as far as you were concerned."

"Still, I should have done something," Jeff stated. "Things might not have gone so far if I had. When I saw Brendan pull his gun on you, I didn't have any choice but to shoot. I couldn't let him plug a man in the back . . . I just couldn't."

Jeff's voice broke, and he buried his face in his hands, sobbing. It took him several minutes to regain his composure.

"I'm sorry," he finally murmured.

"There's no reason for you to be ashamed for cryin'," Jim assured him. "I'd be doin' the same if I were in your boots."

"I appreciate that," Jeff answered.

They sat in silence while Charlie finished ministering to Jim's wound.

"There, Dad, I'm finished," he said, taping the last strip of bandage in place. "You can put your shirt back on. And I still say you shouldn't go after Tom Foley, at least not by yourself."

"Chip's right," Ty agreed. "We should go with you, or at least one of us should."

"Boys, I appreciate your concern," Jim answered. "But this is personal between Tom and me. It's somethin' I have to do alone. I hope you understand."

"I reckon I do, but that doesn't mean I have to like it," Charlie replied.

"Good. Now let's take care of the horses, then get some shut-eye. I'll be leavin' at sunup. Jeff, you mind if we find spots in the bunkhouse? I'd like to explain everything to your men before we call it a night."

"You sure you wouldn't rather spend the night here in the house?" Jeff answered. "There's plenty of room, and besides, don't you want Doc Withers to look at that shoulder?"

"No, Charlie did just fine patchin' me up," Jim said. "Far as where we bed down, it'll be easier all around if we stay in the bunkhouse. Charlie and Ty'll be stayin' here until I return, and I'll stop by and see you before I head out if that's what you'd like."

"I'd appreciate that, Jim," Jeff said.

"Then I'll see you in the morning. G'night, Jeff."

"G'night to all of you."

The Rangers' horses were rubbed down and turned into a corral, where they were fed and watered. Before turning in, Jim explained to the Bar 7 hands everything which had led up to the confrontation with Brendan Nichols and Bill Hennessey. Once he had answered their questions, he, Charlie, and Ty found empty bunks, undressed, and stretched out on the straw mattresses. Jim could hear Charlie murmuring his evening prayers, while he did the same. One by one, the men drifted off to sleep, until Jim was the only one still awake. He would remain that way for several hours, lying on his back and staring at the ceiling, contemplating finally facing Tom Foley over his gunsight.

Jim hit the trail shortly after sunrise the next morning, keeping Sizzle at a steady pace once the big horse had warmed up. The long-legged gelding's lope fairly ate up the miles. Jim stopped to allow the paint an occasional breather, letting him nibble at the grass or taking a short drink from the cool, clear waters of the Frio. The day was not excessively hot, and the ride alongside the river was pleasant. In several spots the trail crossed the Frio, Sizzle splashing his way through the generally shallow waters. Just before noon, Jim spotted the canyon Hennessey had described. "This has gotta be the place, Siz," he remarked to his horse. "Hennessey described it to a T. Now let's see if we can find our way in there."

Jim dropped from the gelding's back, his feet landing in slowly-flowing, ankle-deep water. It only took a moment for him to find what appeared to be a mere hollow formed by fallen rocks. A closer inspection revealed this was indeed the entrance Hennessey had meant.

"Let's head on in, Siz," Jim said. "It's gonna be a real tight squeeze. This is one time I'm gonna wish you were a bit smaller, fella."

He gave Sizzle a peppermint, then allowed the paint to nuzzle his cheek. Just inside the entrance, he located a length of dead mesquite, which he lit to use as a makeshift torch. Moving slowly, he edged his way through the narrow, low, tunnel, sweat pouring off his brow and plastering his shirt to his back. More than once Sizzle snorted nervously, but willingly followed Jim's gentle pull on his reins.

"Light up ahead. We're almost through this, pard," Jim reassured the horse, when he spotted a brightness just ahead. He reached the end of the tunnel, shoved the torch into the sand, and stood blinking, his eyes readjusting to the bright daylight.

"Let's move on, Siz," Jim ordered, once his

vision had returned. He put his left hand on the horn and left foot in the stirrup, preparing to remount, then stopped at the sound of an approaching horse and rider. Before he could even react, Tom Foley appeared, in the saddle of his black gelding. Behind Foley were two bulging saddlebags.

"Jim!" Foley shouted, at the same time grabbing for his six-gun. Jim leapt back from Sizzle, also clawing for his pistol. Both men got off one hasty shot, each missing badly. Foley then spun his black and raked the horse cruelly with his spurs, sending the gelding leaping forward into a dead run.

Jim sprung onto Sizzle's back and leaned low over his neck, speaking encouragingly to the paint while he pushed him into a full gallop.

"C'mon, Siz, let's show that black what runnin' really is," he urged. "Looks like Foley decided he wasn't gonna wait for his pardners after all. Those alforjas have gotta be full of cash, I'd bet my hat on it. Appears we got here just in time. C'mon, boy, pick up your feet."

Despite the long miles of the past several days, Sizzle responded with a fresh burst of speed. Slowly, inexorably, he narrowed the gap between himself and Foley's black.

"We're gainin' on him, Siz!" Jim exclaimed. "Just a little more, please."

Somehow, the exhausted, sweat-streaked horse

dug down deep inside and pushed even harder, every muscle straining in his race to catch Foley's swift black.

Foley pounded past the line shack, heading for the canyon's back wall. Hidden somewhere there, out of Jim's sight, was a trail out of the apparent dead end. If Foley reached that trail, he would most likely be able to elude the pursuing Ranger, or hole up and kill him from ambush.

Foley's horse reached the slope at the head-wall's base, slowing as he started to climb. The black stumbled when he hit a soft spot, nearly going down. Foley left the saddle, rolled to his knees, and sent two quick shots in Jim's direction. Jim dove from Sizzle's back, wincing when the impact sent pain tearing through his still-healing gut and freshly wounded shoulder, and crawled behind a low rock shelf. He poked his head up to send a return shot at Foley, who scrambled for shelter against the canyon's rough wall. He shoved himself into a crevice, protected somewhat from Jim's bullets by an erosion-carved overhanging ledge.

Both men fired several more shots, emptying their pistols in a futile effort to hit the other with a lucky shot.

"Tom!" Jim called as he punched empty shells from his Colt and reloaded.

"What is it, Jim?" Foley shouted back.

"You know I've gotta ask you to give yourself up," Jim replied.

"Just like you know I've gotta say there's not a chance in Hell of that," Foley retorted. He finished reloading, waited patiently for Jim to poke up his head, then sent another bullet ricocheting off the shelf, his shot just missing to the Ranger's right.

"Tom," Jim called again. "I have to know why you turned renegade. You were a mighty fine lawman, and a good friend. We had some real good times when we rode together. What happened to change you?"

"Money, what else?" Foley returned. "You know how little Rangers are paid. Look at you, you've been a Ranger for a lot longer'n I have, and what've you got to show for all those years of riskin' your life for next to nothin'? A rundown little horse ranch, that's all."

"There's a lotta things more important than money," Jim answered. "Like pride in a job well done, and feelin' good about yourself at the end of the day. Besides my ranch, I've also got a fine wife and son, don't forget, not to mention my self-respect. I wouldn't trade any of that for all the money in the vaults of every bank in Texas."

"Mebbe that's good enough for you, but not for me," Foley retorted. "I like livin' high on the hog, with plenty of good whiskey and pretty women for company, so when I saw the chance to grab some real loot, I took it. I'm sure you figured out by now why I never asked to be transferred back from the border country. I had a real lucrative scheme workin' for quite a few years, movin' cattle and smugglin' goods both ways across the Rio. In another year or two I'd figured on takin' life easy, down Coahuila way."

"Why'd you kill Captain Trumbull, then plug me and leave me for dead?" Jim continued.

"Trumbull finally got suspicious and started doin' some checking," Foley explained. "He dug up enough evidence to send me to prison for the rest of my life. He confronted me with it in his office that day, so I had no choice but to kill him. As far as you're concerned, I sure didn't plan on shootin' you, but when you surprised me I had no choice. Should've made sure of you. I ought to have known two slugs wouldn't be enough to finish you off, Jim."

"Tom, your pardner Brendan Nichols is dead, and Bill Hennessey's in custody, with a bullet-shattered leg. I'm gonna give you one last chance to surrender."

"For what? To face a noose?" Foley harshly laughed. "No sir, Jim, I figure I've still got good odds of ridin' out of here with my hide in one piece."

He fired two more shots at Jim, who returned Foley's bullets with two of his own.

"Tom," Jim called yet again.

"What is it now, Jim?" Foley answered.

"I've got a proposal."

"Which is?"

"Instead of wastin' lead like this, let's face each other, man-to-man," Jim offered.

"You mean, see who's faster on the draw?" Foley questioned.

"Yep, that's exactly what I mean," Jim replied. "Just like in the dime novels, we'll holster our guns, face off, then draw. If you plug me, you'll be able to ride away, free and clear. You'll be in Mexico long before anyone figures out what's happened."

"You must've been readin' too many of those things, Jim," Foley retorted. "However, let's say I take your challenge. What's in it for me?"

"A decent burial if I plug you," Jim answered.

"Jim, you're plumb loco," Foley said. "Then again, I reckon I am too. You say I can ride away free and clear if I put a bullet through you?"

"There'll be nobody to stop you, long as you steer clear of any towns until you reach the border," Jim said.

"I always did wonder which one of us was better with a gun, so I'm gonna take you up on this, which means one thing for certain. One of us is gonna die like some made-up, phony gunslinger in the pages of cheap fiction," Foley stated. "Reload first? I'd hate to run out of bullets, although I don't plan on usin' more'n one this time. I'm gonna drill you right through the center of your chest. You won't come back from the dead twice."

"Sure, we'll reload first," Jim agreed. "No sneakin' in a shot before we're both ready, though. Agreed?"

"Agreed."

Both men reloaded their guns and emerged from their shelter, then stepped toward each other, not halting until they were less than twenty feet apart. Foley's dark eyes seemed to bore through the Ranger, while Jim's blue ones glittered with an icy anger. Jim suddenly realized that sometime in the past weeks Foley had shaved off his bushy mustache. It always struck him as odd, the little details a man noticed at a time like this.

They stood facing each other, Foley's right hand ready to reach across his body and yank his butt-forward gun in a cross-draw from the holster on his left hip, a style which many swore was faster than the conventional draw. Jim's left hand hovered an inch over the heavy Colt Peacemaker on his hip, his fingers slightly flexed.

As if by some unheard signal, both men went for their guns, the reports sounding almost as one. Foley's bullet plowed into the ground between Jim's feet. Dust puffed from his shirt where Jim's bullet took him in the left breast, nicking the edge of the renegade Ranger's heart. Jim kept his gun at the ready while he watched Foley's right arm fall, his Colt, still trailing smoke, dropping from his hand. Foley pressed his left hand to his bullet-torn breast, blood seeping between his outspread fingers as he spun a half-circle, his knees buckling, then toppled face-down to the dirt.

Jim stalked up to Foley and kicked the Colt out of his reach. Using the toe of his boot, he rolled the downed man onto his back. Foley stared up at him, his lips mouthing a word Jim couldn't quite catch.

"That was for Hank Trumbull," Jim said.

Tom Foley's eyes glazed, he gave one final long sigh, and breathed his last.

"I reckon it's finally over," Jim muttered. He reloaded his pistol, then slid it back in its holster. Now that Hank Trumbull had been avenged, Jim felt a deep weariness, clear to his bones. He also felt a great sense of sadness and loss, looking down at the body of a man who had been his friend and riding partner, a man who had in fact once saved his life.

Jim whispered a silent prayer over Foley, asking the Lord's mercy on his soul. Maybe God would consider all the good things Tom had done, balance them against the bad, and forgive his sins. Perhaps someday Jim also would be able to find forgiveness in his heart for Tom, but not yet. The murder of Hank Trumbull was still too fresh in his memory, and the bullet still lodged in Jim's chest would be a lifelong reminder of

Foley's treachery. At this moment, Jim fervently hoped Tom was shaking hands with the devil.

"Still enough daylight to make it back to the Bar 7, if I don't waste time," Jim murmured. He looked around for the horses, spying Sizzle and Indigo, Foley's black, nibbling at some grass a short distance away.

Jim whistled shrilly, and Sizzle picked up his head, whinnied, and trotted up to the Ranger. As Jim had hoped, Indigo, not wanting to be left alone, followed his horse.

"Easy, boys," Jim said, in a calm voice. He pulled two peppermints from his pocket, gave one to Sizzle, then offered the other to Indigo. The black sniffed uncertainly at the unfamiliar treat, took it gingerly between his lips, then crunched down on the candy, tossing his head up and down as he tasted peppermint for the first time.

"Tastes pretty good, huh fella?" Jim asked the black, patting his muzzle. He looked at the bloody spurs gouges marring Indigo's flanks, and shook his head sadly. The Tom Foley he'd known would never have mistreated a horse like that.

"I'll take care of those cuts soon as we get back to the Bar 7," Jim promised the gelding. "Let's see what's inside here," he continued. Jim opened one of Foley's saddlebags, as he'd expected finding it stuffed with Mexican five and ten peso coins. He softly whistled.

"This is quite a haul here. Looks like Tom had no intention of returnin'."

He picked up Indigo's reins and led him to where Foley's body lay. When the horse shied at the sight of his dead rider and the smell of blood, Jim spoke soothingly to him, gently stroking his neck, and soon had the black calmed down. Indigo danced sideways a few steps when Jim lifted the dead man, but with Jim's encouragement reluctantly allowed the Ranger to drape Foley over his back.

"Can't tie Tom to the saddle, or we'll never fit through that tunnel," Jim spoke to the horses. "I don't have anything to bury him with here, and don't have time for that anyway. Hate to do it, but I'll have to drag him through that opening. Figure I'll take Tom back to the Bar 7 and bury him there, mebbe in a spot overlookin' the river. He'd probably like that."

Jim stiffly climbed into his own saddle and rode back to the cabin. He dismounted and went inside, where he performed a cursory inspection of the shack. As he suspected, there was nothing of worth left behind, the pesos in Foley's saddlebags apparently all the valuables which had been there when Foley decided to head for Mexico.

"Nothin' here," he muttered. "Might as well quit dawdlin'."

He headed back outside and remounted, then walked the horses away from the cabin. Once he reached the narrow exit from the canyon, he swung out of his saddle and untied his lariat, tying one end to Indigo's saddlehorn. He lowered Foley's body to the ground and wrapped the other end of his rope around Foley's chest.

"Easy, boy," he reassured Indigo, picking up the black's reins and looping them over the horse's neck. "It's just like ropin' a cow critter."

Jim removed Sizzle's lead rope from his saddlebags, attached one end to Indigo's bridle and tied the other to Sizzle's saddlehorn. He found and relit the length of mesquite torch, picked up Sizzle's reins, and led the horses into the narrow passageway. Foley's body bumped and thudded against the rocks when his nervous horse broke into a trot, the only thing stopping him from breaking into a panicked runaway being Sizzle blocking his way.

"We'll be through this in a minute," Jim promised.

Once they reached daylight, Jim had to cross the river before he could take Foley's body and lash it belly-down over his black.

"Time to start for home."

Jim breathed a sigh of relief once he climbed back into his saddle and put Sizzle into a trot.

Chapter Fifteen

Jim, Charlie, and Ty spent several more days at the Bar 7, going over the ranch's records and tying up loose ends. Jim's examination of the Bar 7's books turned up no connection between Jeff Nichols and the rustling and smuggling ring headed by his brother and Tom Foley. Between the records and Bill Hennessey's declaration of Jeff's innocence, the younger Nichols was completely exonerated of complicity with his brother's misdeeds.

Now, five days after leaving the Bar 7, the Rangers were approaching San Leanna. Jim had decided they would head for home first, spend the night there, then go in to Ranger Headquarters the next day to file their reports.

"It's sure gonna be good to get home again, Lieutenant," Ty remarked.

"It sure is, Ty . . . but how many times have I gotta remind you to call me 'Jim', not Lieutenant? Jim answered.

"I'm sorry, Lieutenant . . . I mean, Jim," Ty apologized. "It's just that after so many years callin' you Ranger Blawcyzk it's hard for me to get used to callin' you Jim."

"My mom can call him anything she wants,

long as she doesn't call him late to supper," Charlie laughed. "Bet a hat on it."

"You can bet a hat you're still not too big for me to give you a smack on your britches, either, if you're not careful, Ranger," Jim retorted. "Speakin' of supper, I sure hope your mom has some chicken ready to fry."

"We won't find out if we don't pick up the pace," Charlie answered. He heeled Ted into an easy lope. Jim and Ty matched their horses' pace to his.

An hour later, they rode through the JB Bar's gate to find several people gathered on the front porch, along with Julia. Pal, Charlie's collie, spotted the approaching riders, bounded off the porch, and raced across the yard to greet them, barking joyously.

"Hi, Pal," Charlie shouted. "It's great to see you, boy."

"Looks like we've got a reception committee waitin' for us," Jim remarked.

"Sure does," Ty agreed. "I see my folks. There's Captain Huggins also. I don't recognize the hombre next to him."

"I do," Jim said. "Son of a gun, there's Smoky McCue and his wife, too. That sure eases my mind, seein' the ol' Smoke back home."

Jim left the saddle before Sizzle had even come to a full stop, letting the reins trail as Julia hurried down the steps to meet her husband and son.

Charlie dismounted almost as quickly, so Julia hugged them both, wrapping her arms around them and holding them tightly.

"Jim, Charlie, I'm so happy to see you again. I was so worried, until Captain Huggins told me he'd gotten a telegram from you saying Charlie and Ty were both safe, and you'd be home in a few days," Julia said.

"What're all these folks doin' here?" Jim asked.

"Your wire said you'd be home today, so everyone decided they'd like to be here to welcome you back," Julia explained. "I've missed you both so much, and would have preferred to spend some time alone with you first, but I couldn't say no to them."

"I missed you an awful lot too, Mom," Charlie answered.

"Enough that you'll quit being a Ranger?" Julia asked.

"Sorry, Mom, not quite that much," Charlie replied, with a grin.

"He's just like his father that way," Jim Huggins remarked. He'd left the porch to join them. Alongside him was another Ranger, tall and swarthy, with jet black hair and penetrating dark eyes.

"Jim, you did a fine job, from what you've told me so far," Huggins stated. "That goes for Chip and Ty, also. We'll forget about the incidents down in Mexico, since Wilfredo Herrera has smoothed things over with the authorities down there. It also didn't hurt that when the rurales searched Foley's hacienda and Bernardo Jalisco's warehouse, they recovered a whole passel of smuggled goods."

"Thanks, Captain," Jim answered.

"Uh-uh." Huggins shook his head. "It's not Captain Huggins any longer. I'm just a plain old Texas Ranger again . . . well, except I am gettin' to keep the rank of Lieutenant. Jim, you recall Earl Storm, don't you?"

"Sure do," Jim confirmed, shaking Storm's hand. "Howdy, Earl. It's been a long time."

"Far too long," Storm agreed. "Welcome home, Jim."

"Earl's been appointed to replace Hank Trumbull, permanently," Huggins explained. "He's our new commanding officer, and not a minute too soon. I've been stuck in that office for what seems like most of my life. I'm headin' back to Centerville tomorrow. It's been far too long since I've seen Cora, and Dan's got some leave comin' so he'll be headin' home too."

Huggins' son Dan was also a Ranger, stationed in Laredo.

"Congratulations, Earl," Jim said. "You've sure earned that appointment."

"Thanks, Jim," Storm answered. "I've got some mighty big boots to fill."

"You'll do just fine," Jim assured him.

"I hope you're right," Storm said, laughing. "Although if I don't let you get back to your wife, I might not live long enough to try out the job."

"Jim might not live much longer if he doesn't come up for an explanation about that black horse he's got with him," Julia smiled. "What about him?"

"Honey, that's Indigo, Tom Foley's horse. He needed a home, so I just couldn't leave him behind."

"Jim, we don't need any more horses," Julia protested.

"Don't listen to her, Jim," Smoky called from the porch. "I'm gonna show you something."

"Smoky, you promised," Julia cried.

"I fibbed," Smoky chuckled. "C'mon, Cindy, let's go get Julia's new friend."

"I can hardly wait for Jim to see it," Cindy Lou his wife, smiled. She and Smoky headed for the barn. A moment later, they led a blaze-faced bay gelding out of his stall. The horse spied Julia, nickered, and broke free from Smoky's grasp, trotting up to Julia and nuzzling her cheek.

"That's Cactus!" Jim exclaimed. "What in blue blazes is he doing here?"

"When Duffy got shot, before he died he asked Chip to make sure Cactus was cared for," Smoky explained. "Chip promised Duffy he'd bring Cactus home and let him do nothing for the rest of his days. So, when I was released by Doc Torres, since y'all were still down along the border, I brought him home with me. Seems like he's sure taken a shine to Julia."

"So, we don't need any more horses," Jim grinned.

"Well, perhaps one or two more," Julia answered, blushing.

"Julia, dinner's just about ready," Michele Tremblay called from the porch. "Have your menfolk clean up so we can eat."

"Before Ty gets it all," his sister, Brianna, added.

"Dinner?" Charlie said.

"Yes," his mother answered. "We've made a huge roast, plus mashed potatoes, corn on the cob, and peach cobbler. I thought you'd probably be tired of your father's bacon and beans by now."

"Boy howdy, ain't that the truth," Charlie exclaimed. "Sorry, Dad."

"There's no need to apologize," Jim answered. "I get pretty sick of my cookin' too. C'mon, Charlie, let's put our horses away and go wash up."

Sam, Sizzle, and Ted, along with Indigo and Ty's horse, Bandit, were unsaddled, given a quick currying, and turned into a corral, with plenty of hay and water. Once that was done, Jim, Charlie, and Ty washed up, then joined the others for dinner. Charlie, as usual, led the Grace, adding a prayer of thanks for their safe return home, and another for the eternal repose of Duffy McGlynn's soul. The meal was a particularly joyous occasion, with its celebration of the rescue of the two young Rangers.

After the dishes were done, everyone went onto the porch to socialize for a while. The Tremblays were the first to leave, Ty being anxious to sleep in his own bed once again.

"We'll swing by on our way to Austin," Jim told him. "Be ready about seven-thirty."

"I will be," Ty assured him.

"Jim, I want to thank you again for bringing Ty home in one piece," Mark Tremblay said.

"Nothing you wouldn't have done," Jim answered.

"Yeah, but I'm sure glad I didn't have to," Mark smiled.

"And here I was all ready to redecorate his room and move in," Brianna teased.

"Sis, if you really want my room, it's yours," Ty answered. "I won't be home all that much, long as I'm a Ranger."

"Really? Thanks, my favorite brother," Brianna answered.

"He's your only brother, Brianna," Charlie pointed out.

"Which makes it easier to choose my favorite," Brianna retorted.

"Mark, children, let's go," Michele ordered.

"Jim and his family have a lot to catch up on. Julia, I'll stop by in a day or two."

"I'm always happy to see you," Julia answered.

After the Tremblays departed, the rest of the guests drifted away, one by one.

"Finally," Julia sighed, once Jim Huggins and Earl Storm rode out. "I was glad for the company, but even happier to see them go."

An hour after their last guest had left, Jim and Julia were sitting in their rockers on the front porch, with Charlie seated on the steps. Jim glanced up at the sound of an approaching horse and buggy.

"Not more company," he groaned. "Who could that be?"

"I believe that's the Jarratt's rig," Julia said, recognizing the dapple-gray mare pulling the buggy.

"It certainly is," Charlie exclaimed, jumping to his feet. "Sure hope that's Mary Jane drivin' it."

A moment later, the horse was pulled to a stop. Mary Jane Jarratt stepped out, removed the iron weight which was attached to the horse's harness from the buggy, and dropped it to the ground. The anchor would hold the horse in place as effectively as tying it to a hitching post.

"Mary Jane!" Charlie exclaimed. He rushed to take her into his arms, then stopped, flushing bright red.

"I mean, good afternoon, Mary Jane. It's certainly a pleasure to see you."

"Hello, Charlie. May I say the same? I wish I could have been here sooner, but the store was extremely busy, since it's banking day for the ranchers and farmers. Lieutenant Blawcyzk, Mrs. Blawcyzk, my parents send their apologies for not being able to visit today."

"That's perfectly all right, Mary Jane," Julia assured her. "I know they would have been here if it were at all possible."

"Charlie, I baked you an apple pie, all by myself," Mary Jane said. "It's in the buggy."

"You did? That's great, Mary Jane, but we just finished a huge meal a short time ago. I'm stuffed."

"Do you mean you don't want to sample my pie, after all my hard work, Charles Blawcyzk?" Mary Jane indignantly questioned.

"No, I don't mean that at all," Charlie answered. "I just want to wait a while, so I can truly enjoy that pie. I've got an idea. Why don't we go for a ride? We can talk, then a little later I'll eat the entire pie, plate and all. Bet a hat on it."

"I'm not sure," Mary Jane hesitated. "What will your parents say?"

"His parents say go, and have a good time," Julia said.

"You mean that, Mom?" Charlie asked.

"Of course I do," Julia confirmed.

"Thanks, Mom."

Charlie and Mary Jane hurried to the buggy. He helped her onto the seat, returned the anchor to its place, then also got into the buggy and picked up the reins. He slapped them on the gray's rump, putting the mare into a smart trot. Julia and Jim watched until the rig disappeared from sight.

"Alone at last," Julia sighed. She leaned over to give Jim a kiss.

"Except for Pal," Jim laughed, when Charlie's collie stuck his nose in between them, begging to be petted.

"Get, Pal!" Julia ordered. "Go chase a jackrabbit or something."

Pal yelped, then dashed across the yard, scattering chickens in every direction.

"That should keep him busy," Jim chuckled.

"It will if he knows what's good for him," Julia answered.

Charlie parked the buggy on a low rise overlooking the creek, where there was a clear view to the eastern horizon. He and Mary Jane talked for over two hours, while Charlie recounted his adventures in Mexico and south Texas. As the sky faded to indigo, then black, the glow of the rising moon brightened the landscape.

"It's gonna be a full moon tonight, Mary Jane," Charlie noted, pulling her closer.

"It certainly is a beautiful sight," Mary Jane agreed. "Would you care for some more pie, Charlie?"

"It was delicious, but I can't take another bite," Charlie answered.

"You could eat like this all the time if you stayed here in San Leanna," Mary Jane offered. "I missed you so much while you were away, and I worried about you the whole time."

"I missed you an awful lot too," Charlie murmured.

"Enough to resign from the Rangers, so you could be with me all the time?"

Charlie thought before carefully framing his response.

"Mary Jane, you're the only gal in the world for me, you know that. But, all my life I've wanted nothing so much as to be a Texas Ranger, just like my dad. Now that I've got that chance, I can't give it up, not just yet, anyway. Can you understand that?"

Mary Jane sighed, and a single tear trickled down her cheek.

"Charlie, I knew that would be your answer, even before I asked the question. I have to say, I really can't understand why you have to be a Ranger. I also know there's nothing I can say or do to change your mind. I'm trying to accept your decision, but it's hard."

"I know it is," Charlie said. "But if you love

me as much as I love you, you can be a lawman's wife. Look at my mom and dad, or Smoky and Cindy McCue. They've been married for a long time. Sure, it's difficult, but it can work."

"I know it can, but I'm not quite ready to try," Mary Jane answered. "Will you give me the time I need to make certain I can be happy married to a Texas Ranger? Can you promise me that?"

"Of course I will, Mary Jane," Charlie said. He pulled her closer and kissed her full on the lips.

"Does that show you how much I love you?" he asked.

"I'm not certain," Mary Jane smiled. "Perhaps you should show me again."

"Julia, it's gettin' awful late," Jim remarked. "I'm worried about the kids. Mebbe I'd better try'n find 'em."

He and Julia were sitting side by side on the porch swing.

"Jim, there's not a thing to worry about," Julia tried to reassure him. "Charlie and Mary Jane are young, and unless I miss my guess they're in love."

"In love?" Jim exclaimed, jumping to his feet. "Those kids are far too young to be in love."

"They certainly are not," Julia answered. "Charlie's nearly eighteen, and Mary Jane's only a few months younger. Some of their friends are already engaged. I wouldn't be surprised if

Charlie asks Mary Jane to marry him before long."

"They still shouldn't be out there all alone, especially with that full moon," Jim fretted.

"Doesn't that moon give you an idea, Jim?" Julia hinted.

"It sure does, and it's probably givin' Charlie the same one," Jim answered. "Now I know for certain I'm goin' to find those two, bet a hat on it."

"Jim, you'll stay right here with me, and watch the moon," Julia ordered. "Don't you remember how it was when we were courting?"

"I sure do," Jim smiled. "Wait a minute! We never courted. You dragged me out of the street, half-dead, and patched me up. We were married right after that, by the first priest we could find."

"Then perhaps you should try courting me right now," Julia suggested. She patted the seat next to her.

"What about Charlie and Mary Jane?" Jim insisted.

"I think they can do their own courting, without your interference," Julia answered. "Sit down, Jim."

"Are you sure?" Jim persisted.

"I'm positive," Julia said. "Now sit by me."

"All right," Jim conceded. He sat by her side.

"Jim . . . ?"

"Yes, Julia?"

"Aren't you going to kiss me?"

"If I start, I won't be able to stop at just one kiss," Jim cautioned her.

"That's exactly what I'm counting on, Ranger," Julia answered.

"Don't say I didn't warn you, lady," Jim responded, taking her in his arms. "We could be here all night."

"Aren't you worried about the kids?" Julia asked.

"What kids?" Jim retorted, then crushed his lips to hers.

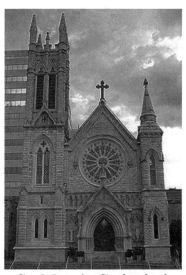

St. Mary's Cathedral

The history of St. Mary's Church—now Cathedral—in Austin dates back to 1852, when the Catholic community in Austin, at that time the temporary state capital with a population of approximately 600, built a small stone church called St. Patrick's at the corner of 9th and Brazos Streets. In 1866 the church was renamed St. Mary's. In 1872, after Austin was made the permanent capital of Texas, the cornerstone for a new church was laid one block north of the original location, at 10th and Brazos Streets.

In 1948, when the new Diocese of Austin was formed from the Diocese of Galveston, St. Mary's became the church from which the new bishop would preside, changing from Church to Cathedral. Today it is the mother church of the Diocese of Austin, which serves over 450,000 Catholics.

—Diocese of Austin,
History of St. Mary's Cathedral

Center Point Large Print
600 Brooks Road / PO Box 1
Thorndike, ME 04986-0001 USA

(207) 568-3717

US & Canada:
1 800 929-9108
www.centerpointlargeprint.com